her
aussie
holiday

her
aussie
holiday

USA TODAY BESTSELLING AUTHOR

STEFANIE
LONDON

Entangled Publishing, LLC
10940 S Parker Road
Suite 327
Parker, CO 80134
Visit our website at www.entangledpublishing.com.

Amara is an imprint of Entangled Publishing, LLC.

Edited by Stacy Abrams
Cover design by Elizabeth Turner Stokes
Cover art by Photopixel/Shutterstock
AtSkwongPhoto/Shutterstock
Ljupco Smokovski/Shutterstock
Interior design by Toni Kerr

Print ISBN 978-1-64063-9089
ebook ISBN 978-1-64063-9096

Manufactured in the United States of America

First Edition September 2020

ALSO BY STEFANIE LONDON

THE PATTERSON'S BLUFF SERIES

The Aussie Next Door

THE BEHIND THE BAR SERIES

The Rules According to Gracie
Pretend It's Love
Betting the Bad Boy

OTHER ROMANTIC COMEDIES

How To Win a Fiancé
How to Lose a Fiancé
Trouble Next Door
Loving the Odds
Millionaire Under the Mistletoe
Taken By the CEO

*To all the creatives,
don't let anybody dull your shine.*

CHAPTER ONE

Cora Cabot knew three important things about Australia:

1. The men were hotter Down Under (Chris Hemsworth, Hugh Jackman, the other Hemsworth…)
2. It was hot. Period.
3. Pretty much every animal could kill you.

Okay, so maybe not *every* animal could kill you. But a country that prided itself on having the deadliest snakes in the world was not a country to be trifled with. Add to that spiders—of the hairy and poisonous variety—sharks, stingrays (RIP Steve Irwin), all kinds of creepy crawlies, and Cora knew she would have to be on high alert at all times.

But standing outside a slightly run-down yet utterly charming house surrounded by huge, swaying trees whose leaves rustled in the dry, sea-salted air made Cora instantly understand why Aussies put up with their infamous critters. It was truly beautiful here.

She walked up the unfinished driveway, careful to avoid the dozens of small, podlike things littering the ground. Her suitcase bumped behind her, wheels rattling and lock jangling with each step.

So what *was* a dyed-in-the-wool city girl—a New Yorker, no less—doing thousands of miles from the nearest Saks?

Healing…escaping.

It sounded a little melodramatic, sure. But Cora wasn't exactly opposed to a little melodrama. After all, one did not grow up with a mother famous for her daytime television relationship therapy segments without developing a passing interest in the theatrical and over the top. But right now, Cora needed to get as *far* away from that stuff as possible. A whole hemisphere away, in fact.

Pausing at the front door, she sucked in a breath. Finally, after what felt like an eternity of airports and immigration lines and endless road, she was here. Alone. The sound of nature enveloped her—birds and leaves and wind and the ocean creating a soothing cacophony that melted into her bones.

This was *exactly* what she needed.

Cora slipped a carefully folded piece of paper out of her bag and flipped it open.

Dear Cora,

I am so excited for our house swap! Seriously, thank you. You've saved my butt. I had no idea how I was going to afford to rent a place in Manhattan for a month without going totally broke. Anyway, my little place isn't anywhere near as fancy or glamorous as yours, but I hope you find it comfortable. A few things:

1. *The bathroom pipes rattle terribly. Give them a second to run and the noise will eventually stop. If they're too annoying, let me know and I'll have my brother come by*

to work on them.

2. *There's a cockatoo (noisy white bird with a gold crest) who likes to pop in. I call him Joe and keep some bird feed by the back door. He's very friendly!*

3. *Print this email out because reception is terrible, and you'll need the access code to get the key. There's a little box under a red pot. The code is: 2513.*

Now get to work on your novel! When you become a famous author, I'm going to rent this place out as a tourist attraction and charge people a fortune to visit the creative retreat of the great Cora Cabot, literary genius.

Love, Liv.

Cora cringed. Why had she even told Liv she was working on a novel?

Maybe it was a moment of giddy excitement at typing those fabled words: The End. But clearly she should have curbed her enthusiasm long enough for her literary agent father to cut down any delusions of grandeur. He'd called her book *unpublishable*, her lead character *unsympathetic*.

And then he'd declined to represent her.

Of course the feedback wasn't intended to hurt her feelings—she knew that. Her father had a black belt in tough love, and his criticism was meant to help her grow and improve. To make her a better writer. And she absolutely intended to rise to that challenge.

But right now, she had more pressing concerns…like liberating the front door key from its hiding place.

"Please, please, *please* don't be hiding anything more than a key," she said as she crouched down, reaching for the pot described in Liv's email.

Cora felt like Dorothy in *The Wizard of Oz*. Only instead of lions, and tigers, and bears, *oh my!* it was more like snakes, and bugs, and poisonous, hairy, eight-legged freaks of nature waiting to suck your blood like B-movie vampires.

Too squeamish to pick up the pot, she nudged it over and hoped nothing would scuttle or slither out. Thankfully, the only thing underneath was a plastic box containing the key. The simple gold thing didn't look secure enough to protect much. Cora's New York apartment had a twenty-four-seven doorman, a concierge, swipe key, and two physical keys to get inside.

But maybe around these parts, people trusted one another. What a thought.

Cora unlocked the front door and dragged her suitcase inside. The house was in the middle of renovations, as Liv had previously warned. On one side there was a kitchen, gleaming and modern with white subway tiles and a soft-white granite countertop with pretty silver and charcoal veining. The family room, on the other hand, was older-looking and well-loved with a heaving bookshelf and big couch in faded blue.

There was a section of floral wallpaper. It looked vintage, but not in a good way. More like in a "grandma was a pack-a-day smoker" kind of way.

But her friend Liv had thrown her own *joie de vivre* onto the weary canvas, with a collection of colorful mismatched cushions on the couch, quirky wall hangings and photos of her family dotting several surfaces. This was a house with love embedded in the walls and floors and shining in through the windows.

A *real* home.

Liv had been worried it might not be up to Cora's standards, but frankly, luxury furniture and expensive art handpicked by New York's best interior designer hadn't made her happy. And it had become painfully obvious that the fancy handbags and red-soled shoes her mother had taught her to covet were a poor substitute for the things that actually mattered in life. Cora would trade it all in for the real deal: a loving husband, a family who supported one another, a career that made her soul sing.

"Oh, bloody hell!"

Cora jumped and whirled around, pressing her palm to her heart. "Who's there?"

"Bugger off!"

The noise was coming from the kitchen, where a window facing the back of the property was totally open. Gee, they *really* didn't worry about security here. A white bird sat on the windowsill, staring at her. Its golden crest fanned out above its head, demanding her attention.

"You must be Joe," Cora said, narrowing her eyes. So much for friendly. She was pretty sure being told to *bugger off* wasn't a nice thing in this country. But she also understood that it was easy to say something you didn't mean if you were "hangry." It happened to her all the time. "You want something to eat, little guy?"

The bird squawked, as if offended at being called little. But then he bobbed his head in this strange boppy dance, and Cora couldn't help but laugh.

"I'll take that as a yes."

It took her a few minutes to locate a sack of bird seed, which had a note taped to it: *1 x small handful. He'll eat from your hand, or scatter into the backyard.*

Cora looked at the bird's curved, pointed-tipped talons—the damn things looked sharp enough to carve a Thanksgiving turkey. So that was a hard pass on the hand feeding. Joe chattered away, clicking and chirping and making all kinds of funny noises while he waited for his lunch.

"All right, mate! Who's a pretty boy?"

In spite of her trepidation and emotional exhaustion, Cora found herself feeling lighter than she had in weeks. Hell, maybe in months.

Don't fool yourself—it's been years. You don't get this messed up without a solid foundation of BS from way back.

Her snarky inner voice was cut off when Joe whistled at her in a way that sounded a whole lot like a catcall. Now *who* had taught him to do that?

"Sorry, little guy, this vacation does *not* include a fling. I've only got eyes for fictional men right now. Book boyfriends all the way."

She tossed the seed through the window, and it scattered across the grassy area behind the house. Joe immediately flapped his wings, swooping down to collect the bounty and trying to intimidate a couple of smaller birds looking to join the meal. He puffed his chest out and stomped around, claiming the territory.

"You guys are all the same, only after a free lunch," she said, shaking her head.

Being wealthy wasn't uncommon in Manhattan, not by a long stretch. Coming from a famous family wasn't, either. But that didn't stop the opportunists and users from piling up.

Warning: Traffic conditions in Cora Cabot's life are dire. A collision containing one ex-fiancé and one narcissistic mother have created untenable conditions in New York City. Watch out for the ego spill on Fifth Avenue. Get out while you can.

For the next month, Cora would forget all about her fame-hungry mother, her string of failed relationships, and her unfulfilling job. She was going to enjoy being away from the drama and having a beautiful location to work on achieving her dream: producing a novel worthy of publication.

Right now, that was the only thing that mattered.

Cora's nose wrinkled at the smell of something unappealing and, with horror, figured out it was *her*. Looked like her grand life reset would have to wait until after a very long, very hot shower.

• • •

Trent Walters's ute navigated the winding, overgrown road to his sister's house. Although calling it a road seemed a little generous. More like a root-infested, teeth-rattling, wild, life-dodging driving "experience." Why his adorable, social butterfly baby sister had chosen to purchase a home so secluded was beyond him.

But Liv had her own house and he didn't, so who was he to judge? Being a builder by trade and a general handyman by hobby, Trent wanted the perfect house with the perfect view. Unfortunately, despite securing the ideal block of land upon which to build his dream home some time ago, he'd yet to make a start. Too many other commitments kept getting in the way.

To make matters worse, his best mate had decided to move his girlfriend into their shared house, and the nightly squeaking bedsprings and cries of "yes baby, do it harder" had finally become too much.

All of that was to say, Trent's living situation was…fluid. For now, he would camp at his sister's place while she was away. It was the perfect opportunity to get some extra work done on her renovations without her standing over his shoulder. First up: fix the shitty plumbing. The old pipes rattled like that angry, chained-up ghost in *The Muppet Christmas Carol*. It was like the Ghost of Bad DIYs Past. How Liv put up with the sound, he'd never know.

So he'd taken the plumbing apart earlier that morning in the hopes that he'd get it all fixed up by lunchtime tomorrow. Then he could *finally* have a shower without the walls moaning and groaning.

Never mind that Liv had told him to pause the work while she was away—*that* was an advantage. The less she suspected, the more impact the surprise would have. He was already picturing the big smile on her face when he did the "grand reveal" like he was on some home improvement reality show.

Trent eased the ute around the sharp corner to where his sister's house was nestled among the bushland. Warm, salty air washed over him as he pushed the door open and hopped out onto the ground. He was covered in grime from spending the morning on a construction site for a new home overlooking the Patterson's Bluff shoreline. It had an *amazing* view. They could see the smooth, calm waters of Port Phillip Bay and on a good day, the view would stretch endlessly, as if they could see all the way to the edge of the world.

Trent's heavy steel-capped boots crunched over the path, crushing gum nuts and twigs as he headed toward the house. From the outside, it didn't look like much, but by the time he was done with the inside…well, it would be an oasis for his little sister.

He kicked off his boots before heading inside. It was hot and stuffy in that typical late-summer way, with the kind of heat that could feel oppressive if you hadn't grown up with it. Especially if you were inside with no air conditioning. Feeling sticky already, Trent pulled his T-shirt and socks off and dropped them into the hamper by the laundry. A funny feeling settled into his gut as he padded barefoot into the kitchen.

Something was off.

For starters, the kitchen window was closed. *That* would explain why the house felt so warm. The new air-con unit wasn't due to arrive until later that week, so leaving the windows open was the only way to keep the place cool. He'd planned to fit the flyscreen after work so he could leave it open overnight without getting eaten alive by mozzies.

Maybe he'd accidentally closed the window without thinking. Shaking his head, he wrapped his hand around the refrigerator door. But something froze him in place. A sound. More specifically, a sound he should *not* be hearing.

Running water.

"What the…?" Trent abandoned his plans for a cold beer and headed toward the master bedroom.

Liv's tiny en suite bathroom had the worst pipes Trent had ever seen. Whichever bozo had built this house originally had no idea what he was doing, Trent was sure of it. Not only were many elements *not* up to current—or former—building codes, the finishings had a DIY feel…and not in a creative, handmade, one-of-a-kind way, either. More in the "I have no idea what the hell I'm doing" kind of way.

"Liv?" Trent poked his head into the bedroom. His sister had flown out yesterday, texting the family's WhatsApp group earlier to say she'd landed safely at JFK Airport.

Now that he looked closer, he saw a suitcase sitting by the bed. It wasn't the one his sister used—which had been a hand-me-down from their mother, tied with a ratty red polka dot ribbon at the handle to distinguish it from the thousands of other beat-up black wheeled boxes that graced the airport's luggage carousel.

This suitcase looked expensive.

But Trent's concerns about figuring out who was showering in his sister's house were suddenly overtaken by a much larger concern.

"Oh shit!"

Without giving a moment's thought to what he might see in the bathroom, he rushed toward the door and yanked it back. Just as he thought, the place was entirely flooded.

CHAPTER TWO

Cora held her hands over the open pipe, attempting to stem the aggressive flow of water into the bathroom. But she was failing miserably. And moistly.

"No, no, *no*!"

The water kept coming, like a tsunami of bad luck manifested. What *else* could possibly go wrong? She was soaked from head to toe, her hair dripping and hanging like a heavy sheet around her shoulders. Strands stuck to her arms and her cheeks as the water pounded her in the face.

Cora coughed and turned her face away, but the stream sprayed her ear and she winced. How the hell had she missed the gaping hole in the wall where the sink should have been? What else did she need, a giant flashing sign?

She'd been drawn zombie-like to the deep bathtub and the promise of feeling clean after her long flight. Nothing like being stuck in a flying tuna can for fourteen hours to make you crave running water and a bar of soap. That's what she got for not stopping to freshen up at the airline's lounge before the two-hour drive from the airport to Patterson's Bluff.

Are you feeling fresh now?

"Stop already!" She squeezed her eyes shut as more water came, pushing past her fingertips and spilling onto the floor. It rose up to where her knees pressed into a soggy bathmat. Her dress would be ruined.

Everything would be ruined.

Cora hadn't even stripped out of her clothing before disaster hit. She'd been here all of five freaking minutes and she'd ruined her friend's house.

How can you be this much of a disaster with even the simplest thing?

The water kept coming, and now she had so much in her eyes that she couldn't even open them to look around. She hadn't been able to figure out how to make it stop, and no amount of twisting the bathtub's taps had worked.

This was the end. She was going to flood the entire house, have nowhere to stay, and her only real friend was going to hate her forever.

RIP, Cora Cabot. She didn't live long, but she owned a lot of pretty shoes.

"What the hell are you doing?" An angry voice boomed over the sound of rushing water, and Cora squeaked, surprise causing her to yank her hands back from the open pipe. Mistake! The water gushed out harder, and she immediately tried to cover it again.

"What are *you* doing?" she shouted, her voice shaking. Great, now, on top of being a complete hot mess, she was going to get murdered by some stranger while she looked like a drowned rat and smelled like a dead one. "Who are you?"

"Who are *you*?"

Cora could barely keep her eyes open long enough to see who was shouting at her because water droplets kept finding their way in. Should she run? How far would she get on this slippery floor? And where would she even run to? This place was in the middle of nowhere.

"You stay there—I'm going to shut the water main off." The sound of footsteps sloshing through water faded.

Minutes later, as sheer helplessness almost overwhelmed her, the water mercifully stopped. She withdrew her hands and used her forearm to push her hair out of her face so she could survey the damage. The entire bathroom was soaked. Totally and thoroughly soaked. The fuzzy pink mat made a squelching sound as she stood, her feet sinking into the sodden material. Her suede ballet flats lay ruined next to where the door opened up into the bedroom, and beyond that, the powder-blue carpet had a huge dark patch stretching all the way to the foot of the bed.

For a moment, Cora stood still as a tree, her heart pounding in her ears. The place was silent except for the drip, drip, drip of water sliding from her fingertips and her hair. Catching sight of herself in the mirror, she cringed.

She looked like that freaky little girl from *The Ring*.

As she stepped onto the carpet, water pooled around her feet. A cute pink cardboard box sitting on the floor next to Liv's chest of drawers was ruined. The cardboard had warped, softening and losing shape so that the box leaned precariously to one side. Biting down on her lip, Cora peeked inside and sighed with a heavy heart.

It contained a scrapbook that said "Happy 40th Wedding Anniversary" on the front with a picture of a man and woman who looked a *lot* like Liv. On top of ruining her friend's carpet and her bathroom, she'd also ruined a handmade gift. Cora swallowed against the sadness tinged with green-eyed envy climbing up the back of her throat. It was clear her friend had put a lot of time and thought into it. And even more than that, it was clear she had the kind of family where such a thing would be appreciated. Where a gift of time was worth more than a swinging price tag containing as many zeros as possible.

Pressing the heels of her palms to her eyes, Cora let out a strangled noise of frustration. This was her life at the moment, one ridiculous problem after the next.

"You'd better tell me who the hell you are and what you're doing in my sister's house." The angry voice was back, booming through the quiet room.

The man was barefoot and shirtless and bronzed, with water dotting his skin like glimmering freckles. His hair flopped over his forehead and he raked it back, biceps flexing with the movement. There were muscles…everywhere. Like his muscles had muscles in some kind of mind-bending hot guy trick. For a moment, Cora was convinced she'd actually drowned, and this was some weird earth-to-heaven transitory phase.

Sexy limbo.

Crap. This was Liv's older brother? He looked pissed. Apparently, her day *could* get worse.

She pressed a hand to her chest in the hopes of

slowing her thundering heart. Though only part of the accelerated beat was due to getting pummeled in the face with water. "Don't you know it's rude to sneak up on a person like that? What if I'd been holding a weapon? I could have hurt you."

"Explain to me how you would have been holding a weapon while you were occupied with a flooding pipe?" He came closer. Now she could see his eyes were blue—a perfect sky-at-noon blue. Almost too vibrant to be real. "And what was your plan, anyway? To hold your hands over the pipe until the world ran out of water?"

Shame flushed through Cora's face, heating her cheeks until she was certain she resembled a tomato. Okay, sure, she wasn't the handiest person around. She didn't know how to do things like fixing leaks or sanding wood or…hammering nails or whatever other handy things people did to their houses.

"I was taking a moment to think," she said, folding her arms over her chest. A water droplet ran down her forehead, racing along the line of her nose and then clinging to the tip. But she refused to wipe it away, because on some silly level, that felt like showing weakness.

Yeah, like pretending not to be a drowned rat is going to make a difference.

Drip.

"How was that going for you, huh?" The man shoved his hands into his pockets, and the action drew Cora's eyes down to where denim stretched across his crotch. Snapping her eyes back up to his, she caught the tail end of a fleeting smirk. If she'd thought her cheeks were hot before, they were twin blazing suns now.

Could you maybe not *ogle his man bits for five seconds and figure out what's going on here?*

"It's going…poorly," she admitted.

"So, question number one is who are you?" He came closer still, sauntering toward her like some silver-screen cowboy but with the most delicious accent she'd ever heard. The vowels were broad and lazy, like a scorching summer day.

"Cora Cabot," she replied, swallowing back the strange fluttering feeling wreaking havoc inside her. "I…I'm friends with Liv."

Judging by the raised brow, Mr. Bronzed and Shirtless had not been expecting anyone at the house. All Cora knew about Liv's family was that she was the youngest of five, with four rough-and-tumble older brothers, each one more protective than the last. From the tidbits she'd shared and the anecdotal evidence of the scrapbook, Liv's family seemed close-knit. Loving. Like how Cora had always hoped her family might be.

"You're friends with Liv," he repeated, looking confused. "She's not in the country at the moment."

"I know that. She's in Manhattan, staying in *my* apartment," Cora said. "When she told me about her internship, we agreed to a house swap. She didn't mention it?"

• • •

Trent scanned his memory for information of a friend staying at Liv's house, but nothing sprang to mind. Although, to be fair, his sister liked to blow up the family group chat with long messages that made Trent's head spin. He was more of a two-word-response kinda guy. The occasional emoji. Precise. To the point.

Liv liked to recreate *War and Peace* every time she got on her phone.

"If she did, I don't remember," Trent said.

"I have an email from your sister." The woman picked up a small bag perched on top of his sister's bed that had a long gold chain attached and a fancy-looking clasp made out of two Cs. "She sent me some instructions and the code to get into the house."

She thrust the piece of paper in his direction, her wet hands blurring the ink in places. But there was his sister's email address, clear as day at the top, *and* the pin code for the spare key.

Cora stood, her hands knotted in front of her. Her long hair was soaked through, and it stuck to her shoulders and arms. She wore a fitted black dress, which, now that it was wet, clung to her body like a second skin. He could see every contour, every mouth-watering line, from her shapely legs to the subtle dip at her waist to the enticing flare of her hips. He could even see the texture of a lacy bra covering her perky breasts. Her blue eyes were icy pale, and they stared at him unwaveringly.

"You're here for a month?" He scrubbed a hand over his face, wondering how in the hell Liv hadn't thought to *tell* him about her house swap. She knew he never checked his emails and group messages.

Who had time for that? "That might pose a problem."

"You mean aside from the flood damage?" She attempted a smile that was so sweet, a little part of him softened.

"Didn't it occur to you that there was a reason pieces of pipe were lying all over the ground?" He'd have a hell of a mess to clean up now, not to mention that in the height of summer, they had to keep an eye on water usage. Australia was abundant in many things, but rain was not one of them. "You've made my job a whole lot harder now."

"I can't believe I did that," she said with a sigh. "I honestly was so tired from the flight, and all I wanted was a soak in the tub. I didn't even notice there was anything off. It was like I had blinders on. I'm so sorry."

It would have been easy to rule Cora out as an oblivious princess with her designer luggage and fancy handbag and a dress that looked more suited to a cocktail party than an international flight. But she looked genuinely distressed.

"Oh…" She bit down on her lip and scrunched up her face. "There's one more problem."

"What else?" Trent tipped his head back and looked at the ceiling, as if he might find strength there.

"This." Cora reached into a sad-looking box that had lost all structural integrity due to extensive water damage and pulled out a book covered with silver and gold material. The edges of the pages were crinkled with moisture, and the thick black letters spelling out "Happy 40th Wedding Anniversary" had bled ink everywhere.

"Oh no." Trent's shoulders sagged. "Liv is going to be devastated."

His sister had been working on the scrapbook for *months*, collecting old photos and writing out fond memories and even interviewing people who had known their parents when they were first dating. Trent held his hands out, and Cora handed over the sodden mess. The pages had soaked up water like greedy plants after a drought. When he flipped open the cover, a picture of him and his siblings from when they were kids stared up at him. He counted five sets of baby blues and gap-toothed smiles. Five lots of gangly limbs and sun-streaked hair. Five hands sticky with half-melted ice creams.

A perfect memory captured forever.

The paper disintegrated under his touch, a piece of it tearing right off and splitting Trent away from his siblings. Thank god Liv hadn't used all originals. They were photocopies that could be replaced, but hours of flipping through albums, photocopying and cutting and pasting and drawing decorations, were now for nothing.

"Do you think we can save it?" Cora asked hopefully.

"If by *save* you mean start the whole thing completely from scratch, then yeah." He tossed the ruined gift onto the ground, and it landed with a moist *splat*. "But my more immediate concern is where you're going to sleep tonight. We need to get the water sucked out of this carpet and bring the dehumidifiers in. You can't breathe this damp air all night. It's not safe. *And* we've got to prevent mold from growing. My brother and his wife run a bed and breakfast—"

"I'm staying here to help," Cora said, folding her arms over her chest, a determined set to her jaw. "I made this mess, and I'm going to clean it up."

Trent raised a brow. Cora didn't look like the kind of person who'd done manual labor a day in her life. "This is a job for the professionals, I'm afraid. I'll need to call my crew in."

"Then I'll make coffee and snacks. I can go through the scrapbook and make a list of everything in there so we can start putting it back together."

He laughed. "We?"

"The only reason water came out of the pipes was because you didn't turn off the main before you took the bathroom apart," she pointed out.

Well, *touché.* Maybe Little Miss City Slicker wasn't so clueless after all. "I didn't anticipate having a stranger in the house who'd mess up all my plans."

"And yet, here we are." She looked him dead in the eye, and Trent had to admire the woman's resolve. She was stubborn; he'd give her that. It wasn't a quality that had a good reputation, but Trent liked stubborn people. People who stuck to their guns and followed through on their promises. People whose words meant something.

"You'd better be willing to put your money where your mouth is," he said, shaking his head.

"You really want to help?"

Her pale gaze held him captive, unwavering and daring him to challenge her. "I really do."

"Then I hope you know how to use a glue gun."

CHAPTER THREE

Spoiler alert: Cora did *not* know how to use a glue gun.

Because glue guns were for people with normal childhoods that involved regular-kid things like arts and crafts, video games, and playing hide and seek. It went along with homemade Halloween costumes and school plays where kids fumbled their lines without consequence and sleepovers spent swooning over Zac Efron.

Cora's childhood could be best summed up as: *may result in therapy.*

Instead of mud pies and Scrabble, it was dressage and cotillion. Instead of movie nights with popcorn, it was a rotating army of nannies and cooks and maids. For someone who'd grown up completely surrounded by people at all times, she'd been so lonely that her only solace was hanging out with fictional characters. Ah, but to the glamorous Mrs. Catriona Cabot, having a socially awkward bookworm for a daughter was *not* acceptable. God, what her mother would think of her writing a book.

Fiction is for people whose real lives provide no excitement, her mother had said. *How will you ever get married if you're so boring, you have to hang out with imaginary people?*

Cora shoved the unpleasant thoughts aside. The whole point of coming here was to get distance from her mother's derision, not to spend time thinking about it. Besides, Cora liked having an imagination. As far as she was concerned, it was one of her better qualities.

And sure, her vacation hadn't gotten off to the most amazing start—*understatement of the century*—but she was going to make the best of it. Because in crappy times, the only thing in her control was her attitude. It was an important lesson she'd learned, and one that held her in good stead. Her life might be in shambles right now, but that didn't mean she had to let her mind be the same.

While Trent's friends worked on the house, getting the water sucked out of the carpet with some noisy vacuum-type thing and finishing off the plumbing so this disaster would be a one-time-only deal, she sat at the dining table. Her pen scratched diligently across the pages of the notebook she always carried with her, jotting notes as she slowly worked her way through the scrapbook.

- Page five: *the early years.* 1 x photo of Mr. and Mrs. Walters dated 1985. Pregnant with baby #1. Decorations: photocopy of ultrasound photo (is this the real ultrasound? To be confirmed.)
- Page eleven: *the early years continued…* Blue ribbon, picture of Mrs. Walters in the hospital bed with Baby #2 and a blue teddy bear.
- Page twenty-two: *all the babies.* Picture of baby #5 sleeping in bassinet. Letter from Mrs. Walters to her pen pal in England talking about the pregnancy.

It would take a lot of effort to get the scrapbook recreated, but Cora vowed to stay up all night, every night until it was done. She would not let Liv down.

Trent strode out into the living area and headed toward her. He'd put a T-shirt on now, thank God. It was impossible to concentrate on anything at all with those muscles staring her in the face. But frankly, the T-shirt wasn't much better. It was fitted and showed off his broad, work-honed shoulders and trim waist to perfection. He'd also changed into a pair of fresh jeans, and his unruly blond hair had dried into wavy perfection.

All the stories about Australia are true. The men are *hotter Down Under!*

"How's the damage?" he asked, nodding at the scrapbook.

"Thorough." She sighed. "It sucked the water up like a sponge. But thankfully most of the images are clear enough that I've made a list of everything Liv included. Hopefully, we can get all the pictures copied again. I'm assuming the originals are with your parents?"

Trent nodded. "I'll make sure they're out of the house so we can get the copies in secret."

"It looks like Liv put a lot of love and care into this." Cora touched her fingertip to a picture of Trent's mother smiling as her hands cradled a large baby bump. "You have a beautiful family."

"They're not bad," he said with a cavalier wink. Now that he wasn't trying to figure out why there was a stranger in the house, he seemed to have relaxed.

"How's the bathroom?" she asked, almost not wanting to hear the answer.

"It'll be okay. The crew's working on the carpet now, but I think we got to it quick enough that we don't have to worry about any permanent damage. And Liv was planning on ripping up the carpet to put down some hardwood, anyway." He raked a hand through his hair. "Uh, about before. Sorry if I was a bit harsh."

"I don't blame you. You came home to a stranger and a flood." Cora mustered a smile, still feeling so mortified about the whole damn thing. "And I'm glad you did, because I had no idea what to do. I probably would have sat there with my hands over the pipe until I drowned."

"I'm glad that didn't happen."

Was it her imagination, or was there an appreciative gleam in his eye? Definitely not. The only reason he was being nice was because of her relationship with Liv. He was probably teasing her.

"I'm not sure I could have handled the disposal of a body as well as the flood damage," he added with a smirk.

Okay, yeah. He was *definitely* teasing her.

"Ha-ha," she drawled.

"The blokes are going to do their thing for a bit longer, and apparently I'm not required. Do you want to grab a drink at the pub? Maybe get some food?" Her eyes must have lit up so much that he laughed. "I'll take that as a yes."

"My body doesn't even know what time zone I'm in anymore," she admitted, abandoning her duties and grabbing her handbag. Then she remembered that she hadn't showered since leaving her house almost twenty-four hours ago. After the "incident," she'd changed into a bikini and thrown a loose dress over the top, wanting to be comfortable in the muggy heat inside the non-air-conditioned house. "I should get changed."

"No need. The pub is casual," he said. "You'll fit right in. I figure we can stop by and use the beach showers on the way back, freshen up a bit."

She almost sighed in ecstasy at the thought of it. The quick swipe at her armpits with a facial wipe had done only so much to stem the scent of international travel. "You're speaking my language."

"I haven't even mentioned the possibility of ice cream yet." He laughed, and the sound ran like liquid heat through her veins. Damn, even laughter sounded better in this country.

"Aren't you a good host," she said, slinging her bag over one shoulder.

As they walked out the front of the house, she tried to smooth her hair back into a ponytail—but Cora's shiny, sleek locks were not a natural feature. Oh no, they were the product of keratin treatments and a love affair with her flat iron. When exposed to moisture, Cora's hair tended to pouf out, kinking and frizzing into a fluffy mess.

"Eh, I figured we didn't start out on the best foot and, more importantly, my sister will have my left nut if I don't make you feel welcome." Trent hit the remote to unlock a dusty silver pickup truck sitting in front of the house. "I hope you're okay riding in the ute. It's not super comfy, but it does the job."

"Ute?"

"Short for utility vehicle. What do you call them?"

"Pickup trucks." Not that you would see too many of those around where she lived. "And it's no problem. If you promised me a cold beer, I would ride a kangaroo to get there."

"You know we don't really do that here, right?" His lip twitched in a way that belied the deadpan tone of his voice. "But we do eat them."

"You what?" Cora gasped. "They're on your passports, for crying out loud."

Trent shrugged. "They're tasty *and* a very lean, healthy source of protein."

"Well, *I* won't be eating one, thank you very much." That would be like eating a bald eagle. It seemed weird to treat a national symbol as a meal, but maybe they didn't worry about things like that here.

"Not adventurous with your food, are you?" he teased. The pickup truck—sorry, *ute*—roared to life, and Trent executed a tight turn in the driveway that had them on a gravelly little road surrounded by dense bushland.

"I'm plenty adventurous. Manhattan has some of the best cuisine in the whole world, but I'm not about to pretend I'm on an episode of *Survivor*."

"So witchetty grubs are off the menu as well, then?"

Cora pressed a hand to her stomach. "Keep talking like this and I won't even *need* a menu."

Trent chuckled, and the ute bounced along the unfinished road, kicking up dust and stones behind them. Every time one hit the side, it made a little *chink* sound. The scent of something sweet and floral drifted into the car through the open windows, mingling with the salty tang of the ocean. Eventually, they exited onto a busier road with more houses sprouting up. Every so often, when the houses broke, the ocean could be seen like a beautiful aqua line along the horizon.

"So how do you know Liv?" he asked.

It stung a little that Liv had never mentioned Cora to her family—but she had to remind herself that Liv was the kind of person who made friends everywhere she went. She was vivacious and gregarious and outgoing and probably had dozens of people in her closest circle.

"Actually, we met online," Cora said. "We were both in a copywriting course and we hit it off. Then we started swapping work for critiques and Skyping every other week."

Liv might not know it, but she'd been Cora's lifeline in a time when everything seemed to be failing her. Hearing the familiar chime of the Skype ringtone on her MacBook had always filled Cora with a sense of relief, because for the hour or two that they talked, she could feel like she mattered to someone.

Liv had listened to her cry over her breakup with her fiancé, she'd commiserated when her parents announced they were getting a divorce, and she'd been the one to text Cora randomly through the day and night, little heart emojis and "I'm thinking of you" cheer-up messages.

"Eventually we ended up meeting in London, of

all places."

"Oh right." Trent snapped his finger. "She went for a friend's wedding."

"I happened to be there for work, so it was kind of serendipitous." Meeting Liv in person had been like meeting a long-lost sister. "And now I'm staying in her house and she's staying in mine. I consider her a real friend, even if most of our conversations happen via the internet."

Trent navigated the smooth corner, and suddenly they were on what appeared to be Patterson's Bluff's main drag. The town was capital-A adorable. Neat rows of shops were bustling with people, many of whom walked dogs or had children in tow. Cora spotted a sweet little bakery and an ice cream store with an old-fashioned blue and white striped awning and—oh!—a yoga studio. The street was dotted with big, sweeping trees and cute wrought-iron benches.

It was postcard-picture perfect.

"Welcome to the White Crest," Trent said as he eased into a parking spot. An old building sat like a monument on the corner, guarding the rest of the street like a father watching over his children. It had a white balcony on the second level where people had gathered, laughing and drinking. "Most important place in Patterson's Bluff. Home to the best brew this side of the Peninsula *and* the spot where you can catch pretty much anyone in town. If you need to find someone, this is your first port of call."

They got out of the car and walked into the pub. Inside, the place was decorated as one would expect from a seaside town. There was exposed, sun-bleached wood everywhere and big windows that allowed the afternoon light to flood in. The tables were high and round, once painted white but now had that delightfully worn-in and rustic look. And the bar appeared to have been carved from a single tree—the beautifully gnarled edges making for a stunning feature that flowed like a wave along its length.

"I love it already," she replied with a grin.

Maybe the disastrous first part of her vacation was nothing more than a glitch. A speed bump. Perhaps from here on out, everything would go according to plan.

. . .

Trent tried not to notice the enticing way Cora's short, loose-fitting dress shifted as she climbed onto a stool at one of the high tables, flashing hints of toned thighs. The dress exposed thin, white bikini straps at her shoulders that looked barely solid enough to withstand a strong breeze. Or a tug. The very thought of it—taking a strap between his fingers and pulling until the knot unraveled—had him shifting on the spot, battling a sudden surge of attraction that was so strong and so swift, it felt like a zap of electricity.

She probably thinks you're a jerk after the way you spoke to her this afternoon.

Ugh, he owed her a beer for that.

Plumbing rule number one was *always* turn off the mains. Total rookie move. The guys he'd called in to help were never going to let him live that one down.

It wasn't like him to be quick to anger—Trent was the smile-through-a-crisis kinda guy. The one who could be counted on to crack jokes even if the walls were crumbling down around them. But he'd had this instinctive reaction to Cora, a visceral gut churning that knocked him off-kilter and upended his usually calm-blue-ocean approach to things.

Maybe it was because she was a dead ringer for his ex. Like, long-lost-sister levels of similarity. If not for her accent, he might have been suckered into believing that she *was* the woman who'd shattered his heart only three years ago.

That's why you're attracted to her. It's like… muscle memory.

Which was precisely why he'd repeat that over and over in his head as a reminder of why it was a terrible idea to ogle his sister's houseguest, even if her dress stirred up all kinds of dark and dirty images with each indecent little flick of fabric. If there was one thing Trent *wasn't* looking for, it was any kind of romantic entanglement.

Especially not one that spelled trouble in flashing neon letters.

Trent left Cora for a moment to order a couple of beers and a hearty mound of the herb and garlic chips that were his bar snack of choice. When he brought them back to the table, balancing everything with the expertise of someone who'd been doing bar runs all his adult life, she immediately reached for her bag.

"Snacks are on me," he said, setting everything

down on the table. "If you flew in today, then you've probably had nothing but shitty airplane food for the last twenty-four hours. The least I can do is make sure you're fed."

"Thank you. These look good." She reached for a chip and bit down on the end. "Oh yeah, that's the stuff."

"We're not big into fries here," he said. The piping-hot, thick-cut potato planks were like salty morsels of goodness, and the *perfect* accompaniment to a crisp, cold lager. "But I've yet to meet a person who didn't love these."

"I can see why," she said, reaching for another.

"Cheers." Trent held his beer in the air and Cora clinked her glass against his. "So, a house swap, huh?"

She nodded. "Liv emailed me asking for recommendations of where she might be able to stay that would be walking distance to her internship. My place happens to be around the corner, so it seemed like the perfect solution. I was well overdue for a vacation anyway."

"What do you do for work?" He took a long pull on his beer, almost missing the way Cora's expression shifted from easy and relaxed to something that seemed a whole lot…tighter.

"I'm an office manager," she said. "For a literary agency."

"And what does an office manager for a literary agency do?" Trent had zero experience with anything that involved the words "office," "management," *or* "literary." He'd avoided the cube-farm workplaces inhabited by several of his friends, going straight into hands-on dirt-under-his-fingernails work the second he walked out of school on his sixteenth birthday.

"Oh, lots of things," she said. "I help with on-boarding new hires, running our summer internship program, coordinating company-wide initiatives for all kinds of things like corporate health and well-being, information security, workplace culture… that kind of thing."

Trent nodded like he had a single clue what any of that meant, which he most certainly did not. "Literary agency, like for books?"

"That's right. It's a relatively small company. Most of our staff members are agents who represent authors and try to help them get publishing contracts. They do other things, too, like helping authors manage their careers, speaking at events, and keeping a pulse on what's happening in the publishing industry." She munched on a chip. "We have some pretty big clients, too. Names you might have heard of."

Trent doubted it. The last time he read a book was…high school, most likely. The main thing he read these days was his brother's comic strip—because it was awesome and hilarious. But between working his regular construction job, helping friends and family with an endless stream of handyman tasks, playing cricket with his mates, *and* maintaining a healthy social life, reading time didn't really factor in all that much. Hell, Trent barely even watched television unless the footy was on.

That's the kind of guy he was—he'd much

rather be out with people, soaking up the rays or doing something active rather than being at home alone.

"I'm not up to date with what's hot in the book world, I'm afraid," he admitted.

"I'm going to take a stab and say you work with your hands." Cora's pale eyes twinkled with amusement.

"That obvious, huh?" Trent looked at his hand, which was wrapped around the pint glass containing his beer.

He had blue-collar hands—they were a bit beat up. Calloused and rough from hours of hard yakka. He had a bandage around his pinkie finger from where he'd sliced it on some plastic piping, and the hairs on his hands and arms were bleached white-blond from being outdoors every day. He loved his work—loved the satisfaction of taking raw materials and turning them into something solid. Loved the ability to create a place where people would build their lives and make memories.

Was it corny? A little. Would he ever say that aloud in front of his work mates? Hell, no. But he had a sentimental streak, even if he refused to show it to anyone.

"Just a bit," Cora replied. Her eyes skated over him, curiosity unconcealed in a way that made Trent want to reciprocate. It wasn't unusual for him to bask in the glow of admiration of the opposite sex—some *might* call him an attention whore.

It wouldn't be totally incorrect.

But there was something about Cora that made him want to watch his step. Whether it was because she was a friend of Liv's or because of the resemblance to his ex, he wasn't sure. But Cora had an air about her that screamed: *don't get too close.*

"I work in construction," he explained. "Mostly residential developments, new builds, and the odd extension here and there. Every so often I'll do a retail fit-out as well."

"And renovations?"

"For my family, yeah. Liv got that house for a steal, and she needed to fix it up on a tight budget, so I'm helping her out as best I can. Pays to have a brother willing to work for free." He popped a chip into his mouth and enjoyed the salty taste and crispy texture. "Well, in exchange for accommodation."

"You're staying there?" Cora's eyes widened. "I had no idea. Liv said the house wasn't occupied."

"Might have been a bit of a miscommunication," he said sheepishly. "My previous living situation became…not ideal."

Cora raised a brow and sipped her beer.

"My roommate's girlfriend moved in."

"Oh, I see." She wrinkled her nose. "Bedposts banging against the wall?"

"You got it. Squeaky bedsprings and all kinds of sounds that I never want to hear unless they're coming from *my* room." He laughed. "You learn *way* too much about a friend in that situation. I do not need to know that he likes his hair being pulled."

Cora snorted and then clamped a hand over her mouth. "Oh no!"

"Oh yes, as it was most commonly screamed."

Cora's cheeks flushed the prettiest shade of pink, and she scrubbed a hand over her face. "I think I'm getting secondhand embarrassment for you."

"I appreciate the commiseration." He grinned. "Needless to say, it was time to get the hell out of there. I figured, since Liv's place was going to be empty I could kill two birds with one stone—have a peaceful night's sleep *and* get some extra work done on her place so she'd be surprised when she came back."

"That's very sweet," Cora said with a smile. "And only a little self-serving."

"Exactly the kind of balance I like to maintain." He rested his forearms against the edge of the table. "So tell me, why on earth did you agree to a house swap when you'd have to holiday here of all places?"

Not that Patterson's Bluff was a bad place to visit. Every summer, tourists flooded in, seeking out the clean, endlessly stretching beaches and the sun-drenched lifestyle that was the ultimate antidote for city life. Trent adored this town and everything it offered. But it wasn't exactly going to top any lists of "most amazing" places to visit in Australia.

He got the impression that Cora could have gone anywhere. So why was she here, in his little town—at the end of tourist season, no less, when nothing much would be happening—if she could be snorkeling in the Great Barrier Reef or climbing the Sydney Harbour Bridge and having cocktails overlooking the Opera House? She could be exploring Melbourne's endless maze of alleys and funky bars or seeing the incredible natural magnificence that was Uluru.

"It seemed like fun," Cora said with a noncommittal shrug. "Liv has always spoken very highly of her hometown, and I wanted to see what it was like."

That was a big steaming pile of BS if Trent ever heard it. But it wasn't his business, and he didn't want to pry. So he decided to drop it.

There you go, another *reason to stay well away. That fancy trunk wasn't the only baggage she brought with her.*

"So, uh…what does this mean for living arrangements?" Cora asked.

There was no way in hell Trent was going back to Hale's place—besides, he was pretty sure the girlfriend had already taken over his old room. She'd been eyeing it off as he packed his things. Staying at Liv's was meant to be temporary anyway. Just long enough for him to secure an architect to start work on his house plans. Then he was going to live on-site in a caravan when building started.

He *could* stay in the family home, but that wasn't ideal. As much as he loved his folks, they drove him absolutely bananas. And there was no way he'd mooch off Adam and his wife by staying with them. But Cora might enjoy some good old-fashioned Aussie hospitality.

"You sure you don't want to stay at the bed and breakfast?" Trent suggested. "Seriously, my brother and sister-in-law will take great care of you. It's a beautiful little place, and I'm not just saying that because I helped them refurbish it."

"I can't leave you with the mess from today," Cora said, taking a long pull on her beer. "There're two bedrooms, right? Do you think we could share the space without getting in each other's way?"

"There's going to be noise and dust while I work on it. Not to mention other contractors possibly coming in and out."

"I don't mind."

"But I'm sure you were expecting something more relaxing. This is your holiday, after all. Don't worry about the accommodation bill, either. I'll cover it—"

"I *said* I don't mind," she repeated firmly. Cora's eyes met his so unwaveringly, with so much conviction, it was obvious her desires were all but chiseled in stone. "I'd like to stay, if I won't get in the way of things."

Trent sighed. There wasn't much more he could say without seeming like a jerk for kicking her out when *he* was the one who'd decided to camp there, without permission. "You promise to keep it a secret from Liv? I wanted the reno to be a surprise when she came home. She worked her butt off to buy that place, and I plan to make it perfect for her."

A sweet smile drifted over Cora's lips, and she made a locking motion with one hand. "Your secret is totally safe with me."

"So we're roommates, then?"

"Yes. And I won't keep you up with squeaking bedsprings and screaming in the middle of the night." Her eyes twinkled mischievously, and for a hot minute, Trent felt *very* disappointed that he wouldn't hear those sounds coming out of her mouth. "No requests for hair pulling or anything like that, I promise."

"Well, how could I possibly refuse a deal like that?" He held out his hand, and Cora slipped her palm against his, their agreement sealed. "Welcome to Patterson's Bluff."

CHAPTER FOUR

After chips and beers, Cora suggested they order a proper meal, and Trent was more than happy to oblige. The food at the White Crest was good, hearty fare, and he was perfectly content to sit with Cora and chat. They kept things light and impersonal—skirting topics about her motivations for coming to Australia and why she seemed determined to have the "local" experience. Trent had the feeling Cora was like an onion, one layer of complexity after another with the real her buried far beneath.

Still, Trent found himself enjoying her company, and before they knew it, the pub was filling up around them. So they fixed up their bill and decided to head to the beach to use the showers there.

"So what are your plans after your sister gets back?" Cora asked as they headed along the main drag. The sun was low on the horizon, laying a rich, orange-gold filter over the world. It picked up on the burnished tones in Cora's highlighted hair.

"I'm going to build my own place," he replied. "I've got the perfect piece of land and everything waiting for me to find the right time to get started."

But there always seemed to be something delaying him—renovations on Liv's house, fixing up the back decking around his parents' place, overtime at the day job, accepting a rush contract for the yoga studio's expansion when the other building company pulled out last minute. But those things were important to him. As his dad always said, "our family helps others." It was the Walters' way.

And who would he be if he didn't adhere to the family credo?

"That must be nice," she mused. A salt-drenched breeze ruffled her dress, swirling the hem around her thighs as they walked.

"Building a house?"

"Hunting out a piece of land. There's something primal about that, don't you think? Laying claim to the dirt and soil, building a home on top of it." She had a dreamy expression on her face. "I've never had a backyard."

Trent blinked. "You've never had a backyard?"

"Nope." She shook her head. "I'm a born and raised Manhattan gal, remember? We're not exactly flush with extra space there. The best I ever got was a terrace."

"But…even as a kid?" He balked. He couldn't imagine his childhood without the feeling of springy grass between his toes and sprinklers cooling him down on hot summer days. "How did you play sports with your friends? How did you have sleepovers under the stars? What about water gun fights in the summer?"

"Well, we'd go to the Hamptons in the summer and we had plenty of space there. But that wasn't home." A dark look crossed over her face. "And I was never allowed to play sports as a kid."

"Why the hell not?"

Cora sighed. "My mother preferred me to take up more 'ladylike' pursuits like playing the violin and flute. She wanted me to pursue a music performance career."

"I'm guessing you didn't."

"The truth was…I was only ever mediocre, and I get terrible nerves in front of a crowd. My mother threw all the money she could at it. She even donated a huge sum so I'd be accepted into an elite performing arts conservatory, but everyone there knew I'd bought my way in. I wasn't as good as they were." She sucked on the inside of her cheek. "Eventually I couldn't take it anymore. So I quit."

Cora's expression told Trent very clearly how *that* action had gone down. "And then you went to work for a literary agency."

"That's right."

"Did you ever take up any sports?" They rounded a corner to the road that would bring them to the beach—cars lined each side, people with sand-covered legs and feet brushing themselves down as they packed their things away.

"Does going to spin class count?" she joked.

Trent shot her a look.

"Then, no. I have officially never played any kind of competitive sport." She held up her hand. "Don't judge me."

"I'm not judging you. But I *am* incredibly sad for your childhood." He raked a hand through his hair. How could someone deprive their kid of such a fundamental childhood experience? "You've never known the sweet taste of victory in winning a game that was neck and neck the whole way through. You've never known that rush when your team is down, and something happens to put you back in the lead."

Cora laughed, and the sound was like wind-chimes and champagne bubbles. When she laughed, all the worry in her body seemed to evaporate. The crease of her brows relaxed, her shoulders dropped, and her eyes seemed to glow. "Maybe I'm not competitive."

"Everyone is competitive," he said. "It's human nature. Survival of the fittest and all that."

"I guess I'm going to get eaten by a lion out in the wild," she quipped.

"I won't let that happen. How would Liv feel knowing I sent you out into the wild, ill-equipped to deal with any lions you might come across?" He grinned. "Besides, my cricket team is one down. We need another girl to play with us."

"Oh no." Cora shook her head vigorously. "I'm *not* going to take on that level of responsibility."

"It's a very chill team, trust me. And besides, you *did* say you wanted the local experience," he pointed out. They reached the short wooden steps that would take them down to the beach, and Cora kicked off her sandals when they got to the bottom. They dangled from her hand as she wriggled her toes into the grainy white sand. "Think of it as payment for the flooding incident."

"That's a cheap shot." Her eyes skated over him, equal parts curious and distrusting.

"What can I say? I fight dirty. I promise it will be fun." He nudged her with his elbow, and she laughed, shaking her head.

"Does anybody ever say no to you?"

"Not usually." That was the truth. Trent might not have been the kid with the academic smarts, but he'd learned from a young age that he could make up for a lot of shortcomings with the right words. With the right smile. Charm was his greatest skill, and his weapon against the world. "Come on. I'll be your personal coach and everything. Give Childhood Cora what she always wanted."

Cora tipped her face up to the sky and sucked in a long breath, her eyes crinkling. "I know I'm going to regret this…"

"But?"

"But yes, I will pay my dues by being the worst cricket player your team has ever seen."

"You're going to have a blast."

They approached the beach's outdoor showers, which were designed for people to quickly wash the sand and seawater from their bodies before heading to their cars. A teenage boy with a boogie board stood under one shower and a mother occupied the one closest to the car park, wrangling two chubby-limbed youngsters so deftly, Trent wondered if she had extra arms.

"After you," he said, motioning for Cora to take the last unoccupied shower.

"I've been waiting *all* day for this." Cora set her bag and sandals down next to Trent and then stripped her dress over her head.

Underneath, she wore a white bikini with little gold beads dangling from the ties at her shoulders and hips. Trent almost tripped over his own feet at the sight of it. Cora might not have ever played sports, but spin class was *definitely* working for her.

Her body was lean and strong, with legs that seemed to go on forever. And an ass that filled out her bikini bottoms to perfection.

Clearing his throat, he pretended to look at his phone as she strode toward the last shower. The teenage boy next to her did a double take so comical, it looked almost as if it could have been staged. Cora was oblivious, driven by the desire she'd mentioned to wash the long flight from her skin. The water streamed over her, soaking her hair and gliding over her body. Making her glisten. Streams ran in rivulets along her back, over the curve of her butt, and down the backs of her thighs.

Trent's mouth was suddenly drier than the sandy ground beneath his feet. Lust gripped him at the base of his spine, an instant need pulsing in time with his accelerated heartbeat. He dragged his eyes away—but not quickly enough. He'd need to be careful of that.

"I never knew a shower could make me feel *that* good," Cora said with a blissful sigh.

Trent nodded, keeping his eyes on the crashing waves. Maybe if he counted them as they rolled in, his body would calm down enough that he could look Cora in the eye without thinking anything inappropriate.

"I feel like a brand-new human being," she added.

Trent glanced back in her direction to see she'd turned around. Now the flat plane of her stomach was exposed, and the sight of her perky breasts barely kept in place by the skimpy white triangles was enough to melt him like ice cream on a summer's day. He caught sight of a small tattoo on her upper thigh, something black and white that was small and a little difficult to make out. He would never have pegged her to be the kind of girl hiding some ink under her skirt.

The teenage boy was scurrying in the direction of the car park now, averting his eyes from Cora's body and strategically holding his boogie board in front of him.

I feel your pain, buddy.

"Nice tat," Trent said, determined to keep his mind on a subject that felt safe, rather than letting his thoughts wander to how easily he could snap those bikini strings with his teeth.

She's your sister's friend, dude. Not cool.

"Oh, thanks." Cora turned the taps off and squeezed the water out of her long hair. "It's in the perfect hide-from-your-parents place."

"They're not a fan of sports *or* ink?"

"Just two items in a long list of many things I was never supposed to indulge in," she said drily. When she came closer, he could see it was a small creature—a caterpillar. It was inked in fine black lines, almost minimalist in design. It seemed an unusual choice.

"I've seen a lot of butterfly tattoos in my day, but not many caterpillars."

"I have a theory on that," she said, pulling her dress over her head. Since her body was damp, it stuck to her in places, but the fabric was thin and the balmy breeze would have her dry in no time at all. "Lots of people choose the butterfly as the representation for metamorphosis, because it's the end state. The goal. And so many people want to be the butterfly now. They want the beauty and the admiration, without putting in the work required of the caterpillar. Yet without the caterpillar, there is no butterfly."

"That's very profound."

"I guess I'd rather be at a point where there's still hope and good things in front of me, than wishing to rush to the end." Cora's cheeks flushed. "But that was probably *way* more information than you wanted."

She gave him a gentle shove toward the showers, her pale-blue gaze not quite meeting his. Trent wasn't sure he'd ever met someone where his initial impression had been so swiftly turned on its heel.

And, against his better judgment, Cora Cabot had him officially intrigued.

CHAPTER FIVE

Cora woke the next morning, her back tight from sleeping at an awkward angle. Trent had advised it would be best to give Liv's room another day or two to fully dry out, since he was concerned about her breathing in anything harmful before the post-flooding treatment process was complete. He'd offered her the spare bed—aka the one he'd been sleeping in the past few days—but she'd refused.

Frankly, she was having a hard enough time keeping her eyes off Trent without sleeping in a bed with sheets that probably smelled like hot Aussie man. The comfy blue couch seemed like a *much* safer option. A much *smarter* option. Especially considering she'd already given so much away about herself—talking about her family's brow-raising quirks and sharing the story of her tattoo.

Like someone as charming as him gave a crap about metamorphosis.

Cora scrubbed a hand over her face. She'd probably sounded like a total weirdo. For all her mother's efforts to turn her into the perfect young lady of society, she was still a little too thoughtful and a little too strange and a little too introverted for her own good sometimes. She looked at the tattoo, peeking out from the hem of her sleep shorts. She'd drawn the original design herself, keeping it simple and stark with the crisp black lines and minimal shading.

At the time she'd been desperate for change—stuck in a toxic battle of wills with her mother, failing her classes, struggling to get out of bed in the mornings with dread weighing her limbs down. She'd numbed it all for a while, going out for cocktails with her friends most nights of the week and ordering mimosas at brunch every weekend. It was surprisingly easy to make the excessive drinking socially acceptable. Because she wasn't keeping a bottle of Johnnie Walker in her purse or necking something covered in a paper bag.

Her drinks were ordered at classy bars. She rotated her friends so nobody knew exactly how often she was out, downing martinis like water. She'd headed home nightly, teetering on her heels with a glassy look in her eyes, and covered it all with concealer the next morning.

Thankfully, that time hadn't lasted long, and Cora had gotten herself out of that hole before things got too bad. But she remembered the day she'd trekked out to Brooklyn to get her tattoo, palms sweaty while she gnawed on the inside of her lip. Only the scratch of the needle had been a welcome blessing, the pain reminding her that she had the capacity to feel. To take charge of her life.

She traced the design with her fingertip. The image reminded her that she wasn't done growing yet, that she could always do something to push herself in the right direction. That it wasn't too late.

And life had gone better after that...until it hadn't.

A clatter in the kitchen startled Cora out of her

reverie. The noise was followed by a muffled curse, and she shifted on the couch to look out across the room. From her vantage point, she could see Trent reaching into the cupboard above the coffee maker, his strong, lean body on full display. A pair of shorts rode low on his hips, and he was topless. The muscles in his back and shoulders worked as he pulled a bag of ground coffee down from the top shelf.

The man was magnificent. Top shelf, A-plus, and gold stars all around. Not to mention that he seemed to spend more time with his top off than on.

No complaints here.

The fact that she was looking at Trent with hunger stoking a small fire in her belly was progress. Not that she was going to do anything about it, mind you. One, she wasn't taking advantage of her friend's generosity only to screw her brother. Literally. Two, the whole point of this trip was to find some direction for her novel…and that did not involve getting distracted by feelings of lust.

"Want a coffee?"

Trent's voice startled Cora so much that she yelped and almost fell off the couch. Snatching the blanket up over her chest—like *that* would make a difference—she cringed as her cheeks filled with heat. How did he know she was awake? Had he caught her staring at him like he was a hot fudge sundae with extra whipped cream?

"There's a mirror on the wall." Trent pointed to a circular, decorative mirror that was framed in a gold sun-like design. "I could see that you were awake. Sorry, didn't mean to startle you."

"It's fine." She pushed up into a sitting position and released the blanket. "And I would love a coffee, thanks."

Oh God, he *had* been able to see that she was staring. How embarrassing. Cora's track record with men wasn't the greatest. In fact, if she were to write an autobiography centered on her love life, it could be called *How to End a Date Early for All the Wrong Reasons*.

Which was exactly why she'd been thrilled to find a guy who "got" her—being in a relationship meant she no longer had to suffer through awkward first meetings and fumbled kisses and that sinking, disappointed feeling she got when it was clear that a limp cucumber had more chemistry than her date.

"What's the plan for today?" she asked, folding the blanket and setting it neatly on the couch.

"I've got a mate coming around this morning to help me fix the plumbing and check on the water damage. Then I figured we should get to work on trying to put this bloody scrapbook back together." He shook his head. "I'll never understand why Liv couldn't get them a voucher to a nice restaurant. Or buy them a plant or something. She turns everything into a fanfare."

"I think it's sweet." Cora headed into the little open-concept kitchen where Trent was making the coffee. He placed one steaming mug in front of her along with a carton of milk and a bowl of sugar with a small, gold spoon sticking out of it. "She clearly put a lot of effort into it."

"A lot of effort that *we* will have to replicate."

Cora smiled at his use of "we." It felt like they were a team in this, despite their dramatic first introduction. And being on someone's team wasn't a feeling she'd had in a really long time. "So you weren't big on arts and crafts as a kid?"

"Uh no, that was strictly Liv and Mum's hobby. My brother Jace is a comic book artist, so I guess we could put him in that category, too. Well, minus the glue guns and shit. But the rest of us boys were firmly in the sports and outdoor activities camp." He dumped some milk into his coffee and waded a spoon through it. "Footy, cricket, tennis, surfing. If there was a competition attached—we'd play it."

"Sounds like that would take the whole sibling rivalry thing to the next level."

Trent laughed. "Yeah, you could *definitely* say that. You'll see it in action, anyway. Nick is on our cricket team and Adam fills in sometimes if we're down a player."

"I *really* don't think my being on your team is a good idea." Cora sipped her coffee and tried not to stare at Trent's half-naked form. The man was *literally* physical perfection. And, as someone who had great appreciation for the written word, she didn't use that particular one lightly. "I can promise you the only time I would ever hit a ball would be in self-defense, and only *then* because the planets aligned and I made contact out of sheer coincidence."

Trent shook his head. "You can't be *that* bad."

"Trust me, if I'm a bad person and I go to hell… it'll be some kind of batting practice." She shuddered at the thought. "Growing up, I was that kid with a nose in my book at all times."

Well, when her mother wasn't berating her for being "antisocial."

"It doesn't matter—we're competitive, but we're not sore losers. Besides, the biggest thing at stake is a round of beers afterward." Trent took a long sip of his coffee. "It's a social thing, and it doesn't matter if you're any good. That's not the point of it."

As much as she knew she'd be awful, the thought of spending more time with Trent wasn't exactly *un*appealing, to say the least. Like his sister, he was friendly and down-to-earth. A veritable antidote for the snobby people she'd grown up with, for whom judgment and ridicule were their sports of choice.

"How novel to do something for the fun of it," she said, a bitter tone lacing her words. But then she shook her head, determined not to let her baggage cast a shadow over her time in Australia. "Anyway, if you accept my total lack of skills, then I look forward to footing the bill for beers afterward."

Trent eyed her. Clearly he hadn't missed her little comment—just another thing she'd shown him about herself, and which she should have kept locked away.

A knock at the front door interrupted the conversation, and Cora took the opportunity to duck into Liv's bedroom and change out of her pajamas. If Trent was working on the plumbing, then she'd park herself outside and spend a little time with her manuscript. At least that way she could work on her tan at the same time—multitasking for the win!

She gathered up her laptop and the printout of the feedback letter her father had written for her, on which she'd scrawled a bunch of notes. Trent was talking to another man—a guy with dark hair, a beard, and a full sleeve of tattoos down one arm.

"Cora, this is Hale. He's our local plumber extraordinaire." Trent grinned. "And Cora is a friend of Liv's. They're house swapping at the moment."

"I'm also the source of the water damage," she said, sticking her hand out. Hale clamped his big bear paw of a hand around hers and gave her a firm handshake. He had mischievous brown eyes that crinkled good-naturedly when he smiled.

"Uh no, that blame lies entirely with this clown here for not turning off the mains." He jerked his head toward Trent. "Now, if you'd gotten a *real* plumber to do the job—"

"Yeah, yeah." Trent rolled his eyes. "Enough with the self-promotion."

"Just saying." Hale held up his hands. "If I were here, there wouldn't have been a problem."

"If you hadn't moved your noisy girlfriend into our house, I wouldn't even have been here to start work on the plumbing yet."

Ah, so Hale was the former roommate. To Cora's surprise, the big man blushed. "Well yes, you know…honeymoon period and all that."

"I'm joking. You know I think Aimee is great. I haven't seen you this happy in years," Trent said with a wink. "I won't hold the screaming against either one of you."

Hale shot him a look that said if his friend didn't shut up, he was likely to be *made* to shut up. "I'd say we're square now, seeing as you don't seem to own any shirts."

Cora clamped a hand over her mouth, stifling a laugh.

Hale nudged Trent with his elbow, clearly encouraged by her reaction. "Seriously. If this guy walked around with his shirt off any more, they'd start giving him Matthew McConaughey's movie parts."

"Couldn't come up with a more recent example than that?" Trent laughed.

"What about Channing Tatum?" Cora supplied. She could *very* easily see Trent giving it some Magic Mike action. Rolling hips and rippling abs and that sexy, panty-melting wink.

Ma'am, you need to keep your hormones under control.

"Oh, definitely," Hale said. "Anyway, it's nice to meet you, Cora. I hope you're enjoying our little slice of paradise down here in Patterson's Bluff."

"I landed yesterday, so I haven't seen too much. But from what I can tell so far, I think I'm going to love it here."

"Ah well, good thing you've got the town charmer to show you around."

Cora raised an eyebrow. "Town charmer?"

Now it was Trent's turn to shoot his friend a look. "Hale's jealous I was more popular in high school."

Hale snorted. "Yeah right. And you didn't even finish high school, so I never got the chance to catch you."

Something flashed across Trent's face—so quick and so fleeting, Cora wondered if she'd imagined it. But then he raked his hand through his hair and winked at Cora. "Better to quit when you know there're better things out there, right?"

Hmm. Wasn't that what her ex had said to her? They were from different types of families and no amount of trying was going to change that, so it was better to quit and find a better match. That had cut to the bone. She'd tried *so* hard to be his best match.

"Anyway, I'm not paying you to stand around talking shit," Trent said, slapping a hand down on Hale's back.

"I wasn't aware you were paying me at all," his friend ribbed back. "But yes, let's get this show on the road. I've got a job at twelve that's been rescheduled twice already, so I have to be on time."

"Yell out if you need anything, okay?" Trent smiled at Cora, and it sent a shiver all the way down her spine. When he looked at her, there was an intensity to his gaze—like he saw something more than she wanted him to.

Maybe that's why they call him the town charmer. He makes everyone *feel seen.*

But no matter how good it felt to have a man's attention burning her up, she couldn't get used to that feeling. Cora knew how quickly a fire could burn out—she'd been dumped by every single guy she'd ever dated. Every. Single. One.

Maybe it was time to stop trying.

Cora headed outside to where a deck overlooked the backyard. A table sat with two wicker chairs, lovingly decorated with blue-and-white-striped cushions. The backyard seemed to go on forever, with huge trees on all sides leading into dense bushland. Maybe she'd take a walk later, get in touch with nature. And Central Park, gorgeous as it was, didn't have the same peaceful vibe, what with all the tourists and street performers.

Cora settled down on one of the chairs and looked at the printout of the rejection letter her father had given her, telling her all the ways her manuscript sucked. It stung, of course. But her father only pushed her so that she would be better. He wasn't like her mother, burning down every one of Cora's dreams in order to make her fit some fictional fantasy daughter mold. Her father had a good eye, and she would do everything in her power to make this book good enough that he would take her on as a client of the agency.

Cora, I finished your novel last night. I know you worked very hard on this and I can see you really want to do well. I love you, sweetheart, and it pains me to tell you this book isn't publishable. For starters, a character with such insecurities about her own worth is unsympathetic. People want to be inspired. They don't want to read about a woman who is so desperate to be loved that she has no idea who she is. That woman isn't a heroine.

For some reason, that last sentence made tears prick the backs of Cora's eyes, but she blinked them away. She could do better with her story. She could make her heroine stronger and more resilient. More confident. She could wow her father. Make him proud.

Make him believe in her.

And that was a *way* better thing for her to focus on, instead of how Trent's lingering gaze made her feel more alive than she had in months.

CHAPTER SIX

Trent and Hale stood back and surveyed their work. The plumbing was now in much better shape, with the sink reinstalled and everything sealed up. Trent had the shower running, and only the sound of water rushing against tile could be heard.

No more ghost-in-chains rattling for this house.

"Thank God," Trent said, shutting the taps. "I don't know how Liv has put up with that sound the past few months. It was so loud, it sounded like the whole bloody house was coming apart at the seams."

"Lucky she's got big brother to help her out." Hale crouched down to throw the last of his tools into the heavy metal box with his business name etched into the side. "Are you going to tell her about the flood?"

Trent shrugged. "Why bother her with it? It wasn't Cora's fault, and we've fixed it all now."

"You don't want to get the American in trouble. That's sweet." Hale chuckled and rubbed a hand over his thick, dark beard. "You know, something struck me about her. She looks exactly like—"

"I know."

"Like…a lot. They could be related."

"They're not." He'd know if someone was related to his toxic Venus Flytrap of an ex. Mainly because the family traits included horns and pitchforks. "It's an odd coincidence, nothing more."

"What ever happened to Rochelle?" Hale asked, picking up his tool kit and heading out into the main room.

"She moved to the city, got married, and started popping out kids."

All with the guy Trent had caught her with. In their bed. He remembered the day like it was yesterday—he'd had a funny feeling when he couldn't reach her, so he'd come home early to find her screwing her best friend. The best friend she "thought of as a brother."

One of the many lies she'd told him.

Rule number one of relationships: never trust anything that comes out of someone's mouth unless you can categorically prove it.

Only Trent hadn't wanted to let people know he'd been duped—it had made him feel like a dickhead. He never told *anyone* that she'd cheated on him. Instead, he'd acted like he was bored of her and had avoided anything long-term ever since. He leaned into being the "town charmer" and used his charisma to mask the hurt.

But Trent wouldn't make the mistake of trusting someone ever again. Even the people he cared about most in this world—his family—had hidden things from him. And if he couldn't trust them, he couldn't trust anyone.

After Hale left, Trent spied Cora through the sliding glass doors, sitting outside on the little deck that was badly in need of a sand, stain, and refinish. She sat on one of the wicker chairs, her leg dangling over the arm as she worked. Her toenails were painted a bright, fiery red, and she swung her foot back and forth with a gentle rhythm.

Her hair tumbled down her back, glinting all shades of caramel and toffee and deep gold. Like everything about Cora, it was perfectly styled even if it looked like it wasn't styled at all. Because a woman like that knew how to pay attention to the details.

He'd seen the notes she started putting together on Liv's project—the care and diligence in jotting down every single thing.

"Arck! Ya bastard!"

Trent's head snapped to the open window, where a cockatoo sat, head cocked and crest fully fanned. The damn thing showed up on the daily, looking for the lunch that his sister so happily provided. That was Liv—friend to all, including creatures of any size.

"You're a nuisance," he told the bird. "And rude, too."

Joe the Cockatoo whistled. *"Who's a pretty boy?"*

"You, buddy, you're the pretty boy." He walked over to the windowsill and held out his arm. The bird hopped straight on, happy to be chauffeured to his meal. His big, gray claws gripped Trent's arm, the sharp talons scratching against his skin. "Ease up. I don't want you leaving a mark."

He walked the bird over to the bag of bird seed and dug his free hand in, scooping out a small amount the way he'd seen Liv do. Then he nudged the sliding door open with his foot and headed out onto the deck. Joe squawked in protest. Clearly, he wasn't used to waiting for his food.

"Hey."

Cora almost jumped about ten feet in the air and snapped her laptop closed. "Way to sneak up on me…again."

"Jumpy?" He grinned.

Pressing a hand to her chest, Cora laughed. "I see you brought a friend."

"I'd use the word 'friend' loosely," Trent quipped. "Scavenger, maybe. Or sponge."

Joe snapped his head toward Trent as if to say, *Excuse moi? Scavenger?*

"I think you insulted him." Cora's pale eyes sparkled, and she swung her long legs to the ground.

Trent slowly uncurled the hand containing the seed, and the bird eyed it eagerly. Then he walked all the way up Trent's arm, across his shoulders, and down his other arm, as if using the man's body as his own personal climbing equipment.

"Doesn't that hurt?" Cora watched, fascinated. "I mean, look at those sharp things."

"He's pretty gentle, actually." Trent watched as the bird got a good grip on his hand and bent forward to enjoy his lunch, his beak tickling the inside of Trent's palm. "I suspect he might have been a pet at some point. Possibly belonging to the people who lived here before Liv bought the place."

"And they abandoned him?" Cora's eyes widened. "That's so sad."

"Some people have no idea what trust means," he said darkly.

Um, how did you make this about you?

"I mean…" He scrambled for something to make a connection to that sentence so it didn't seem like he'd shared something too personal. "People dump pets all the time. The shelter here is always full. It's disgusting."

"I agree." Cora stood slowly, so as not to spook Joe. Then she came closer and watched him eat from Trent's palm. "I take it you're an animal lover?"

"I'm not the kind of person to make a menagerie out of my home, but yeah. I have a soft spot for the underdogs of the world." He grinned. "We had guinea pigs growing up, and my parents were always taking in strays and playing babysitter to other people's animals. One time we had a baby goat with his leg in a splint."

"I was never allowed to have pets growing up," Cora said wistfully.

"No pets *and* no sports. What kind of childhood robbery is that?" It sounded like Cora had grown up in quite an unusual environment.

"Like I said, my parents were strict." She shrugged as though it wasn't a big deal, but her face was a smooth, beautiful mask. Hiding her hurt away.

"Want to feed him?" Trent held his arm closer to Cora, and she bit down on her lip, a mixture of excitement and nerves radiating in the air around her.

"He won't take a chunk out of me?"

"Naw. He's a softie." Trent chuckled. "Foul-mouthed, but a softie."

He moved his arm closer to Cora and nudged

the bird so he'd step onto her arm. Joe flapped his wings, his crest fanning out in a flash of brilliant yellow, and Cora sucked in a breath.

"Easy," Trent said. "You're all right."

He tipped the seed into her open palm, and Joe repositioned himself and went back to his lunch. The bird's charcoal beak nudged her palm, burrowing into the little well of seed as he ate.

"It tickles," she said, her voice sparkling with unreleased laughter. "Gee. He's heavy, too."

The pure, childlike wonder on Cora's face made her seem even more gorgeous—because it was something beyond her glossy hair and endless legs and the pearls dangling from her ears. It was more than how incredible she looked in a scant bikini. More, even, than the way her eyes had coasted over him this morning when she thought he couldn't see her watching him. Those things were attractive, sure.

But the look on her face right now was like pure gold.

"Do you really think his family left him behind?" Her eyes drifted up to his. "I can't bear the thought of it."

"He's doing okay." Trent stroked the front of the bird's chest, enjoying the soft, downy feel of his white feathers.

"Did Liv name him Joe? Seems like an odd choice for a bird."

"Oh, she never told you?" Trent chuckled, pulling his phone from the back pocket of his jeans. "Watch this."

He pulled up the YouTube app, searched for the

song "You Can Leave Your Hat On," and pressed play. The sound of Joe Cocker blared out of the phone's tiny speakers and the bird froze, a little seed rolling out of his beak. As the song started playing, he stretched up to full height and fanned out his crest before leaping onto the railing that enclosed the small deck.

"Go on, little guy," Trent encouraged him. "You know you want to."

As the song neared its famous chorus, Jos started bouncing his head and waving his foot up and down in time with the beat. Then he went into full head-banger mode, bowing and rising with the time of the music, giving a little shake every so often as if enjoying the music so much that his whole body was alive with it.

Cora let out a delighted laugh. "Joe Cocker... Joe Cockatoo. Clever."

"I was working on the house not long after Liv bought it, before she'd even moved in, and I had some old rock music blaring. This little guy came to the window and got his groove on." Trent grinned at the memory. "Now I always try to play something for him so he'll come visit."

"I can't believe anyone would leave you behind." Cora made a clucking sound and Joe chirped in response.

"Bugger it!"

Cora laughed and looked at the bird. "I was about to say you were a total sweetheart, but then you had to go and curse me out."

"Seems the previous owner didn't have much of a verbal filter," Trent said. "He's got quite the repertoire."

"Maybe I can teach him a thing or two while I'm here." She rubbed her finger against the bird's feathered breast. "Give him a few nice things to say. Or at least some American curses."

At that moment, Joe decided the hangout was over. He launched himself into the air with a powerful flap of his white wings and, a second later, disappeared into the densely packed trees behind Liv's property. Cora scattered what was left of the seed onto the grass.

"On that note, are you ready for a change of scenery?" Trent asked.

"Sure."

His smile broadened. "Good. Throw your bathers on. I'm taking you to the beach."

●●●

Fifteen minutes later, Cora followed Trent down a set of wooden stairs that led to the Patterson's Bluff beach. The sun was out in full force, and it beat down on her shoulders and back and arms, as if recharging her. There was something so invigorating about the beach, something so... restorative.

The planks were warm beneath her bare feet, and the cool breeze brought the briny scent of sea and sunscreen to her nostrils. There were plenty of people out enjoying the glorious weather. Young families frolicked at the water's edge, and a group of teenagers battered a giant beachball around in the waves. There were even a few dogs enjoying themselves, chasing tennis balls and carrying sticks and doing all kinds of adorable doggy things.

Trent waved to a group farther up the sandy stretch. A group of men and women were all in beach gear—board shorts and swimsuits and bikinis. It was like an Australian tourism ad, bronzed beautiful people with salt-drenched hair and tanned skin and beaming smiles. Suddenly Cora felt like an outsider—like she was intruding on their perfect world.

"I didn't know we were meeting people," she said, suddenly feeling self-conscious. When Trent offered nothing more than a cavalier wink, a sinking feeling settled in the pit of Cora's stomach. *Uh-oh.* "Why do I have a feeling this is sports related?"

He laughed and bumped her arm, walking close to her. He'd showered before they left, and the scent of citrus soap was still fresh on his skin. "You know me so well already. Like I said yesterday, my cricket team is down one."

"You asked them if it was okay for me to join, right?" she said. Back home, in her parents' social circles, everything was invite-only, exclusivity worth even more than money. And turning up unannounced was not only frowned upon, but a quick way to become a social outcast.

Back in the Cabots' world, a person had to earn their place.

Trent looked at her, his brows wrinkled in confusion. "It's a public beach; everyone is welcome here."

"Right." She adjusted her sunglasses. "I just…

You don't have to babysit me, is all. If you want to hang out with your friends, you don't need to let me tag along."

Trent stopped dead in his tracks and turned to her, placing his hands on her upper arms. The warmth of his touch infused her with a lightly sparkling quality, like someone had tipped champagne into her bloodstream.

"You're officially invited, Cora. Besides, I thought you might want to meet some of Liv's friends." His lips pulled up into a devilish smile. "I also want to see if you're as terrible at sport as you predict."

"Well, that's just mean," she said, ducking her head and laughing. "Oh God, this is going to be so embarrassing."

"What's life if you're not embarrassing yourself from time to time, right?" He gave her a gentle shake. "And you'll learn one thing about us Aussies—we don't mind having a laugh at ourselves. In fact, I'd almost go as far as to say it's a national pastime."

Trent was so…unpretentious and kind. He was unlike any of the men she'd met back home, who all seemed to want to know her social pedigree, education level, and employment history before agreeing to a second date.

Yeah, but you're not dating Trent.

Could have fooled her body for all the little fireworks going off in her belly.

"How do you do that?" she asked.

He cocked his head. "What?"

"Make people feel instantly comfortable?"

His eyes searched her face, and she wondered if he felt the little crackle of energy that passed between them. It was fizzy and wonderful and it set her skin ablaze. In only one day, Cora was *feeling* again. That cold, unrelenting numbness she'd been drowning in back in New York was starting to crack and fall away.

God, she would owe Liv forever for this trip.

"It's one of my many talents," Trent said with a shrug. "Come on, let me introduce you to the team. I have a feeling you'll fit right in."

They stepped down onto the sandy beach, and Cora scrunched her feet up to feel the warm grains sliding between her toes. It was heavenly here—a natural paradise. Waves *whoosh*ed to and fro, crashing into foam at the shoreline and racing up the beach to the sound of delighted squeals and the indignant squawk of seagulls. Trent's friends stood around a small blue and white box that looked like a cooler. On the ground was a bat the likes of which Cora had never seen before and a few tennis balls.

"Everyone, this is Cora. She's a friend of Liv's and is staying with us for the month. She has also… never played cricket." Trent stepped back from her with his fingers crossed as if she had a contagious disease, and everyone laughed. "We need to educate her in the way of our nation's greatest sport."

"Nice to meet you all." Cora held her hand up in a shy wave.

"This is my big brother Nick." Trent pointed to a guy Cora could have picked out as Trent's sibling even without the introduction—they had the same blue eyes and blond hair and broad smiles. "Then we have Kellen and Leigh, who run the gym on Main Street. Maddy is our resident book pusher—"

"*Happy* to be called that," Maddy said, sticking her hand out. She had long black hair, amber eyes, and brown skin with intricate tattoos running up her left arm. "I run Just One More Chapter near the town hall."

"I love that name so much," Cora said, beaming and already making mental plans to visit.

"Then we have Skye." Trent gestured to a woman in a fire-engine-red bathing suit who had total *Baywatch* vibes, right down to her wavy blond hair. "And her brother, Dean. They're both in service of our great state. Skye works as a constable at the police station off Main Street and Dean works in OH&S out in the Frankston precinct."

"That's a fancy way of saying I help officers get back on their feet after an injury," Dean said. "Since many, like my dear sister here, don't always give a thought to their own well-being in the course of their job."

"Ha." Skye rolled her eyes. "I'm fit as a fiddle."

She wasn't kidding. Skye was lean, with broad shoulders and the kind of definition in her arms that Cora could only ever achieve with a contouring stick. Despite looking like a supermodel, Skye clearly could snap a person over her well-toned thigh if she wanted to.

"Thanks for letting me join your team," Cora said, taking a moment to shake all their hands.

"We were *desperate* for another woman," Skye

said, bringing a water bottle to her lips and tipping her head back. "The team is testosterone heavy enough as it is."

Trent nudged Cora in the ribs. "Told you."

"Well, I hope *you* told *them* that not only have I never played cricket, but that I am probably the worst athlete you'll ever come across." She grimaced. "So apologies in advance."

"We play for fun, right, team?" Maddy said with a twinkle in her eye. "Right, Nick? Kellan?"

The two men grumbled something incoherent, earning them a swat each from Maddy.

"Well, *I* say we play for fun," she said. "And today is an excuse to hang out anyway—we've got our first game of the season next week, so plenty of time for you to practice."

A week was *not* plenty of time. But Cora decided right then and there that her trip to Australia wasn't simply about getting some space from her troubles back home and working on her novel. This time would be a chance for her to let loose, go with the flow, and be spontaneous—all things that she wouldn't *dare* do normally.

Because one thing was certain, whatever she'd been doing for the last several years of her life had gotten her absolutely freaking nowhere. What did she have to show for all that time of trying to win others over? A failed engagement, a job that she'd only gotten because of her father and that came with no advancement opportunities, and a fancy apartment that felt like a gilded cage.

She didn't have to be that person here. She could be anyone. Even herself.

CHAPTER SEVEN

"Okay, this is my beach cricket lesson, speed edition." Trent picked up the bat and handed it to her. The rest of the group were applying sunscreen, drinking water, or chatting among themselves while waiting for the action to get started.

The bat was strange — flat on one side and pointed on the other. She'd heard people say that baseball and cricket were kind of comparable, but she'd only ever seen baseball before. Yankees box seats, through her father's work, and she hadn't paid much attention to the game. Given her minimal interaction with sports as a kid, she found it hard to follow.

But she knew how they held the bat, at least. So she hiked it over her right shoulder, unsure whether the flat or the pointed side was supposed to be facedown.

Trent chuckled. "In cricket, we hold the bat to the ground."

"Oh." Cora's cheeks warmed. "Whoops."

"Let me show you." He guided the bat off her shoulder. "This part is called the toe, but that's basically a fancy way of saying the bottom of the bat. We stand side-on, flat part forward and swing with that toe coming down toward the ground."

Trent executed a movement, pretending he was holding a bat. Cora swallowed. Unlike the others, he still had a T-shirt covering his top half. But the soft white cotton hugged his body in a way that was mouth-wateringly perfect. As he twisted, the movement enhanced the broadness of his shoulders and the trim vee of his waist, and it made the muscles in his arms flex and bulge.

Good Lord. What do they feed the men down here?

"Okay," Cora mumbled, trying to mimic the movement. But clearly, she'd been too busy checking out Trent's cut physique to actually figure out what she was supposed to do, because her swing was clunky and awkward.

"It'll be easier if I help put you into position." He came closer. "Do you mind getting up close and personal for a second?"

"No." The word came out like a dry croak.

Dear *Lord*. Getting up close and personal with Trent wasn't going to help her learn how to play cricket at all. Because her brain was already speeding toward Jell-O territory as it was. But he came around behind her, his hands moving to her wrists. The warmth of him seeped into her body, stoking the fire already burning bright.

"Let's get you into a setup position." He maneuvered her body, making her face to one side. "Start the bat here, with the toe touching the sand. Always have the face—which is the flat bit—facing the front. Then we're going to flex your wrists and bring the bat back a little and then swing through."

He was being a gentleman, keeping some space between them, but it was impossible not to get close with the swinging motion. Trent's thighs grazed her ass and the touch—subtle and innocent as it was—made her blood pulse hard and hot in her veins. She wanted to arch back into him, to feel his body cradle hers.

To feel those strong, muscular arms wrap around her like they might whisk her away from her troubles forever.

"Let's try that again." Trent helped her draw the bat back, flexing her wrists so that the bat was raised and sweeping it down toward the sand and following through as if she'd made connection. "Much better."

When he stepped back, the loss of him was an echo through her body. "I think I've got it…kinda."

"You got it all right." His blue gaze coasted over her, tracking her face and then down her body with a liquid, languid slowness that made her toes curl into the sand. "Want to try a real hit?"

"Sure." She let out a shaky breath.

Trent reached down and plucked a tennis ball from the sand, the granules already clinging to his feet and legs. He had golden hairs dusting his legs and arms, and the sunlight made his head look as if it was covered with an angelic blond cap.

"We play on the harder sand, so the balls will bounce," he explained as he backed up. "I'm going to bowl to you now, but the bounce can be unpredictable. So try your best and don't worry if you miss. No one is judging you."

Cora took up position, placing her bat down and then flexing her wrists back as she waited for Trent to bowl. He grinned at her from several feet away, his eyes delightfully crinkled as he squinted in the sun. When he bowled, she was so struck by how gracefully he moved—with power and speed and an economy of movement that made his body slice through the air as though it took him no effort at all. The ball whizzed straight past her and hit the cooler with a dull *thud*.

She picked the ball up and tossed it back to him. "Let's pretend that didn't happen."

Trent chuckled. "I didn't see a thing, I swear."

"Good." She shuffled her bare feet, setting them hip-width apart and getting her bat into position.

Trent waited a moment and then bowled to her again. She watched the flash of the yellow tennis ball as it flew toward her, then she cocked her hand back and swung clean through the air. *Thump*. The ball hit the cooler again.

Cora made a frustrated growl in the back of her throat. This was ridiculous. He wasn't even bowling that hard; she should be able to make a connection. But the third and fourth bowls were equally as bad, nothing but the *whoosh* of the air as her bat sailed into nothingness.

She felt the weight of everyone watching her, and though no one seemed to be judging her, having an audience was playing into all her old fears. She flashed back to the time she'd choked at her conservatory's annual Christmas performance, almost dying of mortification as the conductor shook his head in disappointment.

"You've got to relax," Trent said. "No point getting frustrated. The ball can smell fear."

She wanted to hand over the damn bat and walk away—maybe go and hide back at Liv's place and refuse to get near a piece of sporting

equipment ever again. But that was New York
Cora speaking—the side of her whose fear of failure was so stifling and intense, she didn't often try
new things.

Cora took a deep breath. She let the sun soothe
her limbs and the sand support her feet. She let the
bat feel comfortable in her hands as she soaked it
all in. Aussie Cora was going to have fun, even if
she was the worst player on the team by a long
shot.

"I'm ready," she said.

Trent bowled again, and Cora narrowed her
gaze, letting the sound of the waves and children
shrieking and gulls crying fade into nothing. She
stepped forward and swung, the ball clipping the
side of the bat and bouncing a ruler's-length away.
It was probably the shittiest hit of all time, but it
was still a hit.

"Yeah!" Trent fist pumped the air. "See, I knew
you'd get it."

"Consider yourself initiated," Nick said with a
grin. "Everyone ready?"

"How about boys against girls?" Maddy suggested with a mischievous gleam in her eye. She
adjusted the straps on her sleek black one-piece.
"But we'll need one male sacrifice to even things
up."

"More than happy to defect." Leigh jogged
over, his longish hair flopping with each stride. "I'm
feeling confident, ladies! Let's smash these blokes."

Cora laughed as Skye swung her arm around
Leigh's shoulders, trying to knuckle his hair. The
rest of the guys hung their heads together, talking

strategy in a loose huddle. But the heat of Trent's gaze bored into her, stronger and more potent than the full sun overhead. It was hard to shake the jittering energy that flowed through her veins, anticipation swirling like a tornado through her body. Tearing up her reason and sensibility and logic.

Trent pulled his T-shirt up, the white cotton making way for toned abs and a broad chest and those delectable vee muscles driving down into the waistband over his board shorts... Well, Cora wondered if maybe there wasn't really anything *so* wrong with indulging every once in a while.

What happens in Australia stays in Australia?

But she quickly brushed the thought off. Getting involved with another guy would be jumping from the frying pan into the fire.

More like into the inferno.

Exactly. A guy like Trent would burn her to ash, and she needed to protect herself right now. Protect her heart and her head, protect all the wounds still raw from her failed-before-it-ever-started marriage.

She wasn't ready to open herself up to anybody yet. Not matter how tempting.

• • •

Several hours later, Cora's statement was confirmed: she *was* the worst cricket player in history. She hadn't hit a single thing.

However, watching her run for the ball, curly hair flying out behind her, smile as wide as the coast, was easily the most beautiful thing Trent had ever seen. When she let go, Cora was joyous. Luminous. She outshone and out-sparkled everything around her.

Now, the whole crew—joined by a few extra friends—were crowded around a collection of tables at the White Crest that they'd jammed together to fit everyone. Food was being passed around, beer glasses were clinking, and it was as noisy and cheerful as ever.

"So, tell us again how you forgot to turn off the water mains." Dean stuffed a chip into his mouth and munched, shaking his head. "Rookie move, bro. Even *I* know that."

"Yeah, even Dean knows that, and he can't change a bloody lightbulb on his own." Skye rolled her eyes.

"Uh, *not* true. The reason I wouldn't change that bulb was because there was a giant spider in the fixture." Dean shuddered. "Huntsmans are the worst."

"What's a huntsman?" Cora asked, looking on from her seat with interest. She'd piled all her hair on top of her head and a few curls, fortified with saltwater, had fallen out around her face.

An evil grin passed over Skye's lips. "Should I show her a picture?"

"Hell no!" Dean thumped a hand down on the table. "If you start pulling out the spider pictures, I am out of here."

Trent laughed. "How did you survive living in this country for so long with a fear of spiders, mate? They're harmless."

"He squealed like a little girl when I took the light fixture off and the damn thing went scuttling across the roof." Skye laughed as her brother rolled his eyes. "I thought he was going to faint."

"Oh, well, since we're sharing family stories, how about I share the time you freaked out when that moth flew into your bedroom?" Now it was Dean's turn to look evil.

"Moths?" Trent asked. "Really, Skye? I thought you weren't scared of anything."

"Not all moths, just the big ones. They're so… erratic." She shuddered. "I tried to trap it under an empty ice cream container, but its wings were too big."

Poor Cora looked like her eyes were about to pop out of her head.

"Stop it," Leigh said, shaking his head. "You're scaring our guest."

Our guest. Trent winked at Cora across the table, and her lips automatically curved up into a smile. There'd been no doubt in his mind that his mates would accept Cora into their group, even if she was only around for a few weeks. She and Maddy already had plans to grab coffee so she could show Cora around the bookstore.

"Maybe they should issue a survival guide when they check your passport at the airport," Cora said. She'd ordered a Diet Coke and took a long sip on the straw—which made Trent's mouth suddenly run dry. The sight of her pink, glossy lips wrapping around that straw…

He dragged his eyes back to his meal. The chicken parma had barely been touched, save for him snacking on a few of the chips piled to one side.

"Not hungry?" Nick asked with a raised brow. While the statement might appear to be a show of sibling concern, Trent knew better.

"Yes, I'm going to eat it all. Keep your mitts off." Growing up had been like that in their house—always fighting for the leftovers, especially when it came to his three older brothers, who all ate like horses. His mum had cursed the lot of them, saying it was like feeding an army every night.

But that was on her for producing boys over six feet tall. And Liv held her own when it came to her appetite, too.

"So, Cora is staying at Liv's, huh?" Nick asked as he sliced another piece of his half-eaten steak. "How's that working out with you being there, too? Seems odd that Liv would have arranged it like that."

"Uh, she didn't exactly arrange it like that," Trent admitted.

"She doesn't know you're there, does she?" Nick snorted. "You can't move into people's houses without asking first."

"One, I'm doing a crapload of work for her…for free, I might add. Two, did I mention I was working for free?" He speared a few chips onto his fork and dragged them through a small mound of tomato sauce. "Oh and three…she's not paying me."

"Well, you *refused* to take any money from her, so I'd say that's on you."

"She's working hard for not very much. I

remember what that's like." Trent's first few years as an apprentice were tough—minimal pay for long, grinding hours and generally getting treated like a lackey and a grunt. It was worth it in the end, and Liv was the smartest out of all his siblings, but it would still take her a few years to start reaping the rewards and so, in the meantime, if he could help, he would.

"Okay, so you're squatting in her house while she's got a guest staying there." Nick shook his head. "Classic Trent."

Unlike his siblings, Trent was very much a "go with the flow" kinda person. It definitely bucked against the rest of the Walters and their goal-setting, list-making, and rule-following ways. Really, it was one of *many* ways he was the odd one out.

"What? Cora and I talked it over. I told her she could go stay with Adam and Soraya, but she didn't want to." The conversation on the other side of the table had moved on to more Australian wildlife horror stories, and Kellen was recounting the time he had a close encounter with a red kangaroo. "Besides, she seems...like she could use the company."

There was something sensitive about Cora. Something...heavy. Like she was carrying a load on her shoulders.

"I'll bet you're *real* happy to provide her that company." Nick chuckled and took a swig of his beer.

"You make me sound like a creep," Trent protested. "It's not like that."

Except, in his head, it was *definitely* like that.

Maybe inviting Cora to beach cricket hadn't been the smartest move, because watching her bound around in skimpy black bathers had given him way too much late-night inspiration. The beach shower last night had been bad enough; now he had more mental images to keep him awake.

"You know, now that I'm looking at her, she kind of reminds me of—"

"Don't say it." Trent sighed and raked a hand through his hair. "I know, it's weird. I'm trying not to think about it."

Well, *that* was one way to stop his dick from leaping to attention. Thinking about his ex was enough to kill any attraction or positive feelings dead in the water. Ugh. Time to change the topic of conversation.

"How're the plans going for the new development?" Trent asked.

Nick sighed. "The new villas are coming along, but not as quick as I would like."

Nick and his business partners were in the process of seeking approval to build a development of small beachfront properties at the fringe of Patterson's Bluff. He had grand plans for a collection of villas with shared amenities, which would make the area more accessible to people who wanted a beautiful property by the beach but who didn't have huge budgets.

"What's the problem now?" Trent asked.

"We've generated enough 'interest' that we have a group protesting our plans. They think we're going to destroy the natural bushland and all the old trees in that area, to plonk down our...what did they call them? McMansions." Nick's nose wrinkled in disgust. "As if I would ever build a McMansion."

"It sounds like they know nothing about what you're trying to achieve."

"They don't." He shook his head. "And they're holding things up."

That would have to be *killing* Nick. The family joked that Nick's first word was "now" and he'd grown only more impatient ever since. His brain worked at the speed of light and he had a drive and ego to match. He was the family's "big thinker," the guy who always had a strategy for everything. Plan B didn't factor into his vocabulary, because he always got what he wanted first time around.

"So what are you going to do?" Trent asked.

"We're drafting a proposal to send to the council addressing the concerns," he replied. "But I have no intention of caving."

If anyone could figure a way out of that situation, it was Nick. "Well, once you get it all through, you know I'm on board to help with the construction. I think it's going to do great things for Patterson's Bluff."

"Thanks." Nick slapped him lightly on the back. "I'm going to need all the help I can get. I've got grand plans for this one."

"I'd expect nothing less."

Trent's eyes drifted across the table and farther down to where Cora was sitting. She was engaged in an animated discussion with Kellen about something and was gesturing wildly with a chip. That end of the table erupted in laughter, and

Cora's eyes sparkled. For some reason, she looked straight over to Trent then, and it was like being zapped with a live cable. Her cheeks and nose were pink from the sun, making her pale eyes look even more luminous by comparison. Even her teeth were pretty—which seemed like a weird thing to admire about a person. But they were straight and white and when she smiled it was...whoa.

Words couldn't do it justice.

"We need your help to settle an argument," Cora said, leaning forward slightly so her voice carried over to Trent. The pub was louder now—a footy game on in the background that had a row of patrons at the bar yelling intermittently. "What's this?"

She held up a red bottle with a tomato on it.

"Tomato sauce," Trent said.

"See," Kellen said. "Told you we don't say 'ketchup' in this country."

"You called it 'dead horse!'" she accused, laughing. "And I'm pretty sure neither tomato sauce *nor* ketchup is supposed to have horse in it."

"Ah, rhyming slang. Only used by people over the age of sixty...and Kellen," Trent teased. "Don't be fooled by his rippling abs. He's an old man in a young person's body."

"It's true." Kellen shrugged good-naturedly. "I could still kick your ass, though."

"So, day two in our fair country. What do you think so far?" Nick asked, leaning forward slightly so he could be heard by those at the other end. "I hope my little brother isn't giving you a bad impression."

"Says you." Trent snorted. "Who almost took out an innocent bystander by trying to catch a ball today?"

"All's fair in love and cricket." Nick would *never* risk dropping a ball just to prevent an injury.

The rest of the table ignored the brothers' banter—because there wasn't a day in any year where Nick and Trent weren't trading brotherly barbs—and turned toward Cora.

"It's so different to what I'm used to back home," Cora said with an almost shy smile. "You have a real slice of paradise here."

There was a hint of sadness in her tone, a down note that made Trent's protective urges swell. Whatever it was that Cora was hiding out from in Australia, he was going to make it his personal mission to show her a good time. To send her home happier than when she came.

In his mind, life was too short *not* to enjoy every experience you had. Sure, things didn't always go according to plan—he knew that better than anyone. Hell, his whole life had been upended, and at one point he'd questioned everything. His family. His home.

Whether or not he even deserved those things.

But that wasn't an excuse to wallow. How many great things would you miss out on if you were being a sad sack and staying home, alone? So *not* his style. After the breakup with Rochelle, he could have dug a hole for himself, trying to soothe those wounds with solitude and solo drinking.

Instead, he got back on his feet and found something to keep him busy. More work, more sport, more social activities. More, more, more. That way, he wouldn't have a quiet moment alone to let anger and sadness suck him down into a black hole. Eventually, the pain stopped knocking on his door, because it knew there would never be an answer.

Which was why Trent always wore his smile and never let anyone see what was going on inside.

CHAPTER EIGHT

The following day, Cora took the opportunity to explore Patterson's Bluff. Liv had offered Cora her car, and while it was hella scary driving on the other side of the road, there was something *so* freeing about rolling the windows down, blaring music out of the radio, and sucking in ocean air as she drove.

Talk about nature's therapy.

She explored the main drag, popping into the bookstore to visit Maddy, and then settled into one of the cafés facing the beach, where she had three coffees, because they tasted so damn good, and worked on her novel.

That night, however, there was other work to be done. Craft-related work. Trent had swung past his parents' house on the way home from the building site and had picked up a bunch of family albums they needed to start Operation Scrapbook Restoration.

"Do you think we should tell Liv about the… uh, damage?" Cora asked as she eyed the ruined gift, which had dried to a crusty, crunchy mess, with pages rippled by the water and ink bleeding all over the place. "I feel guilty keeping it from her."

"Why don't we tell her *after* we've redone all the work?" he replied. "Better to soften the blow."

"You're very good at handling people, aren't you?" She laughed.

You wouldn't mind if he handled you.

Great. Now even the most innocent of sentences was setting off the dirty-girl alarm in her head. He was wearing one of those tighter-than-should-be-legal T-shirts that should have had "touch me" written all over it. His hair was still damp from the shower, making it look dark gold instead of its usual sun-bleached shade.

"I've got three brothers. A smart one, a creative one, and an ambitious one. That makes me the charming one." He sent her a cavalier grin that Cora felt right down to the tips of her toes.

"How does Liv fit into all this?"

He chuckled. "She's the youngest and the only girl. Nothing else required."

"Ah, the golden child."

"By default." He winked. "Don't tell her I said that."

Cora made a zipping motion across her lips. "I promise."

They settled at the table, and Cora reached eagerly for one of the albums. Maybe it was weird, but she'd always had a strong sense of curiosity about other people's families. It was almost like studying a foreign species. When she was younger, all she ever wanted to do was watch sitcoms like *Malcolm in the Middle*, *Modern Family*, even reruns of *Full House*. These groups of people had trials and tribulations—they fought and butted heads. But they *always* came together in the end to mend hurts and strengthen bonds.

Her house had never been like that.

Catriona Cabot had ruled their house with an

iron fist, and her cold shoulder was frigid enough to chill the entire Upper East Side.

"Oh my gosh, look at you all!" The albums were labeled by year and contained such gems as baby "glamour" shots—cue furry mats and blurred edges—gap-toothed school photos, and cheesy family portraits, hair spiked with cement-strength gel. "Is that… Did you have an eyebrow ring?"

Trent groaned as he settled into the seat next to her. "It was a phase. A bad one."

Now that she looked at Trent closely, she noticed the little scar intersecting his eyebrow. In the picture, he sported a silver bar through one brow and a stud in the opposite ear. His blond hair was sun-bleached and spiked, and he wore baggy jeans. "You look like a Backstreet Boys member."

"One, seventeen-year-old Trent would be *most* insulted. It was System of a Down and Rage Against the Machine on my Walkman, thank you very much. And two, yeah… It wasn't a good look."

"Well, I'll raise your eyebrow ring with a belly piercing." Cora laughed when Trent's brows shot up.

"Seriously?"

"Oh yeah." She remembered the pain she'd gone through, hiding it from her mother. That summer she'd developed a preference for one-piece bathing suits and resorted to taping the piercing down so it wouldn't show through the clingy fabric. Eventually her mother had caught her, of course, and demanded Cora take it out on the spot. "I had a glow-in-the-dark one and everything."

He laughed, and it crinkled the corners of his

eyes in the most delightful way. "Hot."

Flushing, she flipped open another photo album. Trent's parents were capital-A adorable. His mother had one of those standard eighties perms, her blond hair fluffed out like a golden cloud around her head. She also sported some serious shoulder pads. His dad, on the other hand, had an epic mustache and huge wire-rimmed glasses.

Another photo showed his mother with her mirror image—another woman with matching fluffy blond hair and the same heart-shaped face. "Is your mother a twin?"

"Yeah." Trent bobbed his head, his expression difficult to read. "She *was* a twin."

"Oh." She traced a fingertip over their smiling faces. "I'm sorry."

"It happened when I was a baby, and Mum doesn't talk about it much."

"Tell me about your parents," Cora said as she picked through the pages, peeling back the clear layer protecting the photos and plucking out the ones they needed to photocopy.

"Dad was an English teacher and Mum taught Home Economics. They met at work, got married, and had a gazillion babies. The end," he said with a laugh. He pulled one album from the stack. Cora's list was in the middle of them, and he flipped the page, looking over her neatly written notes so he knew which photos to look for. "My family is pretty boring."

"Boring?" Cora blanched. "Are you kidding me? I would have *killed* to have a family like yours growing up."

"It's not all sunshine and roses," he said. "We've had our ups and downs."

"Ups and downs are one thing." She flipped over another page and smiled at a picture of Trent's parents holding a newborn baby, swaddled in a blue blanket. That must be baby number one: Adam. "Nationally televised scandals are another."

"Nationally televised?"

"My parents are…famous." She wrinkled her nose. Of all the F words in the world, this one was by *far* the worst. "My mother is a therapist who turned into a TV star by having a relationship segment on daytime TV. Think Dr. Phil but female. My father is a world-renowned literary agent."

"Sounds pretty good so far."

"Being in the public eye is…" She shook her head. "Frankly, I hate it. People are always watching your every move, waiting for you to slip up so they can document your mistakes for a quick buck. It's gross."

Trent watched her curiously, like one might observe something through glass at a zoo exhibit. She hated it when people looked at her like that, like a…specimen. Being the source of someone's curiosity made her uncomfortable.

"That's why you're here?" he asked. "To hide?"

She thought about denying it for a minute, but what was the point? It didn't matter what Trent thought of her. He didn't know her. Nobody did here. And she was taking a break from trying to win people over. "Yeah, basically. My parents are in the process of getting a divorce and it's…ugly."

Like, public screaming matches ugly. They'd

both ended up at a charity gig recently, drunk and mouthing off. Her father had decided to take a date—some sprite of a woman half his age with tits that looked like two half melons glued to her chest. He'd always been a better father than he was a husband, from what Cora could tell.

In any case, Cora's mother had flipped and someone had captured the whole thing on Instagram Live. So embarrassing.

"That really sucks." Trent frowned, and his concern was so genuine, it socked her in the chest. Even her ex hadn't been able to muster up much empathy, instead telling her it was "hardly shocking" they were splitting up.

Sure, it was true…but sometimes she needed a little sympathy and for someone to tell her everything would turn out okay, even if that wasn't 100 percent true.

"Honestly, it's probably for the best." Cora flipped another page open in the album, the smiling faces of the Walters family twisting her heart. "They didn't really love each other. My parents are…difficult. My mother likes to control people, and I think my father had enough of it by the end."

He should never have cheated on her mother, but there were times when Cora understood why he'd wanted out. There was only so long you could put up with someone trying to run your life.

"That's why she never let you have a pet or play sports?"

"And it didn't stop there." Cora felt all her old resentments rushing back up from the depths of her soul. "I couldn't eat anything with sugar in it, because God forbid I put on weight. I couldn't read anything that didn't get her seal of approval—no romance novels or anything like that. Hell, I only got to have my birthday parties the way *she* wanted them."

Cora sucked in a huge breath, suddenly aware that her voice had been getting higher and higher. God, she must sound so sad. What woman in her late twenties was still hanging on to childhood grudges about birthday parties?

But it wasn't about that, not really.

"Most people have only suitcases for baggage." She offered him a rueful, self-deprecating smile. "Looks like I brought something extra with me... and I am totally sucking the fun out of this."

Suddenly she was aware of how close they were sitting—knees and shoulders almost touching—and she wondered what it would feel like to turn her body toward his. To make contact.

You're wondering what it would be like for your knees to touch? Seriously? Did you hop into the DeLorean and travel back to high school?

But that's how he made her feel—young and fun and giddy in the *best* way possible. He made her feel shiny and new. Like her heart hadn't known pain and loss. Like it hadn't been shattered into infinite, irreparable pieces.

"Yeah, because looking at every bad fashion moment I ever had is *much* better," Trent said with a roll of his eyes. "We haven't even gotten to my goth stage yet."

"No!" Cora pressed a hand to her chest. "You're lying."

"I wish I was." He scrubbed a hand over his face.

"Okay, you *have* to show me now."

"Uh, no, all those photos have been disposed of," he said, holding up a hand. "Permanently. And anyone who might still have photos from back then has been threatened with all kinds of bodily harm."

Cora laughed with Trent as they pulled the rest of the photos. Liv's printer had a scanner, so they were able to get copies right away. That way Trent could return the albums before his parents came back from their trip without accidentally spilling the beans about their surprise gift.

Even if this whole thing *was* a disaster, it was proving to be a fun, glittery distraction and exactly what she needed. Not to mention that spending time with Trent was absolutely *not* a hardship. After the copies were done, they spread out all the necessary supplies for their crafting adventure—a scrapbook album with plenty of pages, glue sticks, glitter, tape, scissors with those funny crinkled edges, all "borrowed" from Liv's stash.

"I have a feeling this is going to get embarrassing." Trent picked up a strange implement with a rotating wheel and looked at it as though it were some kind of mystical artifact.

"Why's that?"

"I am the least creative person in my family. Seriously, my Christmas decorations were so bad as a kid, I caught my mum hiding them around the back of the tree whenever we had guests over."

"Oh no." Cora laughed and pressed a hand to her chest. "That's mean."

"I can't blame her. My 'Christmas rocket' really did look like a sparkly dick."

Now Cora laughed so hard, tears came to her eyes. The visual of little blond Trent and his sparkly Christmas dick-rocket was too much. "Okay, rule number one for scrapbooking: no phallic objects. How about I put you on glue duty?"

"The sparkly stuff is for more advanced crafters, is it?"

She grinned. "Let's just say they don't call it the herpes of the craft world for nothing."

It sounded like she knew exactly what she was doing when, in reality, any knowledge she had was taken from watching reruns of *Craft Wars* after her breakup. Because what could possibly say "my life is falling apart" more than watching reruns of *anything* with Tori Spelling in it?

"Okay, we've got reference material here—" She pointed to the now crinkled and crusty original version. "And photos here. All we have to do is recreate. I'm going to work on the heading, and you can work on the photos."

Trent cut the images out and applied glue to the back. It was amusing to see the dainty glue stick in his large, construction-worker hands. He even did that adorable thing where he stuck his tongue out of the side of his mouth in concentration.

"So you were never into art as a kid?" she asked as she filled in one of the letters with short, precise strokes.

"Not really." He leaned closer to stick the pictures down onto the pages, smoothing the edges with his thumbs. With the two of them working on the same thing, they were getting in each other's space, and Cora didn't mind one bit. "I always enjoyed working with my hands, but I preferred making things that people could use rather than things to be looked at. It's why I ended up leaving school—the idea of being able to get my hands dirty and spend all day outside was way too appealing."

"How did your parents take it?"

"Well, as I said before, they're both teachers. So…" He chuckled and raked a hand through his hair. "They weren't thrilled at first. But a family friend gave me a job and showed me the ropes, and I was always better at building things than I was sitting still in a classroom. They understood that."

"Your parents sound really supportive."

"They're realistic. Plus, they had four other kids pulling good grades, so what's one lost cause in the grand scheme of things?" he joked.

"Did they compare you?"

"It's only natural. People do it to siblings all the time, and we're so close in age that I guess it came with the territory," he said, sticking a photo down onto the scrapbook page. "But I'm not like my siblings."

There was something strange about his tone, a hint of emotion underneath the words that pricked Cora's ears up. As someone who created characters, she was always looking for the chink in someone's armor, the contradiction behind the mask they presented to the world. And even though Trent had appeared nothing less than perfect in the past forty-eight hours, those five simple words hinted at something less-than-perfect beneath the surface.

"I might not have inherited their desire for straight A's, but I'm still the reigning family champion at both Jenga and table tennis. I'm also better at cricket than Nick." Trent smiled and the unabashed cockiness made Cora laugh. "Not that he'd ever admit it."

"Your family seems so wonderful." Cora leaned back to look at her lettering. It wasn't as good as Liv's but it would pass muster. "I'm officially jealous."

"Stay a while. Maybe they'll adopt you."

"Don't tempt me," she muttered with a rueful smile. "Now, how the hell do you think we do this?"

Liv had made some little, flat ruffled thing to go along the bottom of baby Adam's photo. It looked like it was made out of washi tape, which she could identify thanks to Tori Spelling's craft tutelage. But that was based on Cora's very limited hands-on experience and, thus, couldn't be entirely trusted.

Trent looked at her with a blank expression. "I'm hoping that's a rhetorical question and not you expecting me to have a bloody clue about how we're supposed to do any of this."

Hmm.

"You hold it and I'm going to do the ruffling part." She pulled a strip of washi tape and handed the end to Trent. "Hold it straight."

"Yes, boss." His charming smile sent a jolt of lust right through her. How was she supposed to do anything with that expression aimed in her direction? Could neurons even exist around a smile like that?

She focused on trying to make the ruffles with the tape. Fold, stick, fold, stick, fold, stick.

"I don't think that looks right," Trent said, his nose wrinkled.

"Shh. I got this." Fold, stick, fold, stick.

"But aren't they supposed to be…even?"

Cora sighed and looked at her handiwork. Yeah, it wouldn't even pass kindergarten QA. But what else could they do?

"It's fine, we'll stick it on and sprinkle some glitter over the top." She bit down on her lip. "Glitter fixes everything."

"Hang on, I thought glitter was herpes? And that most definitely does *not* fix everything." Trent looked confused.

"No, that's because… Oh, never mind." She reached for the container of silver and gold glitter. "In this case, glitter is a good thing."

"Whatever you say."

She unscrewed the lid, and a little plume of shimmer mushroomed into the air—like a tiny, sparkling dust bomb. All she had to do was carefully sprinkle it over the washi tape, and…

Her nose twitched. Oh no. Cora had been voted "most likely to wake the dead with her sneeze" back in middle school. Her sneezes were no joke. They could wake a baby three houses down and had the velocity of a high-powered sportscar. Twitch, twitch.

It's okay, just put the container—

"Achoo!"

Glitter went flying…right into Trent's face.

For a moment, he didn't even move. He sat

there, like some fabulous drag version of the Tin Man from *The Wizard of Oz*. Silver and gold glitter coated his entire face, his hair…and everything. The container was now three-quarters empty, and Cora couldn't seem to budge her lips from their shocked *O* shape.

"You gave me sexually transmitted glitter," Trent said, eyes still closed.

"Don't blink." Cora set the container down and shoved her chair back, sending another fine cloud of glitter shimmering to the floor. Shit. "Craft glitter isn't meant for use around the eyes because it can scratch your cornea."

She could thank Tori Spelling for that tip.

"Excellent," Trent drawled. "Now how am I supposed to get this stuff off me?"

"Ummm…" Cora's mind spun. "I think water might be best, at least for most of it."

"Is it in my hair?"

Cora pressed a hand over her mouth at the sight of Trent's gorgeous blond locks looking like they'd been attacked by an angry gang of My Little Ponies. "Uh-huh."

"Shower might be best," he said, pushing up from his chair. He moved, hands outstretched, and almost walked straight into the sideboard. "If this was my old place, I'd know where everything was without needing to see."

"Let me help." Cora got up and took Trent by the hands. Walking backward, she guided him to the main bathroom and turned the taps on. Unfortunately, the shower was one of those tub-combo things. "I, uh… You might need a hand getting *into* the tub. I don't want you to slip and fall."

But it seemed he wasn't as perturbed by that idea as she was, and Trent had already ripped his T-shirt over his head, sprinkling glitter all over the bath mat. Then his belt buckle clanked as he yanked it open. The sound of his zipper lowering was like a knife through the thick air, and Cora's knees almost gave out on her as he shoved the denim down over his hips.

Holy *shit*.

There was perfection and *then* there was Trent's ass. Clearly cricket and whatever he did at work were doing amazing things to his body. The board shorts he'd worn to the beach didn't do it justice *at all*.

"Don't worry, I'm not going to take my jocks off," he said, sticking his hands out again. Cora helped him step one foot and then the other into the bath, where he bent forward slightly and stuck his head under the spray.

She tried *really* hard not to look down at the water running in rivulets over his body. Not to mention the bulge in the front of his underwear. Did the guy carry some extra stuffing down there for good measure? Good Lord!

Wrenching her gaze away and feeling hot enough to rival the surface of the sun, Cora made her exit from the bathroom under the guise of finding some coconut oil to help get the glitter out of his hair. That's apparently what all the girls used post-Coachella.

When she passed the table in the living area, she

cringed. Glitter was liberally dusted all over the carpet and table, with a hefty sprinkling on the scrapbook itself. Was she destined to ruin everything in this house?

Scouring the kitchen, she found a tub of coconut oil in the pantry and a roll of paper towels on the countertop. Now all she had to do was face Trent again and try not to ogle his junk. No biggie.

It was definitely a biggie.

She needed to stop that, right now. This whole situation was a disaster because Cora seemed to attract hot messes wherever she went.

"What's the common denominator, huh? Maybe *you're* the hot mess." She knocked on the bathroom door, and Trent called for her to come in. "Don't look at his junk, don't look at his junk, don't look at his junk…"

With a deep breath, she pushed the door open and found Trent still under the spray. He was magnificent…and shining like a Christmas tree ornament.

"I feel like I'm pushing it around," he said with a frustrated growl. "How is there more glitter now than when I started?"

She stifled a laugh, because this was all her fault and really, laughing would be like salt in the wound. "Turn the water off. I think we need to get some oil onto it and then try wiping it off with tissues."

"First you make me look like a cupcake and now you want to oil me down?" He raised a brow but complied with her instructions and wrenched the taps off. "Is this some weird kink you have?"

"Just wait until I bring out the horse bit and the tail," she quipped.

Trent threw his head back and laughed. "I guess I opened myself up to that one, huh?"

"You sure did." Cora went to the edge of the tub. "It's probably best if you stay there while you do the oil thing so you can wash off any residue afterward."

"This is going to be delightful." Trent groaned. "Told you arts and I don't go well together."

Cora dug out a glob of the oil and mushed it onto some paper towel. "Here, rub this over the glitter until it starts to stick and then use the towel to collect it all."

"This is ridiculous," Trent muttered, but he did as he was told.

Eventually most of the glitter was removed, and Trent looked like an oiled-up body builder minus the fake tan and bulging veins. Cora had turned to the side, so she wasn't tempted to stare, carrying on a conversation with Trent and handing him new paper towels and globs of oil as required. She'd gotten him into this glittery mess, and so she had to help him get out of it.

"I feel like a grease slick." He squirted some body wash into his hand and lathered it up over his chest. "And I am officially banning glitter from this project."

"Wait until you see the damage we did to the carpet."

"We?" He smirked. "Really? What do you have against carpets, anyway?"

"I'm just a klutz, apparently." So much for all

the years of charm school her parents had forced her through—she was still that bumbling, awkward girl who regularly dropped her books and never knew what to say.

Maybe it was a good thing she was repelling Trent with her awkwardness, because he was *way* out of her league. Who sneezed glitter all over the hot guy? Ugh. It was like a bad high school flashback. Like that one time she'd made a Valentine's card for her crush in history class and then tripped and fallen flat on her face while trying to stealthily slip it into his locker.

She'd never lived that one down.

"I'll, uh…start vacuuming the living room," she said, bundling up all the paper towels and backing out of the bathroom, keeping her eyes studiously averted from Trent's almost-naked form. Would it be possible for her to get through any more of this vacation *without* embarrassing herself?

Not likely.

CHAPTER NINE

As much as Trent loved his job—getting his hands dirty and seeing the fruits of his labor rise up from the ground, something he was *damn* good at—there was one thing he hated: the early starts. Even now, having worked for more than a decade in the construction industry, getting up before sunrise was a kick in the nuts.

He padded through his sister's quiet house. It was still dark outside, the dusky twilight casting a purple-tinted filter over the world. Soon the magpies would be warbling and rousing Patterson's Bluff from sleep.

Cora's door was closed, and not a sound came from the room. She'd crashed early last night, still thrown off by jetlag and—more likely—avoiding him after the glitter incident. Despite his telling her it wasn't her fault, Cora seemed determined to take responsibility. The poor woman had spent more than an hour trying to clean up the mess, vacuuming and wiping the table down and washing the bath mat and towel that had also been tainted with sparkles. He'd tried to help…but no dice.

It was a rare quality, he'd found. Most people seemed eager to toss blame onto the person next to them, passing it along like a game of hot potato. But not Cora.

By the time Trent made it to the building site, the sun was finally peeking above the horizon. The light was reddish and warm, predicting it was going to be another scorcher of a day. At the hottest part of the year in Australia—February, which was also known as the "holy shit everything is melting" month—construction work started early and finished early.

Trent's boots crunched over the loose gravel and soil as he walked from his ute onto the site. Nick was already pacing, speaking firmly into the mobile phone he white-knuckled beside his head. It didn't take a genius to figure out he was bitching out some supplier who'd failed him.

Woe *anybody* who failed Nick Walters.

"Bad day?" Trent asked when Nick hung up the phone.

His brother tipped his head back and looked up at the rapidly lightening sky as though God might poke his head out from behind a cloud and offer some advice. "Like every other bloody day on this job."

"You love it." Trent slapped a hand down on his back. "I don't know what you'd do with yourself if there wasn't someone to bark orders at."

"Good thing I've got you around," Nick said with a rueful smile. "Speaking of which, when are we getting started on *your* place?"

Ah, this old chestnut. "You know I've got a lot on my plate at the moment. I need to finish up with Liv's place before I even *think* about starting."

"Bullshit."

"It's not bullshit. Just because you're the kind of person who wants everything done yesterday doesn't mean I'm going to shirk my responsibilities to rush into my own project. Besides, I haven't found a design I like yet."

"I thought you met with that architect I recommended," Nick said, frowning.

"I did."

"And what tiny little flaw did you find with this guy, huh?" Trent's brother rolled his eyes with the kind of exasperation he often leveled at people who didn't match his breakneck speed. "The last one was too modern. The one before that was too traditional. And the one before *that* was too much of a mix of both."

"If I'm going to be laying down a few hundred grand and a year of my life for a house, I want it to be right." Trent shrugged. "What's wrong with that? I thought you were Team Never Settle."

"There's a difference between settling and being so picky that you don't move forward with anything." Nick reached for his silver thermos that was perched on a clipboard sitting atop a foldout chair. "If I didn't know any better, I'd say you were scared."

Trent snorted. Of all the big brother tactics Nick liked to pull as second-eldest of the Walters family, this one was *not* going to work. "If you're not a *little* scared of that level of commitment, then I'd question your understanding of how money works."

"Of course Mr. I Like To Keep My Options Open is worried about commitment. Why would I expect any different?"

Trent was used to Nick and his oldest brother, Adam, ribbing him about this. After all, Trent was the only one who'd hightailed it out of school, who never stuck to one sport, who liked to change his tastes so he could enjoy any passing whim. Hence the goth phase of 2009. Adam, on the other hand, had married his university sweetheart. Nick was married to his job. And his middle brother, Jace... well, Jace disliked change more than all of them.

But today, Nick's comments got under his skin. Maybe it was all the memories he'd dredged up yesterday by looking at old photos. Most of the time, he didn't like being reminded of the past... even if it looked happy on the outside.

And of course, looking at Cora was basically like looking into the past.

"Says you," Trent replied peevishly. "I don't see you in a hurry to get yourself hitched and settle down for the three-point-two-kid life."

"Fuck no." Nick wrinkled his nose like he'd smelled a combination of chicken shit, rotten eggs, *and* month-old milk. If Trent wasn't so annoyed, he would have laughed at the comical reaction. "But that's not because I'm afraid of commitment. It's because I don't want anyone to get in the way of my career goals. I've got bigger dreams than finding a wife and making babies."

Yeah, world domination. In reality, it was probably a good thing Nick wasn't interested in a relationship, because he would be hard-pressed to find someone who'd put up with him.

No living woman has that much patience. He'd be searching for a needle-sized unicorn in a haystack.

"Then you should be busy enough that you don't have time to keep harassing me about my life," Trent said. "Besides, I thought you'd be happy with how dedicated I am to my job. And really? You've been helping Liv out, too. We all have, because she deserves it."

"So long as you don't keep using other people's houses as an excuse not to build your own," Nick pointed out. The comment was a thorn.

Okay, sure. Trent was the kind of guy who liked to help people. Maybe it was a crutch, so he didn't have to confront the things about himself he wasn't so proud of. Maybe there was part of him that felt like he needed to earn his place in the world.

Or maybe he was just living by the Walters Way principle his father had drummed into him. Helping others was important. Being selfish made you an asshole.

And Trent did not aspire to being an asshole.

"It's not an excuse." He reached over and stole his brother's thermos right out of his hand and took a long swig. Ugh, mistake. Nick took his coffee like most things in his life—as intense as possible and without anything to make the process easier. Trent pulled a face. "How do you drink this stuff? It's like liquid masochism."

"Milk is for cheaters, bro." Nick winked. "Now, seriously. I've got another guy for you to check out. He designed that cool place in Portsea that we visited a few months back. I can put you in touch."

And of course by "can" Nick meant "will."

"I'll look at him," Trent conceded. "But I'm not going to pull the trigger because you're putting the peer pressure on."

His brother observed him for a moment, brows

furrowed. All the Walters siblings shared the same blue eyes from their mother's side of the family—a striking feature Trent had regularly used to his advantage with the opposite sex. They also shared the same skin that tanned and freckled the second the sun came out and the same naturally broad, muscular frames.

But despite sharing so many features with his siblings, Trent was different in other fundamental ways. Adam, Nick, Jace, and Liv all seemed to have such strong visions for their lives, such crystal-clear goals...even if sometimes those goals *did* change, like when Jace decided he didn't want to be a hermit anymore and now had a wife and *four* puppies to keep him busy.

But they all knew what they wanted. They were ambitious. Sure of their positions in the world.

Trent, on the other hand, was a bit of a drifter. A wanderer. A go-with-the-flow-er. The idea of making too many decisions and locking himself into something permanent seemed...more trouble than it was worth. He knew what it was like to have everything you thought you knew suddenly crumble in your palms. He knew that certainty could be shaken and cracked open, like dry earth in the middle of an earthquake.

His siblings didn't understand that. They were different than him.

Fundamentally.

"Careful," Trent drawled, deciding to go with his most comfortable tactic and joke his way out of emotions he didn't want to deal with. "The wind might change and you'll be stuck with an uglier mug than you started with."

Nick sighed. "You're a lost cause, mate."

"I'm enjoying life." He gestured to the site around them. "New tools to play with, new shit to build. New mounds of dirt to conquer."

"And new problems to be solved," Nick grumbled. "Because we won't be building anything today if these panes don't come in soon. We're supposed to be at lockup already."

"You worry too much." Trent folded his arms.

"And you don't worry *enough*." Nick was back looking at his phone again, his brain already skipping ahead to the next thing. Good. The deeper he got sucked into work, the less brain space he'd have to stick his nose into Trent's business. "If this delivery doesn't come in the next hour, I am going to lose it."

"Everything will be fine, you'll see."

But Nick was already walking away, head bowed as he tapped furiously at his phone. A second later, something vibrated in the depths of Trent's utility shorts. He pulled his phone out to find a message from his brother with the link to the new architect's website.

Maybe he'd take a closer look later. Or maybe he'd forget all about it and let Future Trent worry about where he was going to live when his sister returned.

• • •

Cora woke up around nine a.m., startled out of sleep by the sound of knocking against her window.

For a minute she sat there, clutching the bedsheets to her chest. The knocking persisted. Liv's house wasn't exactly surrounded by people, which meant that if someone had approached the house and Trent was already at work…then she was totally alone.

Shit.

Knock. Knock, knock, knock.

Were the spiders big enough to knock here? It certainly sounded that way from all the urban legends she'd heard. What if they crept up to quiet houses and tapped on the window to lure unsuspecting victims to their venomous death?

Come out, come out wherever you are…

She shuddered. The knocking only got louder. Maybe it was a kid from a nearby house or someone who'd gotten lost on the road? She swung her legs over the edge of the bed and padded quietly to the window. She couldn't see any shadowy figures through the gaps in the slatted blinds.

With a tentative hand, she reached for the lift cord.

"Come on," she said to herself. "Don't be such a chicken."

She yanked on the blinds and was met with… nothing. *Knock, knock, knock.*

Her gaze dropped to the ground outside, where a rather indignant-looking cockatoo stared at her as if to say *finally*. If birds could cross their arms and stamp their feet, then Joe would absolutely have been doing that. Instead, he gave her the most epic side-eye of all time, then stomped off in the direction of the back door.

"Well, excuse me for sleeping in," Cora muttered. The jetlag had hit her pretty hard, and she'd barely made it past nine p.m. before crashing faster than a toddler coming down from a sugar high.

She pulled her silky robe from the bench at the end of the bed and wrapped it around herself as she walked out of the bedroom and toward the back door, picking up her book along the way. When she opened the door, Joe made a ton of noise, fanning his crest and stomping around like he couldn't believe he was forced into the indignity of waiting.

"You're a demanding little guy," she said as she dove her hand into the bag of seed by the back door.

No longer afraid to feed the bird by hand, she walked onto the back deck and dropped onto the wicker chair, uncurling her palm. The day was pleasantly cool and a welcome reprieve from the persistent, beating sun that had been present since she arrived.

Joe immediately hopped up and started pecking at her palm as if he'd been left to starve...which she knew wasn't true. But clearly the little guy had an appetite. "No need to be greedy."

He squawked. *"She'll be right! Fair dinkum."*

"I don't know what any of that means." Cora laughed. They sat for a while in the quiet, Joe eating from her hand, the natural beauty of Liv's garden spread out before them. When he was done, the bird hopped onto the arm of the wicker chair and climbed up next to Cora's head. She wasn't intimidated by his talons now that she knew he was gentle...for the most part.

"Have you come for a hug, sweet thing?" She stroked the bird's downy chest and he made some happy-sounding bird noises. "Do you want some company as well as a meal?"

Joe seemed content to climb up and down the arm of the chair, trying to pull at the silk tie around her waist. Eventually he settled, seemingly happy to sit and soak up the atmosphere like she was. Cora reached for the romance novel she'd picked up at Maddy's bookstore the day before. The colorful font and half-naked man on the cover made her feel almost...giddy. Indulgent. Her mother hated Cora reading too much in general, but she'd expressly forbidden romance novels, so reading one now felt gloriously defiant.

Something about this vacation was making her want to try new things. After the game of cricket, where she had sucked beyond belief, nothing bad had happened. Nobody had laughed at her. Nobody had teased her or excluded her.

In fact, at the pub afterward, they treated her like she'd been the best player on the team. They'd made her feel welcome, valued. One of them.

It had given her a spark of confidence that she hadn't known she needed. A spark that she wouldn't waste by doing the same old, same old.

Cora flipped the book over to read the back. According to the blurb, the heroine was a bookish woman on the hunt for a husband to appease her controlling family.

"Well, I'm *not* on the hunt for a husband, but I can totally understand the controlling family and bookworm bit," she said. Joe looked at her with a cocked head. "Want me to read to you, bud? You might like this one."

Joe bobbed up and down, and Cora took that as a good sign.

She cleared her throat. "'Chapter One. Kylie Kirman needed a man, and not just *any* man. A man who was husband material and who was happy to hop, skip, and jump straight to matrimony. No dating, no trying before you buy, no thirty-day warranty.'"

Joe cocked his head as if to say: *this is a recipe for disaster.*

"Tell me about it," she said to the bird. "Who jumps straight into marriage and expects it to work? Hell, I gave Alex *five* years. That's half a decade. And what did I get?"

The bird stayed silent.

"Exactly, nothing. A big fat freaking rejection like I got with all the other guys I dated." She sighed. "I could tell this Kylie chick a thing or two about what a big mess she's going to make for herself."

"Bloody oath!" Joe fanned his crest and bobbed up and down.

"See, even *you* know." She laughed. "I bet you would have pulled the pin before I did."

He gave a little wriggle that Cora could interpret only as his agreement. Great. Even the bird was judging her. Oh well, it was hardly like she deserved any better. She was the one who had stayed with Alex even though he hated her family, and sometimes he'd ask her not to come to important events because he didn't want the media asking about her famous mother and father.

Alex said she stole the spotlight without trying. She'd tried to be a good partner, tried to fit in with his conservative, tailored life by wearing pearls and cardigans, by learning about all his interests and making nice with his friends and his uptight parents. She'd tried to be everything he wanted in a wife-to-be.

But it was never enough.

"'The funny thing was, Kylie had never wanted to get married before,'" Cora continued reading to the bird. "'She was always the independent one, the career-driven one. But now that she'd returned home to Little Creek, a town so small it could be mistaken for a speck of dust on a map, she knew things had to change. Her grandma was dying. And she'd never seen any of her grandkids get married. Not a single one in all fourteen of them.'"

Cora looked at Joe, who turned his head away.

"I'm guessing, judging by the cover, Miss Kylie gets herself tangled up with a fireman," she said to the bird. "But she shouldn't settle for less than love."

Love had always been her goal. Watching her parents' marriage go from rocky, to rockier, to *holy shit the bridge is about to blow!* had been painful. But it all became clear one day when she found her mother in a drunken stupor in their smoking room—which was a ridiculous name, since no one ever smoked in there—rambling about all the mistakes she'd made in her life.

"I should never have done it," her mother had croaked, one talon-tipped hand sliding around the back of Cora's neck as she attempted to lift her mother from the couch. *"I should never have married that sonofabitch. He never loved me and I never loved him."*

The conversation—if you could call it that—had stuck with Cora. Love was important, and settling for anything less would lead only to misery. Too bad Cora seemed to fall for jerks time and time again.

Her BS radar was officially broken.

"But we're not going to think about any of that, are we?" she said to Joe. The white bird swung his head back and forth. It wasn't quite a "no," more like the love child of a yoga stretch and some heavy metal headbanging, but she'd take it.

Just as she was about to dive back into the story, her phone rang. A familiar picture appeared on the screen, and she swiped her thumb across it to answer the call.

"Hi, Dad." She smiled.

"Is that… Are you carrying a parrot on your shoulder?" Her father peered at the camera, getting so close that the image blurred a bit. He wasn't wearing his glasses, as usual. The man could barely see a thing without them, but he was vain as hell about it.

"It's a cockatoo," Cora replied, and Joe made a trilling noise in response. "He says hi."

Her father frowned. He wasn't big on the outdoors, and the whole "no pets" rule was one of the only things he and her mother had actually agreed on.

"Well, anyway," he said. "I wanted to give you a call about the book."

She stifled a smile. That was her dad, always and forever about business. He'd probably forgotten she was even in Australia. Well, if the cockatoo hadn't given it away.

"I was worried when I didn't hear back after I sent that email. I know I can be a tough critic—probably the toughest—but I want you to know it's for your own good, Cora. I would never send you into the industry unprepared."

She bobbed her head. "I know, Dad. I appreciate that you push me."

Even if the hollow ache of his disappointment felt like it might split her in two sometimes. It had taken her *months* to work up the courage to tell him about her manuscript. Months beyond that to show him anything. No matter how Cora tried to brace herself, at the heart of it, she was a sensitive soul, and every rejection cut like a knife.

That's part of being a creative person—you need to draw on that pain for your stories.

"This industry is…" Her father sighed. "It's brutal. I've seen authors come and go. I've seen the rejection tear them apart. Only the most talented and resilient have even a hope of surviving."

"I'm resilient," she protested. Lord knows that resilience was the very thing she'd required to get through her childhood. "And Professor Markham said I had real talent. It's raw, maybe, but I'm a hard worker. I don't mind putting my pedal to the metal if it means a shot at my dreams. I know…I know this story could be something great."

She was *meant* to be a writer. Books were her life, and the time she spent dreaming up worlds and characters to inhabit them was the only time she felt truly like herself. The rest of the time, she was drifting.

"I can do this."

"Cora…" Her father's forehead folded into a deep crease. "You know I want only to protect you, right? I saw what fame and a life in the spotlight did to your mother. The rejection and constant criticism twisted her. It turned her into someone I didn't even know anymore."

The pain in his voice lashed like a whip across her heart. Her mother had been wrong that day—he *had* loved her. They'd loved each other.

Maybe, on some level, he still loved the woman her mother used to be.

"I'm not her," Cora said stubbornly. "Trust me, I spent every waking hour of every day making sure I am the very opposite of who she is as a person."

Her father nodded. For a moment, he said nothing, simply looked at her through the phone screen a whole hemisphere away. Cora wanted to plead with him. Beg him.

Trust me. Believe in me.

But she couldn't open herself up like that. Rejection for her work she could handle, even though it hurt. Rejection of herself, however, was a whole other—deeper—wound.

"I have to get back to work," he said gruffly. "I just wanted to make sure you were okay after I gave my feedback."

"I can handle it," she said, pasting on a cheery smile. In return, she saw some of the worry evaporate from her father's face.

"That's my girl."

The call clicked off, and Cora stared at the tattoo peeking out from where her silky robe had parted over her thigh.

Metamorphosis.

She wanted to be better. To be good enough to do all the things she craved in life—publish a book, fall in love, have a happy marriage strong enough to erase the scars created by her parents' tumultuous one. Eventually she would find the right combination to unlock those things, right?

If only she worked hard enough. If only she kept trying to do her best. Eventually good things would come.

CHAPTER TEN

That night, when Trent came home from work, Cora was still engrossed in the romance novel. She'd taken a break midday to go for a walk around Liv's property, stopping to pick some pretty flowers along the way. The long walk had also taken her past a little corner store, which they called a "milk bar," that had basic things like milk—hence the name—eggs, cereal, bread, etc.

She'd bought enough to make her favorite egg salad and lettuce sandwiches for lunch (secret ingredient: cayenne) and picked up some supplies for dinner. The rest of the afternoon had been spent cutting out the photocopied pictures for the scrapbook, then reading. Despite her belief that poor Kylie was headed for marital disaster, she couldn't stop turning the pages. At this rate, the book wouldn't last her much longer.

The fall of heavy-booted footsteps made Cora sit up. A second later, the door rattled and there was a gruff noise, followed by the jangle of keys. One in the regular lock, then the deadlock.

"Oh wait!" Cora jumped up and ran to the door as Trent tried to push it open, where it yanked against the chain she'd slid across after returning home that afternoon. "You won't get too far with that."

Trent shook his head, laughing as he stepped into the house, his dusty boots abandoned outside.

"City girl, you don't need three locks on the door, you know."

"Well, it's better to be safe," she said, folding her arms across her chest. "And why have the locks in the first place if you're not going to use them?"

"I think the guy who used to live here was paranoid. The only thing you need to worry about round here are the kind of things that aren't stopped by locks."

Spiders. She shuddered. Thankfully no creepy crawlies had come into the house yet, but Cora remained vigilant. She'd raided Liv's pantry of all cans of bug spray and kept them dotted around the house.

She really *was* a city girl.

"I'm only teasing," he said softly. "Picking on city folk is a local sport."

"Well, I'm sure you would struggle with things if you were staying at my place," she said. If Trent wanted to tease her, then she would give it right back.

"Oh yeah, like what?"

"Well, you have your spiders and snakes and things, and we New Yorkers have rats. Big rats." She nodded. "And raccoons."

Trent looked at her skeptically. "Raccoons are adorable."

"No, they are aggressive trash pandas who will rain hellfire down on you with their tiny, angry hands if you get in the way of their meal. They're very dangerous."

Trent snorted. "Whatever you say, city girl."

He walked past her, aiming a panty-melting

smirk in her direction.

There was something so insatiably sexy about a man who worked with his hands for a living. It definitely *wasn't* something she'd ever thought would be attractive—because she'd grown up lusting after suited Wall Street types, lawyers and bankers and hedge fund managers with their Omega watches and smooth, manicured hands.

But seeing Trent like this—his shorts showing off that his legs were grimy and muscular and his skin was tanned and slightly pink from the sun, blond hair bleached almost white in spots—was doing some sexy trickery to her insides. Who would have thought she'd find dirty so incredibly sexy?

"How's the book?" His gaze drifted to her novel sitting on the coffee table, which was already starting to look well-loved from her intense reading session that afternoon.

"It's good. Very engrossing." There'd already been a pretty steamy kiss, and Cora found herself blushing the whole way through, mainly because, as the scene played out, she'd imagined it was *her* kissing *Trent* and doing all those wonderful things—sliding her hands up his chest, pressing her hips against his, feeling the hard length of him through his pants.

"Certainly looks like you've been enjoying it," he said. His eyes were dancing, a smile barely contained on his lips, and Cora knew her face must be beet red. It was obvious from the shirtless man on the cover *exactly* what one would find inside. "Anything you want to share with the class?"

"No," she squeaked. "Just...great character

development."

Trent paused and sniffed. "What's that smell?"

"Dinner. I made my totally *not* world famous but still very delicious pasta sauce." She grinned.

"You didn't have to cook."

"I wanted to." She bit down on her bottom lip. "You've made me feel so welcome and I wanted to say thank you."

Trent's blue gaze locked on hers, and with each second Cora's heart beat a little faster. But then he glanced at the kitchen. "I certainly won't say no to a home-cooked meal, and it looks like you've been working hard all afternoon."

There were pots in the sink and a fine coating of flour on the benchtop from when she rolled the pasta dough out. Not to mention a little spray of red sauce up the backsplash behind the stove. "I'm not the cleanest of cooks," she admitted.

"No, you're not." He reached up and swiped a thumb over her cheek. "You've got flour every-where."

How could he touch her like that—so bare and so fleeting, her mind could be tricked into thinking she'd only imagined it—and yet make her whole body feel gooey and warm like a brownie straight out of the oven? No wonder they called him the town charmer. His charms were *certainly* working on her.

All the more reason to watch your step, Cora. He makes everyone feel like this…not just you. You're not special.

Cora tried to cover her face, but Trent laughed. "You look adorable. Like a kitchen fairy, sprinkling your flour dust all over the place."

She laughed. "I should probably freshen up before we eat."

"Me too."

They were standing close, tension crackling between them like tiny fireworks. Fizzing and popping and snapping. Every time they were together, the chemistry became more combustible, like a bubble swelling. Cora had gone to sleep last night playing the moment at the beach over and over—the way Trent had guided her body, the heat of him standing behind her. Then the scene of him stepping into the shower, water streaming down his work-honed body.

No wonder she'd slept in this morning. He kept her up all night...well, the fantasy of him, anyway.

"Don't forget this spot." His finger brushed her cheek again, and then he turned and headed toward his bedroom, throwing her one searing look over his shoulder.

Cora lingered a moment, feet rooted to the ground by the attraction surging through her. All she wanted was to skip dinner completely and follow Trent into his bedroom.

What is wrong *with you?*

She'd never been the kind of person who struggled to control her urges. Cora was, if nothing else, good at following the rules. *Very* good. Maybe that's why she was feeling so conflicted—her rule system had been shattered. Her ideals that if she tried hard enough, smiled hard enough, did what she was told, then she'd end up with everything she wanted in life.

Yet she still had nothing.

Well, that wasn't true. Compared to many, she was extremely fortunate—she knew that. She'd never worried about her next meal or where she might sleep or how she'd pay her rent. But the stuff that was further up Maslow's Hierarchy of Needs—belonging, love, esteem—was sorely lacking.

Cora went to splash some water on her face. Oh, and she had to get the flour out of her hairline and her ears. It looked like she'd rolled in the damn stuff. No wonder Trent had given her that amused little smirk the second he'd laid eyes on her.

She stared at herself in the mirror. By New York standards, Cora wasn't exactly a knockout. But she wasn't *un*attractive, either. Her best assets were big blue eyes inherited from her father's side of the family and high cheekbones from her mother's side. She had pretty decent boobs, if she did say so herself. But her hair…well, there was not much that could be done with it in summer, and it was too damn hot in this house to plug in her flat iron. So, it was scraped back into a poofy blond-brown ponytail for now. Her eyebrows also had a tendency to go from normal to overgrown shrub overnight. And her nose was a little on the big side.

She was…normal. Despite her mother trying to push her to be more, despite the expectations placed on women to look as good as the touched-up photos on Instagram, Cora was totally and utterly normal. Not amazing, not terrible. And after a lifetime of sucking it in and fluffing it out and turning it up, she was happy to be here with a bottle of wine and a cute guy and some yummy food and to just be herself.

In a world selling perfection, it felt almost rebellious.

You're going to enjoy every single second of this, no matter what comes of it.

She wasn't going to let herself get tangled up by Trent, she wasn't going to place any expectation on whether it should or shouldn't lead anywhere, because *that* was going to make her stress about how many times she'd been rejected before.

They had plans to eat and drink and enjoy the evening. That was it.

Easy, simple, *normal* stuff.

"Be cool," she said to her reflection. "You're making something out of nothing."

She stripped off the clothes that she'd been in all day and pulled on a breezy green dress. The fabric was rumpled, because who wanted to iron on their vacation? It was cool against her skin, and with her hair up and away from her neck, the heat felt a little more manageable. At the last minute, she reached for a slender gold necklace.

"The pasta will only take a few minutes," she said as she walked barefoot through the house, the cool tile a pleasurable contact to her warm skin.

Trent appeared a few minutes later as she was sprinkling salt into the bubbling water on the stove.

"Wow, you went all out." Trent watched as she grabbed the freshly made pasta.

"I really enjoy cooking, and it's not something I get to indulge in very often," she said. "Hardly seems worth the effort for only one person."

The words slipped out before she had a chance

to assess whether they gave too much away. But Trent bobbed his head, a knowing look on his face, and she felt a sense of camaraderie. Maybe he'd been hurt, too.

"Most of the time I eat at the pub or have dinner with whichever one of my siblings is home." Trent grabbed plates and silverware and set the table.

"What are you planning to do when Liv comes back?" she asked, stirring the pasta with a wooden spoon.

Trent shrugged. "I'm going to build a house, but I haven't found the right design yet. It's a big decision."

"Absolutely." Cora watched the water bubble away in the pot, her eyes flicking to the timer on the stovetop every few seconds. "But you still have to live somewhere, right? Do you think you'll stay here until you find a place?"

"You sound like Nick." Trent nudged her with his elbow and, while the gesture was playful, Cora got the impression she'd hit a nerve.

"It's a reasonable question, isn't it?"

"Sure. But I'm not always in search of answers," he replied with a cavalier lift of one shoulder. "People get too hung up on wanting to know how everything will turn out. If we already knew everything, what would be the point to living? I thought you'd agree with that, what with your caterpillar theory."

"I think we should embrace the process of changing, but there's a big difference between being okay with life's uncertainties and not having a place to live." She cocked her head. "Being open to change doesn't necessarily mean not making plans."

Trent winked. "Don't worry about me, I got options."

"I'm sure you do." A man like Trent would have open arms wherever he went—people loved him. That much was already obvious. The people on his cricket team, the woman in the café who spouted his praise when Cora mentioned the Walters name. He was beloved.

Cora drained the pasta, mixed in the sauce, and served their portions into two bowls. "But doesn't it…scare you, not knowing how things will be in a few weeks' time?"

"When I'm relying on myself, I don't have too much to be scared about," he quipped.

Hmm, didn't she feel *that* down to her bones. Relying on yourself was safe… It was everyone else in the world who made things risky.

They settled at the table, and Trent poured the wine into both their glasses. When they clinked them together, the chime rang through the quiet house. It was so peaceful here, with only the rustling trees and the chatter of birds outside as a backdrop.

Maybe she'd feel free and breezy like Trent if she lived somewhere as beautiful and still as this.

He swirled his fork into the pasta and shoved a hearty mouthful between his lips. The sound that followed was enough to melt Cora into a puddle at his feet. "This is *amazing*," he said. "Where did you learn to cook like this?"

"YouTube." She sipped her wine. "There's nothing I love more than picking a topic and watching a bunch of videos so I can teach myself how to do something new."

"I bet you did well in school," he said with a laugh.

"I did," she said matter-of-factly. Music conservatory disaster aside, that was. "I like learning."

"I hated school," he admitted. "I've always been better with my hands than with numbers and words."

The comment drew Cora's gaze down to Trent's hands, and it kicked up the memory of them at the beach—him standing close behind her, rough and yet gentle hands guiding hers, hips at her back. There wasn't a single doubt in her mind that he was good with his hands. Panty-meltingly, brain-numbingly, skin-scorchingly good. Her whole body tingled as though coaxing her to imagine what it would be like to have them sliding over her body—cupping, holding, smoothing, kneading.

"You look a little pink," he said, cocking his head.

"Standing over a stove is…hot."

Thank you, Captain Obvious.

Lordy. No doubt Trent observed every little bit of that fantasy rolling across her face. How was she supposed to hide something like that? Alex had told her once that she had the world's *worst* poker face. Hiding her feelings wasn't a strong suit, and she wanted Trent so badly, it must have been like red ink stamped all over her.

She twirled some pasta onto her fork. "Doesn't

help that this country is basically a giant fireball."

"So that's it, huh? Just the weather?" He was watching her closely, which made it hard to eat. To breathe. Her appetite had morphed and shifted and turned into something else. Suddenly all the food laid out before them wasn't all that appealing, not when other hungers needed attention.

You really want to do this?

Yes. She knew that it was wrong on a bunch of levels—Trent was her friend's brother, and Cora was recently out of a breakup, head and heart still hurting. Mind reeling. Emotions running wild.

But for her whole entire life, Cora had followed the rules. Followed orders. Worked hard.

And that had done nothing but made her feel like a failure, so why *didn't* she deserve to do something reckless for a change? Why couldn't she seize life in the way so many others did without a second thought? Without worrying what people would think? Without making a list of "what ifs" in her brain?

Nobody knew her here, and she didn't need anything from Patterson's Bluff.

The thought was freeing. Here, she could be herself and damn anyone who didn't like her. Damn anyone who rejected her. Damn anyone who didn't accept her.

This was her moment and screw the consequences.

"I'm overheated because I can't stop thinking about what it would be like if you kissed me."

CHAPTER ELEVEN

The words came out in a rush, like a *whoosh* of breath that had been held for too long. It was both a weight off her shoulders and electricity in her veins, the anticipation of his response making her giddy and breathless like a teenager.

She had *never* been the first to admit attraction, had never been the first to make a move—if her awkward, too-fast confession could be counted as such. Her mother had drummed into her that the only way to get a man was to make him chase, make him want by being slightly unavailable. Always a little out of reach.

By playing a game.

So many rules, so many points of etiquette when what she really wanted was to take charge of her own damn life. And if that meant wearing her heart on her sleeve for once, then she would damn well do it.

"Say something," she said, her hands gripping the edge of her chair like it might keep her tethered to earth.

"Wouldn't you rather I *do* something?" His eyes were like twin blue flames, flickering and holding her captive.

He leaned forward, bracing one hand on the back of her chair and closing the distance with a heart-fluttering slowness. She reached up and slid her hand along the sharp line of his jaw, feeling the gentle prickles of his five o'clock shadow against her palm. The friction sent a subtle shiver through her, kicking up fantasies like a sandstorm.

"Yes," she said, her voice barely a whisper.

It was like trying to talk underwater, her voice distorted and sluggish. Time had slowed to a trickle so she could take in every single detail—the widening of his pupils, so black and bottomless and beautiful. The parting of his lips as he came closer. The scent of shampoo in his hair and wine on his breath.

When his lips finally connected with hers, it was bliss—warm, sensual, spiraling bliss.

His mouth was confident as he coaxed hers open, knowing she would melt for him. And she did. His hand was in her hair, fist closing around her ponytail so he could tug her head backward. That grip, so sure and possessive, snapped the last vestige of her control, and she invited him in.

Their tongues met, and she arched toward him, wanting more, more, more. Wanting everything. The awkward seated position didn't allow for much contact, but she didn't dare move, dare twitch, in case it warned him away. Because she could drown in his kiss forever.

In that moment, she felt wanted. Cherished. It was goodness dragged up from the very bottom of her soul, making every cell in her body vibrate.

She fisted her hands in his T-shirt, trying to bring him closer. But it was no use—her body was twisted to the side and her arm pressed painfully into the table. Growling in frustration, Trent broke free and shoved his chair back.

"Come here." The demand was like a lit match, and the sight of him—hair mussed, legs spread in that unabashedly male way, T-shirt rumpled by her hands—was possibly the hottest thing she'd ever seen. "I need you closer."

Cora rose out of her chair, and his strong hands guided her over. She straddled him, her skirt bunched around her waist and her back pinned against the table. If she'd wanted contact, then this was it. This was *everything*. The hard press of him between her legs, lips eagerly seeking hers. He rolled his hips up to rub against her.

Lord. There would be nothing left of her but cinder and bone.

He kissed her hard. Deep. She felt the stubble scratch against her chin and the deliciously soft cotton yield to her fingertips, barely hiding taut muscle beneath. His hands circled around, sliding under her dress to cup her ass. She writhed, so desperate for more, it filled the air like a perfume.

This wasn't a sweet kiss. This wasn't a romantic movie, peck on the doorstep with a foot pop for good measure. Oh no. This kiss was dredged from the darkest of Cora's fantasies. The kind of full-bodied, impolite, totally penetrating kiss that she'd never let herself indulge in on a first date back home.

You haven't even gone on a date.

Cora pulled back for a moment, dazed and aroused and fighting the little voice inside her. Her ponytail was hanging a little loose, some curls springing around her face and brushing her skin. Trent was equally disheveled, but the sexy, unabashed smile on his lips summed up everything she felt right now: good.

Not worried. Not stressed. Not regretful. Not running.

Good.

But when had she *ever* been able to trust that feeling?

• • •

"God, you're beautiful," Trent said, brushing back an errant strand of hair and tucking it behind her ear. Cora glowed—her pale eyes were like stars at twilight and her lips sported a delectable post-kiss flush. Her cheeks and chest were tinted with pink, and the look on her face...bloody hell.

It was the sexiest thing he'd ever seen.

Maybe that was why he was hard enough to drill nails. Or perhaps it was more to do with the way she'd tugged at his shirt, hanging on for dear life like his kiss was the only thing keeping her afloat.

She looked like a mermaid who'd washed up on shore, magical and impossibly beautiful.

Cora's beauty came from something inside her. Sure, she had a great body and a sweet face and a smile that could power a city, but it was her spirit that called to Trent. There was something inside her, like a treasure, that drew him close, that called on him to look deeper.

And he was *never* the kind of guy who looked beyond. Who wanted more than the surface-level stuff. Never the guy who connected with people because connection meant trusting that they wouldn't knife you in the back.

"You're not too bad yourself," she said with a shy smile, ducking her eyes for a moment before flashing those icy blues back at him.

He kissed her again, slower this time. Gentler. And when she responded without hesitation, Trent was filled with a roaring pride. It was a lion in his chest, a king desperate to conquer. To take. He kissed down to her neck, sucking in the honeyed floral scent on her skin and letting the curling tendrils of hair tickle his face.

He could feel the fluttering of her pulse beneath the delicate skin on her neck, and the soft little sigh that escaped her lips when he kissed her there was like a sound bite from heaven.

"Are we forgetting about dinner?" he asked, thumbing the strap of her dress and trailing his lips along her collarbone.

"What is this word, 'dinner?'" she mumbled, letting her head roll back. "I have no idea what you're talking about."

"Good answer." He tugged the strap down over her shoulder. It was thin and delicate, so its removal didn't really add to Cora's nakedness at all. But for some reason, seeing the smooth curve of her shoulder, uninterrupted, freckles free for him to trace with his tongue, churned him up inside.

He pushed the other strap down and then moved to the line of buttons at her front. The shiny white discs popped easily out of the holes and he peeled the fabric away from her chest. As he'd suspected, she wore no bra underneath. Her chest heaved with each ragged breath, cleavage tempting him closer. More buttons were opened, more skin revealed.

"My God," he muttered. There was nothing else he could say and clearly not enough blood left in his brain to be able to fully operate it.

Cora's breasts were perfection. Her nipples were peaked and begging for his attention. They were the prettiest shade of pink, and when he palmed her, swiping a thumb across one stiff nub, she shuddered. He felt the vibration of it all the way through him, and his erection strained against the fly of his jeans. If he got any harder, he wasn't certain his fly would survive it.

"I want to keep kissing you," he murmured, rubbing his palm in slow circles. "Everywhere."

Her fingers threaded into the hair at the back of his head, and she guided him to her breast. No words. Just showing him what she wanted.

His tongue darted out to swipe over her and she gasped, her hands curling and nails scraping over his scalp. *Yes.* He wanted to worship her. Learn her. When he sucked a hard nipple between his lips, tongue flicking, Cora moaned and the sound shot right through him, coiling every muscle in his body.

"Yes." The word was like a hiss of steam, sharp and yet soft. And so hot. She clung to him, the weight of her body in his lap like sweet, sweet torture.

"Sensitive," he murmured, nuzzling her other breast. "Just the lightest little flick…" He swiped his tongue and she arched against him, like a puppet on the end of his strings. "And you're about to boil over."

Her cheeks were flushed as pink as the sunset outside, which was sending rose gold light spilling into the house through the large windows facing the back. It brought out the golden highlights in her hair and the warmth in her skin. She bit down on her lip.

"This, uh… I don't usually rush ahead like this," she said, ducking her eyes. "Three date minimum, that's the rule."

"We can finish our food first, if you want," he teased with a cavalier grin. But when she didn't stop biting down on her lip, he cupped her face and gently tilted her so she was making eye contact again. "Are we moving too fast?"

"Maybe. No…I don't know." She shook her head and folded her arms over her chest, trying to cover herself. "I'm attracted to you, I know that much."

"That's mutual."

"But I'm rebounding… This is a rebound and…" She squeezed her eyes shut. "God, why can't I do something fun and *not* worry about the consequences for once? I'm broken."

"You're not broken." He smoothed his hands up and down her arms, the slow, firm pressure melting some of the tension from her shoulders. "And we don't have to take this any further if it's too soon."

"Do you think it's too soon?"

He smirked. "I'd be lying straight to your face if I said I wasn't thinking about dragging you to my bed, or maybe into the shower, so I could get you out of that dress and keep kissing you all over."

The pink in her cheeks intensified. "So I'm the only one overthinking it?"

"Yep, but that doesn't mean I'm a Neanderthal who's going to drag you off to the nearest dark corner if you're having doubts." He gave her a squeeze. "Personally, I find the whole sex thing *far* more enjoyable if there are no doubts. And life's too short for bad sex."

"Life *is* too short for bad sex," she agreed.

"Maybe we stick to a kiss for now and then you can think it over, see if I'm as attractive in the morning."

"That is *not* the problem, believe me," she said with a laugh. "Your muscles are very distracting."

"That a fact?" He lowered his lips to hers and kissed the corner of her mouth. She sighed and her lips parted, her head turning toward his so her nose bumped against his cheek. "I'm more than a hot body, Cora. I've got feelings, too."

She giggled. "Please, tell me. What feelings are the ones you're experiencing right now?"

"Horniness." He kissed the side of her neck, and she smoothed her hands up his chest, exposing her breasts again to his hands. Oh boy, he would be thinking about those breasts *all* night long, regardless of where this went. Hell, there was a solid chance they'd be imprinted on his brain forever. "Overwhelming sexual attraction. Uhh…being turned on."

"Those are the same as horniness," she pointed out.

"Feeling pretty bloody good about myself that a girl as pretty as you is hot for me," he teased.

"That sounds like a good feeling." She wound her arms around his neck. "Is it okay if I ask you to kiss me again?"

"Just a kiss?"

She nodded. "Yeah, just a kiss."

Can fucking do.

Trent leaned toward her and she met him halfway, her lips parting for him and her arms tightening around his neck. It was sweet at first. A gentle brushing of lips that was so soft and so light, he could easily have passed it off as being a figment of his imagination. But there was no mistaking the second kiss, because Cora's tongue darted out eagerly to meet his, and she rubbed her body against his in a way that made him shudder. Damn. Now he didn't even want to take her to bed—because that was *too far away*. He wanted to reach under her skirt, pull her underwear to one side, and stroke the seam of her with his finger to see if she was ready for him. How easy would it be to pull down his zipper and guide her to his cock?

Too easy.

But he'd meant every word of what he'd said earlier—life was too short for bad sex. And if there were any doubts in Cora's mind, then that was a hard stop. Frankly, it wasn't like Trent had trouble in that area, and he would never settle for a partner who wasn't 100 percent into it. Why shortchange himself and her?

But something told him this wasn't the last time sparks would fly between him and Cora. Because the way she responded to his kiss—with short breaths and soft moans and her body glued to his—it was only a matter of time before a fire like that burned out of control.

• • •

For the next few days, Cora and Trent tiptoed around each other like the floor of Liv's house was littered in eggshells. The kiss replayed in his mind, but the tension between them had turned from burning passion to…well, thick as soup in the worst way possible.

He left early to head to work and she spent her evenings scrapbooking or reading and being so polite to him that Trent wanted to shake her. He *hated* politeness. It was so…impersonal. But he wasn't going to push the issue. Cora had to be the one to bring it up again, to make it clear she wanted to circle back to their mutual attraction. To pick up where they left off.

Maybe he should never have kissed her.

You know there's no point regretting something like that. Besides, would you avoid kissing her if you had a do-over?

Hell no. That kiss had marked him like a tattoo gun scratching over his skin. And speaking of skin, Cora was officially burrowed deep under his.

"This place has every early 2000s cliché," Hale said as he whacked the end of his chisel with a hammer, dislodging another beige tile from the floor. Now that the plumbing was in tiptop shape, it was time to start on some of the cosmetic side of things.

Trent had been up since the crack of dawn,

dismantling what was left of the vanity unit, and now that it was a more "sociable" hour, Hale and another one of his mates, Sean, had come over to help tackle the tiles.

"I swear, you could show me a picture of the bathroom and nothing else and I could tell you exactly what year the house was renovated," he added.

Trent was working on the backsplash section behind where the new unit would be installed. These tiles were smaller and more stubborn. Each one seemed to want to break into three or four pieces.

"That looks like a dog's breakfast," Sean said, shaking his head. "I bet this was a DIY job."

"Isn't *this* a DIY job?" Hale asked, continuing to make speedy progress on the floor. "We've got a plumber, a brickie, and a... What are you again, Sean?"

"Renovation enthusiast, mate. Jack of all trades."

Trent snorted. "And master of none."

"Still sounds like the opening to a joke." Hale neatly chiseled away another tile and tossed it into the growing pile. "What's the plan for the bathroom?"

"Liv really likes that high-end-spa look, so I managed to find some of those big slate tiles for the floor. Nick had a contact and they discontinued the style, so I picked up the rest of their inventory pretty cheap."

"Got enough in case there's any breakages?" Hale asked.

"I didn't come down in the last shower." Trent

rolled his eyes. "No pun intended."

"Says the man who didn't turn the water mains off," his friend muttered under his breath, and Sean stifled a smirk. Trent was *never* going to live that one down.

"Anyway, we're going charcoal and white. Faux marble backsplash and countertop with brushed gold fixtures." He'd shown some of the inspiration pictures to Cora last night and she'd enthusiastically approved...and then immediately started thinking out loud about what funky decorative items could add to the spa vibes. For a moment it was like they were connecting again...until she'd scurried off to her bedroom, book in hand. "Liv will be over the moon. I think she hated the bathroom more than anything else in this place."

"I can see why." Hale wrinkled his nose.

For a guy who spent most of his life in flannel shirts and work boots and who'd been wearing a man bun *before* it became socially acceptable, Hale's taste ran surprisingly far to the champagne end of the spectrum.

"Actually, now that I've got your snobby ass here, I need your help." Trent grinned.

He couldn't sit back and let Cora be awkward for the rest of her trip. It was clear she needed a break from her life, and he'd overheard her Skyping with Liv earlier that morning and some very interesting information had come out: It was Cora's birthday next week.

Hale shot Sean a wary look. "Gee, when he puts it like that, how can I refuse?"

Sean chuckled and went back to his work at the

other end of the bathroom, the *chink* sound of his chisel hitting tile punctuating the air at regular intervals.

"I need Aimee's help with a birthday party," Trent clarified. Aimee ran a party planning business for kids—putting her bubbly personality and sweet face to profitable use, dressing up as everyone from Cinderella to that *Frozen* chick in order to make little kids' birthday dreams come true. "For Cora."

Hale raised a brow. "You know her customers are usually in the five to ten age bracket, right?"

"I know." When Hale's expression didn't shift, Trent figured being vague wasn't going to help. "Cora told me that her parents never allowed her to have a proper birthday party when she was a kid. Her parents are these hoity-toity types and they wanted to force-feed everyone caviar and gold leaf or some crap."

Hale looked even less convinced than before. "So you want to throw her a child's birthday party?"

"Yes," Trent said with a confident nod.

"Okay, when's her birthday?"

"Next weekend."

"Seriously?" Hale scratched his head, his fingers disturbing his hair so it looked even wilder than usual.

"I know it's short notice."

"I don't know if it's even possible, but I'll ask." He sighed. "And you'll owe the both of us beers."

"Tell her I'll do anything. Cora has had a rough time and…I want to help her."

"I bet you do," Sean said, laughing.

Trent wanted to be annoyed at the innuendo but really, what was the point? Anyone who saw him and Cora in the same room for more than five seconds would be able to work out that they were hot for each other. She'd blushed furiously as she'd caught Trent watching her that morning when she was unpacking the dishwasher, bending over in that floaty little dress that was a mere gentle breeze away from showing her undies to the world.

"Trent!" Hale snapped his fingers in front of his friend's face. "Focus, mate. I said, what kind of theme do you want? Aimee will ask me all these questions, and she gets annoyed when I don't have answers."

Hale was so whipped—and so totally bloody smitten—it would be adorable if it wasn't border-line sickening.

"Can't afford to anger the girlfriend with the fairy outfits," Sean teased, and Hale rolled his eyes. "They're real mean behind all that glitter."

"No shit. She's scary when it comes to business," he said. "Seriously, you think she's all sparkle and lightness, but that girl has a five-year plan and a backup five-year plan and a fallback backup five-year plan."

"And don't even get him started on her *ten*-year plans," Sean said with a laugh.

"You think I'm joking?" Hale grunted. "I'm not."

"Which plan does marriage fit into?" Trent asked, knowing he was poking the bear. Hale wasn't super keen on the whole marriage-and-declaring-one's-love-publicly thing. Called it "a

spectacle for people with more money than sense."
Somehow, Trent wasn't sure Hale and Aimee saw
eye to eye on that one.

"I thought we were talking about *your* love
life," Hale shot back. "And your weird child-adult
birthday party plan."

"It's not weird." He chipped away at another
tile, looking up only when it became obvious two
sets of eyes were fixed on him. "I thought it was
sweet."

"Sweet?" Sean asked, his head cocked like a
confused cocker spaniel. He and Hale exchanged
looks like they'd both smelled something bad.

Trent bristled. "What's wrong with sweet?"

"Nothing, but it's not...you." Hale's eyes were
an almost black shade, so unnervingly dark that
sometimes it felt like he could look right into a
person. "You're not falling for her, are you?"

"Don't be a dickhead," he grumbled, avoiding
the accusation. "She's only here for a holiday, so it's
not like that. *And* she's a friend of Liv's, which
means I need to make her feel welcome."

Neither Sean nor Hale looked convinced. In
fact, they looked a hell of a lot like he was speaking
total rubbish.

"Jeez, can't a guy do something nice for a
person without getting the third degree?" he
muttered as he turned back to the backsplash. He
drove his hammer down onto the chisel, and the
tile splintered off an annoyingly small shard.

"All we're worried about is that you've found
yourself Rochelle mark II." Sean frowned. "Did
you notice that she really looks—"

"Yes," Trent and Hale said in unison, although one was a lot more exasperated than the other.

"Okay, okay." Sean held up his hands, still holding the chisel in one and a hammer in the other. "No need to get defensive. I'm just saying, I remember a very drunk, very belligerent Walters man—who is a real prick after a few too many Jägerbombs, I might add—telling me he was never going to make the mistake of falling for a fancy girl ever again."

Fancy girl.

That's what he'd called Rochelle the first time he met her, when it was clear there was attraction but that they were about as different as two people could be. He was a salt-of-the-earth blue-collar guy and she liked little bags with spangly things on them that cost more than his monthly rent. She'd *hated* that her parents had dragged her to some sleepy seaside town, forcing small-town life on her when she wanted to live somewhere more glamorous.

At first he'd found her big dreams and lofty aspirations to be attractive—since he'd never had those himself. But eventually it became clear those lofty aspirations didn't involve settling down with a man who wanted nothing more than to make a simple life by the ocean.

As a kid, he'd always assumed that a family would be part of his life—husband and wife and a few chubby-cheeked kids. But as he'd grown up, life had proved time and time again that you couldn't trust anyone. Not even those closest to you.

"Cora is *nothing* like Rochelle," he said,

probably a little harsher than he'd anticipated. "She's not going around looking down her nose at the folks here. She's not thinking that she's better than the rest of us just because she has her initials printed on her suitcase."

Sure, she was *fancy* in that she came from money and lived in New York City and she *did* have her initials stamped on her luggage. But Cora was proof money didn't make someone a snob. Because Rochelle's money wasn't the thing that made her a bad person... That was something much deeper.

And he could say, without a doubt, Cora didn't have a bad bone in her body.

"Tread carefully. That's all I'm saying." Sean watched him for a minute longer and then bowed his head to start chiseling again. "Hale and I *will* pick you up off the floor again, but I'd rather you didn't get to that point in the first place."

"There's nothing to worry about," Trent said tightly.

He liked Cora. Of course he did—he might be the town charmer, but he didn't want to get physical with someone unless he liked them as a person. Sexual attraction was one thing, but he needed more than that. The right personality. A few laughs. Call it a lesson learned or whatever, but he counted those things as critical these days.

Still, he wasn't under any illusions about Cora. She had baggage, and apparently, she was rebounding... He'd chosen not to delve into that at the time, because he wasn't sure he wanted to reciprocate in the information-sharing department. But all in all, it was a pile of red flags so big and so vibrant, you could see it from space.

So why are you planning her a party and thinking about her 24-7?

Good question.

"I'll let Aimee know you need her help," Hale said, moving the conversation on like the good peacemaker he was. "She'll be happy to hook you up."

Should he be worried that the thought of throwing Cora a birthday party, seeing that glorious smile break across her face like a foamy wave kissing the sandy shoreline, had him feeling all warm and fuzzy?

Maybe you need a little less warm and fuzzy, and a little more hot and steamy. Keep that balance in check.

For a fleeting moment, Trent wondered what it might be like to have both.

CHAPTER TWELVE

"I can't believe you're back again so soon." Maddy had a pile of books at her feet and was carefully sliding them into place on the shelf in front of her.

Cora had decided to get out of the house while the guys were working—all the banging and rock music blaring wasn't helping her frayed edges. Besides, she'd already devoured her romance novel and, since she'd made things *royally* awkward between her and Trent, she'd had to settle for having a robust fictional love life instead of an actual love life.

She really wanted to clear the air—but every time she even *thought* about bringing up their kiss, she totally chickened out. Not because she regretted kissing him. No way! But because she wasn't sure if she could handle knowing whether or not she'd blown her chance with him.

If he rejected her now...ugh. She wasn't sure she could stand seeing him every day knowing that. Maybe it was easier to pretend it never happened.

"Actually, maybe I can." Maddy added with a grin, "Those books are pretty addictive."

"I'm hoping you have the rest of the series," Cora said. "The author did this mean thing where she set up a bunch of characters and now I *have* to know what happens to them."

"Oh, sequel bait. I both love and hate it." Maddy slipped the last book into place and then motioned for Cora to follow her. "We have a few more by this author. If I don't have them in stock, I can see if I can put an order in. How long are you hanging around?"

"Three more weeks."

How had a whole week flown past already? How had it been three whole days since she'd kissed Trent like her life depended on it?

Dammit. Why hadn't she been able to pull the trigger?

She liked Trent—both from a physical perspective *and* because he was a genuinely great guy with a big personality and even bigger heart. She was *super* into kissing him. The attraction was mutual, and they were both grown-ass adults in a private place where they weren't likely to cause a scandal. Well, unless Liv found out. But really, did that matter so much? It wasn't like they were going to defile *her* bed.

So what was the problem?

You're scared.

It was true. Cora had terrible judgment when it came to how others felt about her, which caused her to make bad decisions. Besides, rebounds weren't healthy, and she was still heartbroken over getting dumped, wasn't she? That was a tough one to answer. The wound felt fresh, but when she thought about her ex she got...nothing. Numbness.

Maybe the thing that stung most was the humiliation of it all, rather than losing Alex. Did she want Alex back? Nope. Because he'd tried to blame it on her—all the times her mother interfered, every fight they had because of it. All. Her.

Fault. But that wasn't fair. She hadn't encouraged her mother to interfere with her life. In fact, she'd told her on numerous occasions to stay the hell out of it.

So why couldn't she let herself have a temporary fling with Trent?

"Okay, *Firehouse Hotties…*" They ventured over to the romance section, which was littered with a rainbow selection of spines and covers with everything from sweeping historical gowns to sweetly embracing couples to hunky half-naked men. "Ah, we've got two more in stock. The book you read is actually book three, and we've got one and two here."

She plucked two books from the shelf and handed them to Cora.

"Thanks." Cora grinned and hugged the books to her chest. No matter how old she got, she couldn't stop that funny little habit of welcoming new books into her life.

"I hug my books, too," Maddy said with a laugh. She shoved her hands into the pockets of her denim shorts, which were frayed at the edges, revealing miles of shapely leg and warm brown skin. She had silver bracelets that made chiming music when she gesticulated and three carved silver hoops in her right ear, as well as a stud in her nose.

Cora would kill to be the kind of woman who had that effortlessly cool look, like Maddy did. But alas, some people were born with it and some people, like Cora, were not.

"How're things going at Liv's place?" she asked.

By now, everyone knew Trent was staying there and working on the place, and they were *all* sworn to secrecy.

"It's…good." Oh boy. Could she be any more of an awkward turtle? Cora felt her face grow warm enough to melt an iceberg, and Maddy's dark brown eyes twinkled.

"God, don't tell me he's cast a spell on you, too?" She laughed and shook her head. "I swear that guy has some magical lady voodoo going on. Any female who comes within six feet of him is likely to catch it."

There was no point denying it. Cora was sure her feelings were written all over her face, as usual. "Guilty. But I just got out of a relationship and it was…messy."

And humiliating. And heartbreaking. And infuriating.

"What happened?" Maddy asked.

"What didn't happen?" she muttered. "Our lives were too different. His parents were…serious. His mother is a professor at Cornell and his father's a judge, and they didn't really approve of our being together."

"Why not?"

Cora sighed and leaned against one of the bookshelves, still hugging her romance novels to her chest as though they might infuse her with some of that happily-ever-after goodness that she so desperately wanted. "My parents are high profile, but they've got reputations. My mother… well, she's a fame whore."

There really was no other way of putting it.

"Over the years, she's pulled some stunts for media attention that were less than flattering. My father is more well-respected, but anyone in her orbit is thrust into the spotlight whether they like it or not." Cora bit down on her lip. "My ex came from old money. Like, serious old money. They looked down on us."

"That's horrible." Maddy wrinkled her nose and folded her arms across her chest. "And he broke up with you because his parents didn't like your family."

"It wasn't entirely that," she said with a sigh.

God, should she even be telling Maddy about all this? Airing dirty laundry was so not her style. But frankly, she needed to get it off her chest. She'd been carrying this shameful secret from the moment Alex called off the engagement, and it was weighing her down.

"My mother put a lot of strain on my relationship with my ex," she said. "But I guess I'd been around her antics so long that I was used to her needing to be the center of attention. I was even used to seeing her hit on other men for attention, knowing she didn't actually want sex from them. She just wanted to feel beautiful."

Maddy cringed. "Oh God, tell me this isn't going where I think it's going."

"So, one night we were having a little cocktail party at a family friend's house. My mother had too much to drink and…" Cora shut her eyes for a minute. "She cornered my ex in a hallway and came on to him. She tried to convince him that she 'knew' he'd secretly had a thing for her the whole time we'd been together. Then she tried to kiss him."

"No!" Maddy clamped a hand over her mouth.

"Yep." Cora swallowed back against the bile that rushed up her throat, like it always did whenever she thought of that night. "The worst thing was, everybody could hear her. The main room was only a few steps away, and they were all *staring* at me…"

She'd wanted to sink into the floor and die. It had easily been the most humiliating experience of her whole life.

"Alex brushed it off at the time, but a week later he told me he couldn't do it anymore. He said I was so desperate for my parents' approval that I let them treat me badly and that I never stood up for myself or made my own decisions. He said I was… weak."

"Oh, honey." Maddy pulled Cora in for a big hug, squeezing her hard. "I don't even know what to say. You poor thing!"

Tears sprang to Cora's eyes, but she blinked them away, tipping her face up to the ceiling so they wouldn't fall. She'd shed enough already.

"I was furious that he wanted to punish me for what she did. It's not like I can control her. And… who else do I have besides my family? My social circle is small because my mother scares people off. I work at my father's business."

It sounded so pathetic when she laid it out like that. She had zero control over her life. Zero agency. All because she'd tried for decades to be the glue that held her family together. All because she'd been desperate to recreate that "happy family" scenario that she saw on TV.

"Is that why you came here?" Maddy asked. "To get a break from it all?"

"A much-needed one." She sucked on the inside of her cheek. "I thought parents were supposed to put their children first."

Maddy made a snorting noise. "Uh, not in my experience."

"Sometimes I don't even understand why people bother having kids if they have no intention of loving them. If you want to worship yourself, get a mirror."

Since the breakup, she hadn't talked to anyone about what she was feeling. Instead, she'd bottled it all up and tried to soldier on. Unfortunately, emotions didn't work like that. You could try to keep them down, but eventually the pressure would become too much. It was like shaking up a bottle of Coke and expecting it not to explode.

Confessing to Maddy was surprisingly cathartic.

"Tell me about it," Maddy said. "I've wondered that, myself."

"Are your parents the same?"

The other woman laughed. "Well, my mother isn't going around hitting on anyone's boyfriend, that's for sure. But is she overly opinionated and controlling? Yeah. She thinks I should be settled down now and having kids. I'm not even thirty yet, but she acts like I'm an old spinster who's squandered my youth. What decent man would want to marry someone as old and wrinkled as me?"

It was hilarious, because there wasn't a damn line in Maddy's flawless skin.

"But that's her opinion and I don't need permission from her or anyone else. I love her, but we're very different people. It's taken me a long time to be able to understand why she says the things she does and that I shouldn't place my worth in her opinion of my activities."

"That's very mature."

"See aforementioned comment about being an old spinster." Maddy laughed. "Seriously though, it took a lot of work. There was a period of time that we didn't speak at all, and it was hard. But the time apart made me see that I didn't want to lose her from my life. We needed to find a middle ground."

"I'm not sure there *is* a middle ground with my mother." Cora sighed. "I feel like I've tried everything—confronting her, avoiding her, trying to play nice…"

"Finding middle ground only works if both sides are willing to try. If you've given it all you have and she's still not meeting you halfway…" Maddy shrugged. "As you said, you can't be responsible for her. You need to live your life at some point."

She nodded. "You're right. I came here to do exactly that and I feel like I've spent the whole time thinking about relationship troubles."

"Maybe you need some more distraction, then." Maddy tapped the books in Cora's hands. "A little steamy romance should do the trick."

But the way she said it, with a twinkle in her eye, made Cora wonder if her new friend was talking about more than romance between the pages of a book. Maybe Cora needed some *real* romance. A true no-strings vacation fling. Who knew? Maybe it might even help get her creative juices flowing for her manuscript?

Perhaps it was time to woman up and stop overthinking everything.

And *so what* if it was a bit of a rebound? She deserved some fun for all the heartache she'd been through lately. And really, it's not like there would be any consequences—she wasn't going to stay in Australia past the end of the month, and it didn't seem like Trent was looking for anything serious. Nobody had to know, either. It wasn't anyone's business.

What are you waiting for?

Cora would put her perfect family dream on hold—for the next few weeks there would be no TV-family fantasies. No white-picket-fence visions. No imaginary husband to give her perfect imaginary babies. No desperation to get her father to believe in her.

None. Of. That. Shit.

All that mattered was the here and now and doing stuff that made her feel good. She'd earned it.

CHAPTER THIRTEEN

Cora made her way back to Liv's house, eager to see Trent after making her decision about collecting on their sexual chemistry. Anticipation burned through her veins, churning her up inside. So what if this was about scrubbing the memories of her bad relationships away? So what if it was for nothing more than feeling good and wanted and desired, even if it meant absolutely freaking zip in the long run?

As she drove, her eyes widened at the darkly shifting shapes overhead. Trent had told her summer storms could sneak up quickly, shattering the sky and drenching the earth before disappearing as quickly as they came.

This is not a bad omen. This is not a bad omen.

She barely made it to the house before the storm hit. It was incredible to watch the sky shift from vivid blue with fluffy marshmallow clouds to roiling shades of inky navy and rich, deep purple split only by streaks of pale gold lightning. She jumped out of the car and made a break for the front door, head bowed to the pelting rain. The cool droplets were almost a relief from the heat, but they came so thick and fast that she was drenched in seconds.

Cora gasped as her sandals skidded on the wet concrete, and when she looked up, she saw the front door was open and Trent was standing there.

"Come on," he said. "It caught me, too. I only just beat you home after picking up some tools from Nick."

"This rain is no joke." Cora's breathing came a little hard from the shock of being wet and cold after a long day of bone-melting heat. Her white T-shirt was all but glued to her skin, and her hair trickled chilly droplets down her back as she stepped into the house.

"One of the quirks of the weather here," Trent replied, raking a hand through his hair and shaking off the excess water.

His T-shirt was also glued to him. It clung to every muscle in his work-honed body, from the broad "carry the world" shoulders to the hard pecs, rounded biceps, and rippled abs. She tried to swallow, but her mouth was desert dry. Even his shorts were clingier than normal, the light tan fabric dark in patches. As Trent bent over to take off his boots, Cora couldn't help but stare. She'd never really been sure *why* exactly people used the peach emoji to represent an ass; her flat butt certainly didn't look like a peach.

But now she knew. Trent had peach-ass perfection.

"You all right?" he asked, looking up as he yanked one boot off and then the other.

"Uh-huh." She sucked her bottom lip between her teeth.

"I feel like you're staring at me." There was a hint of amusement in his voice. "Have I torn my pants or something?"

This was it, her crossroads. They were alone in

this house, shielded by the bad weather—and really, *what* was more romantic than a thunderstorm? Was she going to chicken out again and go hide in her room? Or was she going to seize the opportunity to be wild and carefree and totally *not* like herself?

"Your ass looks like the peach emoji," she blurted out. Immediately, she wanted the ground to open up and swallow her whole. "That…didn't come out right."

Maybe she was doomed to be celibate. Whatever gene other women had that made them sexy and sultry and all those good things was obviously lacking in her. No amount of etiquette school had ever really drummed the awkwardness out of her.

"How was it meant to come out?" Trent stood and nudged his boots to the wall with his foot. Water dotted his skin—highlighting the corded muscle in his neck and arms.

"Umm…" Cora smoothed her hands down the front of her stomach, something she tended to do when she was nervous. And right now she was more than a little nervous.

Trent was hot. Like, stick him straight on a magazine cover without any photoshopping kind of hot. His bright blue eyes tracked her every anxious movement, and the corner of his lip hovered somewhere between smile and smirk. He *knew* he was good-looking. Hell, he probably had women with much more finesse and sexual prowess throwing themselves at his feet every damn day.

Women who probably had the first clue about coming on to a man.

"I'm not very good at this," she said, though whether it was to herself or to Trent, she wasn't totally sure.

Maybe this was one of those cases where actions should speak louder than words? Her fingertips drifted to the hem of her T-shirt, and she toyed with it for a second—pros and cons dancing in her mind like sprites—before she peeled the fabric up and away from her skin. She bent her arms, hoisting the T-shirt over her breasts and then her head before releasing the wet fabric so that it landed with a *thud* on the floor.

"I would say you're *damn* good at it," Trent said, swallowing. His eyes were darker now, smokier. Or maybe it was the shifting of the clouds outside, while the rain thundered down, branches scratching against glass and thunder warning them there was more to come. "But I thought you weren't ready."

"Maybe I am now."

Cora slowly toed off her sandals and nudged them to one side, mimicking what he'd done a moment ago. When she reached behind her, feeling for the clasp of her bra, Trent held up a hand to stop her. The disappointment was like a knife to her gut. She could see he was attracted to her—see it in his eyes, in the taut pull of his lips. In the growing outline of his cock behind his wet, clingy shorts.

The sight almost took her breath away. She was a puddle of wanting, of need and desperation and every other type of vibrating energy all twisted together. Her whole body hummed, like each cell was a tuning fork and he was the catalyst for it all.

"Wait." He came closer, hands splaying out across her hips. His fingertips were cold from the rain, but her body was fiery hot. Molten. "You're either ready or you aren't. I don't do maybe."

She swallowed, fear and lust and anticipation a tornado of temptation inside her. Why did she feel so stripped back? So raw? Maybe it was because he wasn't letting her skirt the edges of things. He wasn't letting her get by without voicing her desires, clearly and distinctly. To speak up for what she wanted, which didn't come naturally.

All her life, she'd been told what to want, what to chase, what her dreams and aspirations should be. But Trent wasn't telling her anything.

He was forcing her to be active in her desires instead of passive.

"I *am* ready," she said resolutely. The sureness of her words trickled through her body, giving her strength and determination. Fortifying her. It felt empowering to claim her desires, to state boldly and clearly what she wanted. It made her feel like a new woman. "I want to sleep with you."

"Then I think we're skipping ahead a few steps."

"We are?" She tipped her face up to his.

"Yes." He touched his forehead to hers, warm breath skating over her skin, hands sliding around her back. "We have to start with a sweet kiss."

He brushed his lips over hers, the kiss so soft and gentle, it had no more weight than a memory. His thumb smoothed over her jaw, and Cora wound her arms around his neck. It was like sinking into a warm bath.

"Then something a little sexier," he said.

This time when his lips met hers, the kiss was hot and open. Sensual. Exploratory. His tongue swept the inside of her mouth, and his hands tracked slowly down her back to the curve of her butt. He tasted warm and smooth, smelled like rain and salt and wanting. She melted into him, and it was like she was no longer a person, just a manifestation of her desires. She was liquid and floating, drowning in his kiss.

"What's next?" she gasped when his lips moved to her neck, sucking, nipping, scraping. His chin was rough with stubble, and when he nuzzled the crook of her neck, it was like being showered in sparks.

"Body contact." He drew her close to him, lining her body with his.

Everything was hard...*everything.* From the coiled muscles in his arms to his fingers as he kneaded her backside. To the hard ridge of his erection digging in to her belly. To his kiss, which was deeper and more and perfect.

"I like this bit," she murmured as her head rolled back, letting his hands move over her.

He walked her backward until she hit a wall. No, not a wall. Glass. It was the back window, and she splayed her hands out behind her, palms sliding over cool smoothness as Trent kissed her again. His hips ground against hers and she let it happen, willed it to continue. Begged with her body to go further.

"Are we at the undressing part yet?" she asked, her voice ragged.

Trent laughed, and it was the most gravelly, growly, sexy sound she'd ever heard. "We can be if you want."

She nodded, heart hammering in her chest.

"Can I do the honors?" He traced a fingertip along the line of her bra, and Cora thanked her past self for having the decency not to wear her "comfy" bra today. This one had a touch of lace at the edge and a little bow between her breasts, like the cherry on top of a sundae. It was sweet and it made her feel pretty, but right now she was sure she'd feel better with it off.

"Yes," she breathed. "Please take it off."

Trent palmed her through the lace and satin cups, squishing her boobs together and planting kisses in the line of her cleavage. The rough bristles of his stubble were fire against her delicate skin, but in the best way possible. And when his fingers found the clasp at the back—not fumbling and cursing like her ex always had—she almost sighed in relief when she was set free.

The roughness of his fingers was heaven against her hot skin, and her nipples beaded immediately under his touch. They were tight, aching. Like the inside of her belly and deepest part of her sex and her heart and her lungs. Everything was aching for him.

"You're beautiful," he breathed, lowering himself so he could take her breasts in his hands, thumbs flicking over her nipples. "Everywhere. All places."

"Please," she begged, not even sure exactly what she was asking for.

When his mouth closed around her nipple, she cried out, her voice drowned by the crack of thunder outside. Her body was a riot of sensations, cool glass at her back, hot mouth at her front. The weight of her shorts felt like too much, and the seam of the thick denim rubbed at her most sensitive part when she squeezed her legs together. She rocked back and forth, trying to get the friction she needed there.

His tongue and teeth and lips stoked the fire burning inside her, and when the heel of his palm slipped between her legs, mercifully giving her pressure right where she wanted it, she almost wept with relief.

"That's it," he murmured against her breast, pulling his hand away briefly to lower the zipper of her shorts before snaking his hand inside. "Take what you want."

It wasn't perfect. Her panties were still a barrier, but she was already running toward the cliff edge of release, and nothing could stop her now. He kissed her and ground the heel of his palm against her sex and she rocked, rocked, rocked against him.

Then she was flying, orgasm splintering and fracturing, and she gasped huge lungfuls of air. Her muscles clenched. They pulsed. They sang. When she came, she buried her face in his hair and screwed her eyes shut, blotting out the senses she didn't need so that she could *feel* as much as possible.

When she floated back down to earth, there was nothing but the sound of her own breath and the rain. And the crackle of excitement. Trent's arms were around her, cradling her, as she clung to him.

"I like that bit, too," she said softly, feeling her

cheeks flush. But there was nothing to be embarrassed about. Didn't a woman deserve a ground-shaking orgasm every so often? Didn't a woman deserve to feel wanted and beautiful and powerful?

And she *did* feel that way. Even if she sucked at knowing the right thing to say or how to be sexy or enticing. Even if her scars and insecurities were deep. Even if she'd had fleeting thoughts that her life was going nowhere and nobody would ever love her again…if they ever had in the first place.

"See, and what if we'd rushed straight over all that?" He stretched up to his full height but kept her tucked against him. Wet T-shirt pressed against her cheek. "That would have been a tragedy."

"Agreed." But she wasn't done, not by a long shot. "Unless you want to stop?"

"No bloody way." He tilted her head back and kissed her slowly. "Do you want to stop?"

"No bloody way," she echoed with a grin.

"I'm going to start calling you my little cockatoo if you keep mimicking me," he said.

The nickname warmed her heart, and *that* was a little scary. Because her heart wasn't invited to this dance—neither was her brain. This was strictly a hands and mouth and down-there-bits only kind of occasion.

"I don't care what you call me, so long as you take me to bed." Okay, so maybe she *did* have a few moves up her sleeve. Apparently, all she needed was one orgasm to get her sexy talk on.

"Why don't we watch the storm?"

"Outside?" Her heart skipped a beat.

"Sure. You're not afraid of anyone seeing, are you?" His smile was so wicked, it made her sex clench.

The house was pretty isolated, with its long driveway and densely packed trees and sprawling block. No would see them... Would they?

"Do you have a blanket?" she asked.

He nodded. Lowering himself to his knees in front of her, Trent placed a kiss at her navel and worked her denim shorts over her hips. Then her lace-trimmed panties followed and she was fully naked. He pulled a blanket from the back of the couch and wrapped it around her shoulders, rubbing over her arms and shoulders, as if drying her off.

There was something really gentle about Trent, something caring and sweet that she wouldn't have immediately spotted. Because the first thing one noticed was how strong he was—physically and personality-wise. He knew what to say, knew how to touch her, and did it all with supreme confidence. Trent was a practiced seducer, and he would be a skilled lover beyond what she'd already seen. No doubt about it.

But even though this was nothing but chemistry, he never made her feel like an object. Like he was driving toward his own pleasure and she was just a vehicle.

"You have to get undressed, too," she said, sucking on her lip as she soaked him all in. He was physical perfection from head to toe. And yeah, it was a little intimidating.

His hands went to the hem of his T-shirt, and he

peeled it up, revealing all the ridges of muscle she'd felt only moments ago. Then it was the belt at his waist, and the sound of metal on metal was like a thunderclap in the quiet room. Then his zipper, fabric being pushed over his hips and his socks following. He left his underwear on.

He was even more glorious when mostly naked, but it was the sparkle in his eye that she was most attracted to—the playful, spontaneous, no-holds-barred nature of him. The proof that, he was as good on the inside as on the outside.

"Come here and share that blanket with me." He reached for her, opening the huge piece of fabric and wrapping them both up, skin to skin. "You're like a sexy burrito."

"What? Burritos are *not* sexy." She laughed, squirming when he turned her around so her back was at his front. "They're squishy and messy and…"

"Delicious, just like you." He pressed his lips to her temple.

"Smooth talker," she said, letting his warmth seep into her. "I might have to watch out for you."

Trent could easily fill her head with tempting thoughts and dangerous ideas.

He walked her to the door while they were both still wrapped up, and it was awkward and funny and she laughed harder than she'd ever laughed before. "I feel like I'm in a sack race."

"Stop whinging," he said, nipping at her ear.

"Whinging?"

"Complaining," he said with a teasing tone.

"Oh, you mean whining."

"Nah, mate. We say whinging here."

She giggled. "Mate."

"You *are* a little cockatoo."

Eventually he let her have the blanket and he strode outside to the back deck, his ass perfectly on display in tight black underwear. Peach indeed.

They cuddled up on an oversize wicker chair, which was padded with a big, comfy cushion. The roof out back, which Trent called a veranda, protected them from the rain. It was magical to watch the storm waging its war on the land. She climbed into his lap and draped the blanket over them both, his body protecting her from the chill in the air.

The clouds shifted, like God himself was blowing them across the landscape. When lightning flashed, illuminating all the shapes in the sky, Cora sighed. Even in brutal weather, this place was impossibly beautiful. As they sat, Trent's hands roamed her body beneath the blanket, skating over her shin and her knee, tracing the inside of her thighs. Teasing her.

"Could this *be* any more perfect?" She sighed.

"This was what you wanted, huh?"

"A hot man and a thunderstorm? Hell yeah." She laughed when he waggled his eyebrows. "I'm glad you ended up being here."

The statement popped out before she had a chance to wonder whether it was telling too much, giving too much away. Instead of allowing him time to ponder what she meant—or let herself go into an anxious thought spiral—she turned to him, clasping his face with her hands and bringing his lips down to hers. He tasted like heaven, and the feeling of his strong, rough hands on her body made her want to float away. Taking her time and not rushing straight to what she'd been taught to view as the "finish line" was new. He seemed content to touch and taste and explore, learning her curves and what she liked. And she did the same, raking her nails down his chest and watching for the flare of excitement in his eyes. Shifting so she could reach down and palm the hard length of him through his underwear.

When she freed him, sighing at the feeling of him skin to skin in her hand, the blanket suddenly felt too hot. Shrugging, she let it slip down to her waist. The cool air peaked her already hardened nipples even further, and Trent's hands came to her breasts.

"So good," he said, his eyes rolling back as she stroked him.

She shifted in his lap, turning to straddle him on the big wicker chair. There was room for a whole football team on the damn thing, and she wanted to take full advantage of the space. "It'll feel better when you're inside me," she said huskily.

"How did we go from 'your butt looks like the peach emoji' to *that*?" he teased, catching the edge of her mouth with his thumb and parting her lips. "Holy hell."

"I guess I needed warming up."

"You're not warm, Cora. You're making the sun look like a glacier."

Who *was* this man? And who was she when she was with him—a siren? A seductress?

"I stand by it," she said with a saucy shrug. "Your butt *does* look like the peach emoji."

He laughed and splayed his hands over her thighs, his thumb stroking her tattoo etched into her skin. "And you don't think you're a butterfly yet?"

She looked down, her eyes catching on the ink that she looked at every day, reminding herself there was more to be done. "I'm a work in progress."

"Aren't we all?"

"I think I need more work than most people," she said with a soft laugh.

"Here's the conclusion I've come to," Trent said, continuing to run his hands up and down her legs in that beautifully soothing manner. "Nobody's got life figured out, and the ones who seem like they have are simply better at hiding their shit."

"Their shit, huh?" She smiled. "Is that the technical term?"

"Pretty sure it's what all the top psychologists would say, but what do I know? I'm just a blue-collar guy."

"There's no *just* about it."

Trent was a force—maybe people didn't see that about him because he was so affable and fun-loving and unpretentious. But Cora was the kind of person who looked deeply, who tried to find the true essence of a person under all their disguising layers—layers she knew intimately because she wore them, too. Trent was more than a joker.

"Can we stop talking now?" she asked, leaning forward. "As lovely as this has been, and as much as I'm enjoying this storm, what I really want is…"

He raised a brow, a sexy smirk dancing on his lips. "Tell me."

"You."

He leaned forward, pressing his mouth to hers and coaxing her lips open. His hands drove up into her hair, fingers threading through the strands and cradling her head, making her feel precious and cared for and…loved.

No, not loved. Never loved.

It was a star too high to aim for. All she wanted now was to feel good physically. To feel wanted and desired and to be able to return that want and desire. The rest…well, it had no place here.

Scooping her up, blanket and all, Trent strode into the house, still kissing her. Cora wrapped her arms around his neck, hanging on as she was swept into his bedroom and laid gently down on the bed. He disappeared for a second to grab a condom from his wallet. While she waited, Cora stretched out on the bed, letting herself sink into this delicious fantasy. Letting herself wonder what life might be like here with a man like him. With a passion like this.

When he came back into the room, he stood before her, naked. Inviting. The hard jut of his cock left her mouth dry.

"Good?" he asked in a way that wasn't really a question. Trent *knew* he looked like a last meal and Christmas morning and fireworks rolled into one.

"Do you want me to stroke your ego?" She

beckoned him to the bed.

He took a moment to roll the condom down onto his length, and he tossed the foil packet onto the floor. Awareness raced through her veins as the bed shifted under his weight and he crawled forward, muscles coiled and eyes like a hurricane.

"I want you so bad," he said, his accent even more pronounced with the lust thickening his words. "I wanted you so bad the second you set foot in this house."

"Really?" The word was a whisper.

How could he have wanted her then? She was a mess, a broken woman made of parts barely held together with hope and concealer. She'd been a shadow of herself, a mere sliver.

"Really. The fact that you didn't turn tail and leave, that you wanted to help fix things and do your part, the fact that you were so beautiful and stubborn and sweet... God." He shook his head. "I couldn't resist wanting you."

The revelation made her heart swell. How had he seen something in her then that she couldn't even see in herself? It was like smoothing a balm over her soul, tending to the emotional cuts and bruises in a way that made her feel whole again.

She reached for him, pulling him toward her with an instinctive need to have him close. Her body sank farther into the mattress as he came down on top of her, muscular thighs parting her softer ones.

"Now," she breathed, her body already crying out for more. "I want you."

In the past, Cora had been a little self-conscious in bed, not finding her confidence until she had been with a man a few times and felt more comfortable around him. But Trent had tapped into something deep inside her, like flipping a switch that had needed the cobwebs to be dusted away.

She felt safe with him. Not judged.

"Don't rush me," he drawled, taunting her. One hand ran over her body, cupping her breasts in turn and tracing a line from her navel to her sex.

"Please," she begged. "I need...I need you."

As he pushed inside, her body gave in to him, melting and yielding and turning to liquid pleasure. The weight of him pressing her into his bed consumed it. It burned her up from the inside out because she felt truly beautiful in his arms.

She felt...cherished.

He moaned against her lips, his hips moving back and forth in deep, fluid strokes. Cupping his face, she pulled him to her and kissed him with everything she had. His lips probed hers, tongue delving into her mouth. Bodies fused together, finding a rhythm. His pelvis brushed hers with each stroke, fueling the fire he'd begun with his hands not long ago.

Everything else evaporated. Her past pains and insecurities stripped away as if nothing existed but right now. No past, no future. Only the glorious present.

"Trent, I'm close." She rocked her hips up to meet his, her body quaking again.

Her hands fisted in the sheets and she arched, shattering with him inside her. Her cries echoed off

the walls of his room, and a second later Trent
followed, his face pressed hard against the side of
her neck as he roared in release.

As she lay there, heart full and body sated, she
couldn't help but feel that she wouldn't be leaving
Australia the same person as when she arrived.

CHAPTER FOURTEEN

Later that night, after they'd stopped for refueling and then gotten lost in each other again, Cora was curled up in Trent's bed, drowsy and watching the storm through the bedroom window.

It was quieter now—the rain slowing to a steady pitter-patter against the glass and the lightning flaring across the indigo sky at infrequent intervals. They'd opened a window, and the scent of rain and wet grass and eucalyptus floated into the room, cutting through the haziness of their lust.

From his vantage point in the bedroom doorway, Trent was struck with how similar this image was. Cora's sun-streaked hair was a tangled mess on the pillow, and she lay on her side, her arms curling the blanket up under her chin. She'd dragged his pillow to her side, as if she were building her own squishy fort. He could see her profile—the long, straight nose and shadow created by her high cheekbones and the fan of her thick, dark lashes.

She looked so much like his ex, it was almost like unpicking the stitches he'd thought had long healed on his heart, reminding him that to trust someone was to put yourself in the firing line. To sign up for being betrayed.

This is nothing to do with trust. It's sex. Good *sex, but that's it.*

If he were the type to read into situations a little more closely, Trent might have wondered if this was

the universe trying to tell him he was stagnant…
but he *wasn't* that kind of guy. He didn't believe in
signs or horoscopes or fate or crystals or any of
that bullshit.

Cora and Rochelle were two different people,
and even if their outsides looked a bit—okay, *a
lot*—similar, there was no comparison when it came
to the inside. Cora was kind and sweet and open
and funny. And he didn't need to trust her, because
it wasn't like she was going to be sticking around.

Even if she was, he'd *never* put himself in a
position to be hurt ever again.

"Are you going to keep standing there and
staring?" she asked, cutting into his thoughts. She
raised her head and looked at him with hooded
eyes and a smile that was an invitation to sin. "It's
awful lonely in this big bed all by myself."

"Maybe I should get you a teddy bear," he
drawled, teasing her. Cora laughed and he stood,
feet rooted to the ground like something was
holding him there.

*Get out of your own head. This isn't going
anywhere.*

But Trent couldn't quite shake the feeling that
Cora's being here had a greater significance than
some hotter-than-normal sexual attraction. It was
like something in the air had shifted, but he
couldn't quite put his finger on what, exactly, it was.
All Trent knew was that he didn't want *anything* to
change in his life—he liked being single and free,
liked the ability to change direction as he pleased.

And most of all, he liked knowing that nobody
could get to him.

• • •

The following afternoon, Cora had been hard at work on the scrapbook until she'd hit a speed bump. They were missing photos. Likely, in the chaos of cleaning up after the "glitter incident," some of their photocopies had been accidentally thrown out. And, given Trent's parents were due to return from their trip that evening and he'd already returned the albums after their last scrapbooking session, they had to be quick about replacing them.

Luckily, Nick had let Trent take the day off so they could sort this problem out. It was funny to see two men as big and powerful as the Walters brothers so terrified at the prospect of angering their little sister.

So she and Trent were now cruising with the windows open down the winding, tree-lined streets on the way to his parents' house. The scent she'd come to associate with the town—briny sea air, eucalyptus, and something uniquely floral that she couldn't quite identify—danced in her nostrils. Cora sighed in total and utter contentment.

She'd wanted her vacation to provide some much-needed rest and recuperation, but there was no way she could have anticipated *how* good it would be for her. But maybe that had nothing to do with the vacation itself and *everything* to do with Trent. *He'd* given her the recuperation. He'd breathed life back into her, warming her so the ice thawed around her heart and she slowly started to recognize herself in the mirror.

At one point in her life, she'd been hopeful about her future. And now, under his care and attention and desire, she was becoming hopeful again.

"Have you thought any more about that architect Nick told you about?" she asked, watching the way the wind streamed in through the driver's side window, rippling his blond hair.

"Not really." Hidden by the darkly tinted lenses of his glasses, Trent's eyes stayed on the road. "I've been a little…preoccupied."

Hmm. That made two of them.

"But you're hoping to start work on it soon?" she prodded.

"Well, as soon as I've gotten everything else off my list. Fixing up Liv's place is priority number one. And then Nick's been talking about this big project he wants to get off the ground *and* I promised Jace and Angie I'd give their granny flat a facelift."

"Do you always put everyone else before yourself?"

"Helping my family makes me happy."

"And it's an easy excuse for avoiding making a decision." The words popped out before she had time to think about the consequences.

Having sex with someone does not *give you permission to psychoanalyze them.*

Trent pulled into the driveway of his family home and killed the engine. Turning to her, his eyes still obscured, he tilted his head. "I like to think things through before I make a big decision. I don't know why people find that so strange."

"It's not strange, it's smart…so long as you don't get stuck in the thinking and never get around to the doing."

He pushed the door open to get out of the car, and Cora followed. "You sound like Nick," he said. "He would have bought that land, fixed it up, and sold it for a profit before I even finished working through all the pros and cons."

"You struck me as the spontaneous type," she said, walking up the driveway beside him.

"Commitment should *not* be spontaneous. Learned that one the hard way."

Cora pressed her lips together, trying to keep the barrage of questions inside. Trent hadn't been too forthcoming with information about his relationship past, but then again, neither had she.

"Bad breakup?" she asked, almost immediately cursing herself.

"You could say that."

She wrinkled her nose. She really, *really* shouldn't pry. It wasn't polite to intrude on someone's personal affairs… "How bad?"

Dammit.

Trent let out a sound that was half laugh and half something a whole lot more derisive. "Bad, bad. Like, a whole lot of Jägerbombs and getting hauled out of the pub by security bad."

"Yikes."

"It's a good thing I've got friends who wouldn't let me take it too far." A strange expression crossed over his face, like he was remembering something important. "Anyway, I don't make the same mistake twice."

Cora fingered the fabric of her maxi skirt, knowing she should shut her mouth and leave the topic alone…but being way too curious to actually let it go. "What was the lesson?"

He jangled his keys in his hand before finding the right one and sticking it into the front door. "That relationships aren't for everyone, and I'm not interested in trying to be someone I'm not just to make another person happy."

For some reason, the words settled like a stone in Cora's stomach. She was still playing that eternal tug-of-war between wanting to be her own person and wanting to belong. A string of breakups hadn't changed her desire to find love.

And last night, she'd really felt something.

You went into this knowing it would be a fling. Stop trying to turn everything into forever.

"If it's the right person, then you shouldn't have to be someone you're not," she said.

"I think people are wired to fix things, especially other people, and I don't need fixing." His charming, cavalier smile was back in place—the darker expression blown away like clouds on a windy day. "Anyway, let's get this show on the road. I don't want Mum and Dad arriving home early and catching us in the act."

Cora gulped. She knew what he meant, of course, but that didn't stop her mind sliding right into the gutter. Ignoring the insistent pulse of her blood and the little voice telling her to act on her sexual impulses, she followed Trent into the house.

The place was homey and sweet. Family photos littered the walls and surfaces, and it was all too easy to imagine the five fair-haired Walters siblings racing through the rooms as kids, laughing and teasing and being a strong, cohesive unit. They headed into Trent's father's office, where all the albums were stored in neat, chronological rows on a big bookshelf. Thanks to his mother's meticulous system, it would be easy to find what they needed. They sat on the floor, legs crossed like school kids, and worked quietly.

Cora found herself distracted, but she leafed through the albums, forcing herself to concentrate and failing miserably. One night with Trent and suddenly she wanted to unravel him. To peel back the layers and figure out what made him tick. Alex had hated when she went into "investigator" mode like that, but Cora had always been curious about people. Maybe it was the stifled writer in her; she tried to satiate that need with real people instead of characters.

She flipped over another page, blinking at a photo of Trent that appeared to be from a few years ago. Five max. This was totally the wrong album. Annoyed at her mistake, she went to close the album when a picture caught her eye. Trent had his arm around a girl with blondish-brown hair and blue eyes and high cheekbones and a slightly pointed chin.

Was her brain glitching? The woman in the photo looked so much like Cora, it was like staring into the past. Even down to the little black dress and strand of pearls around her neck, which were in stark contrast to Trent's white T-shirt and loose-fitting jeans and leather cuff on his wrist.

What the…?

"Who's this?" She held the album up and pointed to the picture.

"I thought you were supposed to be looking at 1990," he said, frowning.

"I picked up the wrong one." She shook her head. "Is this…your girlfriend?"

"Was." His tone was flatter than a pancake. "I have no idea why Mum kept that photo."

Maybe because Trent looked blissfully happy in it—his eyes were shining and he was mid laugh, his handsome face beaming with youth and joy, and it was warmer and more delicious than freshly baked bread. The woman beside him smiled prettily, but she didn't have the same energy about her.

But no matter how good Trent looked in that photo, Cora could only stare at the woman. The resemblance was uncanny. Eerie.

Was it possible he'd been attracted to her only because she reminded him of…?

"What's her name?" Cora's voice was barely a croak.

"Rochelle."

For some reason, Cora's throat suddenly felt tight, her stomach twisted and turned like a violent, storming sea. Had he imagined Cora was Rochelle while they were making love? Was he still in love with her and Cora merely a substitute? A way to get closure?

"No," Trent said, though she hadn't even asked a question. He was perceptive like that, she'd noticed, understanding what people needed and what they were thinking. "Whatever that little voice is telling you, it's no."

"There's no voice," she lied.

"Bullshit."

Cora flipped the page and found another photo with a different angle. It was blurry, which made it even easier to see herself in Rochelle's image. To see the similarities and add even more with her imagination.

"Cora." His voice was rough, demanding. It shouldn't have sent a shiver down her spine, but it did. When he said her name, it was like the world wrapped her in a fuzzy blanket. Like she was safe from the shitstorm back home. From her own insecurities.

From everything.

"She looks so much like me...or, I guess I look so much like her." She snapped the album shut, suddenly needing distance from her discovery. For someone who'd felt second best her whole life, always shivering in her mother's shadow, to feel like she was a carbon copy now...

It made her want to be sick.

"Yes, you look alike. But it doesn't mean anything." He watched her closely. "Not to me, anyway."

"But you noticed it when I first arrived?"

"Well...yeah."

Oh God. He'd said it last night—that he'd wanted her the second he saw her. *Before* he knew who she was. Last night those words had meant everything; they'd felt serendipitous and fate-filled and lovely. But now with this new information, with this new lens, it made her feel used.

Now it was a reminder that she was, as always, a means to an end.

Curiosity swirled viciously in her mind. She wanted to know everything—why they broke up. Whether it was her who called it off or him. Whether he still missed her. Still loved her. Whether any of that had come into his head when he decided to kiss her. Was he comparing them while he touched her, putting traits in columns and ranking them?

He's not an asshole, and you know that.

She sucked in a long breath, trying to quell the sick feeling in her gut. This was nothing more than her own issues latching onto something in order to convince her that she was a failure. It was hard to see herself as anything else, given that's what she'd been told her whole life.

It wasn't fair to pile that on Trent's shoulders.

"Don't you find it a bit…weird?" she asked.

He closed the album in his lap and scooted closer to her, shoving things out of the way to create a path. When his hand came to her arm, it was like all her worries suddenly had their volume turned down. "Can I be honest?"

"I'd prefer it if you were."

"I noticed it and…yeah, it was a little weird at first. But here's the thing I've learned: looks don't count for much." He brushed his thumb over the side of her jaw. "And while I like the way you look *very* much because you're smokin' hot, the thing I like most about you is the whole caterpillar versus butterfly thing."

"Metamorphosis," she breathed.

"Yeah." He smiled. "People…just go about their lives, you know. But you *think* about things. You care about things. You've got so much good stuff inside you that…shit, how could I not be attracted to that? You want to change and be better and I think that's beautiful."

Was she being the caterpillar, though? Coming to Australia had been running away, avoidance. Getting entangled with Trent was a rebound. A distraction.

Last night didn't feel like a distraction.

"I know you've got some shit to work through," he said. "We all do. No one's perfect. But a lot of people do blame the bad things in their lives on others instead of taking the bull by the horns. Hell, you could have walked right out of Liv's place that day and left me to fix the carpet *and* the scrapbook. But you stayed."

"I stayed and turned you into a glitter bomb."

"I'm not saying your approach was great," he added with a laugh. "But you're trying, and that's more than most people can say."

"Thanks." Cora's insides were doing a battle—the warm, fuzzy feelings taking up arms against the hard-shelled insecurities and worries. There was something about Trent that drew her in, like he was a warm fire on a cold night.

But to what end? She'd be gone in less than three weeks, and he'd said himself that he didn't want a relationship. That was a dead end if she'd ever seen one.

"Any doubts about whether I was trying to fix the past by being with you?" he asked with a pointed look.

"Maybe a little," she admitted. "But that's on me, not on you."

"I *wasn't* thinking about her." He pulled her closer, touching his forehead to hers in a way that was so tender and sweet, and yet it jacked her pulse up as though he'd slipped a hand under her skirt. "Last night, it was only you. The day we kissed, it was only you. I've got Cora Cabot on the brain 24-7."

"And I've got Trent Walters on the brain 24-7." She tilted her face, kissing him hard and using her lips to coax him open. The kiss was deep, a little emotional. Passion-charged and white-hot. "It's lucky there are no more hours in the day, because you'd be stealing those, too."

He let out a dark and dirty laugh, his hand slipping behind her head and his fingers sliding into her hair. "Good. I want you thinking about me all day, thinking about all the things I want to do to you when I get home from work."

"You're all dirty when you get home from work," she said softly, her pulse fluttering as he kissed the side of her neck.

"And you'll enjoy getting me clean again, don't deny it." The sound of a car door slamming split them apart, and Trent's eyes widened. "Shit."

He jumped up and jogged into the front room, muttering a curse underneath his breath. A second later, he popped his head into the study.

"It's them. They're not supposed to be home until tonight…" He raked a hand through his hair. "I can't let them find this—Liv would *kill* me. I'll distract them if you can finish up quickly."

Cora nodded. "Sure, I need maybe five minutes. We're only missing two pictures."

Trent shut the door, sealing her inside. She quickly located the album with the year of his birth and flipped through the pages, looking for the photo of him in his mother's arms. Melanie Walters had a tradition with her baby photos—when each one was born, she'd have a photo of them in the hospital bed, the same blue teddy bear tucked in beside her. Apparently, the bear was an heirloom and had been part of her "birth bag" for each baby's arrival.

But, for some reason, there was no picture of baby Trent with Melanie and the bear. Cora flicked through the album, which documented his earliest days, but the photo wasn't there. Oh God, what if they'd accidentally thrown it out?

Shaking her head, she went back to the start of the album. It was marked with the year of Trent's birth, so it was definitely the right album, but there were no pictures of him at the hospital. The photo *had* to be there.

Frustrated, Cora shelved the album and searched for the other picture they were still missing—one of Liv on her first birthday, her hands full of chocolate cake—and easily located it. The voices sounded as though they were outside, so she slipped the photo into her pocket so they could copy it at home before returning the original to the album.

She needed to get out, now. But she *really* didn't want to leave without everything they needed to finish the project. Growling under her breath, she scanned the office. This was hopeless—they'd have to leave the scrapbook unfinished.

As Cora slipped her bag over her shoulder, she turned, accidentally clipping a box that was sticking out of the bookshelves that housed all the albums. It fell, the lid flying off and scattering papers and mementos across the floor.

Dammit! If she got them caught, she'd never forgive herself.

"Shit, shit, shit." Cora dropped down to her knees and started hastily shoving everything back inside, her heart thundering as she heard the telltale jangle of keys outside and the sound of voices getting closer.

As she quickly tried to tidy up yet *another* mess she'd made, her hands coasted over a photo featuring a hospital bed, a baby, and blue bear. Yes! She'd found the missing photo. It was like fate had tipped the missing puzzle piece into her hands. Only…

When she looked closer, something was amiss. Instead of Trent's father standing beside the bed like in all the other photos where his handsome face had beamed, mouth capped by various styles of facial hair over the years, there was no man. This photo had the two sisters in it. One in the bed and one standing beside it.

Maybe Trent's father hadn't made it to his birth and so Melanie's twin sister had been there instead?

Only…there was another problem. The woman in the bed, holding the baby, had a distinctive tattoo wrapped around her wrist that wasn't present in any of the other photos. Cora would have noticed it, because she was fascinated by other people's tattoos. The woman standing next to the bed had no ink showing.

Cora blinked, a sinking feeling filtering through her system. The twin faces of the women stared back at her, matching grins and wide, happy eyes. Melanie *wasn't* the woman in the bed; she was the woman standing to one side. The sister.

Which meant that she wasn't Trent's mother.

CHAPTER FIFTEEN

That Thursday, after Trent had finished work, he walked up the path to his brother's house, sucking in a huge lungful of the floral-scented air. The yard had two big wattle trees, adorned with thousands of fluffy yellow blossoms, and they'd been here ever since the house belonged to their grandparents. These days, Jace lived with his wife, Angie, and their brood of adorable puppies.

And yes, *brood* was the right word. Anyone masochistic enough to adopt four puppies at once deserved a medal.

When Trent jabbed at the doorbell, the house erupted in tiny, high-pitched yaps. A second later, the front door swung open and Jace stood there, surrounded by black furballs.

"Hey, come in." He held the door open. Today Jace was wearing a T-shirt with a drawing from one of his comics—*Big Adventures, Little Dogs*—on the front. "Don't mind the furry army."

One of the little black cockapoo puppies slapped her paws up onto Trent's legs. He bent down to scoop up the little thing, which was a mistake. Because the rest of them descended, yipping and licking and begging for attention. They were *all* females, named after the romantic leads in the nineties rom-coms that Jace's wife loved—Drew, Meg, Alicia, and Sandra, Sandy for short.

"Four dogs, bro. Really?"

Jace laughed. "Are you going to say that every time you come to visit? We've had them more than six months now."

"And I still cannot believe my brother, Mr. Routine, adopted four bloody dogs." Trent stood and followed his brother farther into the house, the pups trailing behind them like ducklings.

Jace's house was neat as a pin, as usual. He was the kind of guy who had a place for everything and hated to see things out of order. Even with the furry army.

"Hey, Trent." Angie came out from the kitchen and pulled him in for a hug. She was still in her uniform from the Patterson's Bluff nursing home where she worked as a day manager and event planner. "So nice to see you. Are you staying for dinner?"

"No, I just came to drop off my laptop. Jace said he'd take a look at it again for me."

Jace rolled his eyes. "What I said was you need to replace this hunk of crap because it's old and I can't do much for it now."

"Ah, but not being able to do much implies you can do *something*." Trent stuck his finger into the air. "Right?"

"I'll take a look at it." Jace grumbled as he took the silver beast from Trent's hands and stashed it on the coffee table. "But no promises."

"How's work?" Trent asked Angie.

"Good, busy." She planted a hand on her hip. "I swear the residents there keep me on my toes. We're getting ready to run our second phase of the learning program, and I've been getting suggestions left, right, and center for what type of classes they want to see."

Angie's program was something she'd created while volunteering at the retirement home when she'd first come to live in Patterson's Bluff. Back then she was in the country on a working holiday visa and had been looking for the perfect place to set down roots. She'd rented the granny flat—a little studio unit—behind Jace's house and while he was her landlord, they'd fallen head over heels for each other. Now she was a permanent part of their community.

"What are they asking for?"

"Everything." She laughed. "Meredith is still intent on getting a pole dancing class for seniors, but we've had some pushback with that."

"Too sexy?"

"Too physical. I think management is worried about the insurance." She rolled her eyes. "At this stage we're sticking with burlesque, because chairs seem a bit more manageable than poles. I've also been in touch with Kellen from the gym about running some strength and muscle conditioning workshops, and the owner of House of Cake has offered a decorating class. I hear you might be in the market to teach a class on scrapbooking, too."

Angie's eyes twinkled, and Trent let out a groan. "Is everyone talking about that?"

"Well, if you show up to a construction site with glitter in your hair, there are going to be questions." She laughed. "And it's such a great story."

"I'm *still* finding glitter on me. I swear, I was in the shower this morning and I found some in my armpit."

Jace snorted. "Maybe you should leave the creative work to the rest of us."

"You want to take over the scrapbooking project, be my guest." Trent raked a hand through his hair and sure enough, a little silver fleck stuck to his palm. "I am not built for this shit."

"How *is* the book coming along?" Angie asked.

"Slowly. After the glitter incident, we've been taking a careful and steady approach to things." Trent's lips quirked. "But we've been working together most nights, and it's been…fun."

Things had been a little strange between him and Cora. The night they spent together had been so explosive and passionate, but she was still skittish around him. A few times, it had looked like she wanted to say something, but then she snapped her mouth shut and made an excuse to go and read or tap at her computer.

But he got it. Cora was slowly coming out of her shell, sharing more of her life in New York. She'd told him about her breakup with her fiancé. Trent's family wasn't perfect by any stretch, but there was no way in hell he could imagine *anything* like that happening here.

It made sense she wanted to ease into things… whatever the "thing" was between them.

"Are you worried about what Liv will say?" Jace asked.

"About the scrapbook? I'm assuming she'll be pissed, but there's not much I can do about it now," Trent replied with a shrug. "No point worrying about what might be."

"He never worries about anything," Jace said to his wife with a shake of his head.

"Not true. I only worry when it absolutely counts, and most things don't. Trust me, when you work with stuff that could literally crush a man to death, *then* you know when to worry and when to be cool."

Angie laughed. "You guys are like chalk and cheese. Well, I hope Liv isn't too upset. Your parents are back now, right? I was thinking we should have a family barbecue or something. I'd love to meet Cora." She gave her trademark sunny smile and slipped an arm around her husband's waist. They were obnoxiously adorable. "It'll be nice not to be the only non-Aussie at the table. Although I might end up convincing her to stay. I couldn't imagine living in a big city now after being here."

"Who knows, maybe you'll start a business bringing single American women out to meet their matches Down Under." Jace chuckled to himself as though he'd made a really good joke.

"I'm sure the male residents would certainly appreciate it," Trent said, his mind immediately sliding back to the night he'd spent with Cora. Dammit. He really needed to put a lid on that, otherwise he'd have to walk around with a folder in front of his crotch 24-7. "Help a few single brothers out."

"You're single *and* loving it," Angie teased, not picking up on the fact that he *wasn't* talking about himself. "Unless you've got some secret plans to settle down and have kids like the rest of us."

The second the words were out of her mouth, Angie's eyes had gone wide like she'd said too much. Trent narrowed his gaze at her. "Excuse me, what?"

"I thought we weren't telling anyone yet," Jace said with a frown.

"Are you...?" Trent's eyes dropped down to Angie's flat stomach.

"No, I'm not pregnant." She wrung her hands. "But I *do* have a big mouth."

"We're trying," Jace clarified.

"Trying just means you're having sex." Trent knocked his brother with his elbow, and Angie wrinkled her nose.

"This is why we weren't going to say anything," Jace reminded her with a sigh. He was a private guy by nature and rarely shared his plans about anything with the family before they were carved in stone. "Don't tell anyone, especially not Mum and Dad. We don't want them asking questions or prying."

"My lips are sealed," Trent promised. "But seriously? You're trying for a baby?"

"We are. I lured him in with puppies first," Angie said, shining a beaming smile up at her husband. "And he's such a good fur dad."

Trent watched his brother's face for any signs of how he felt about the whole thing—he'd learned early on to do that, since his brother didn't always voice how he felt. Jace looked equal parts excited and worried. He'd said in the past that he wasn't sure about the whole "having kids" thing. Being a parent would result in a lot of upheaval, and being autistic meant change was a big challenge for Jace. For the longest time, marriage and family weren't on his radar. But having Angie come into his life *had* changed his view of the world.

"There's a lot for us to think about," Jace said with a nod.

"For starters, I don't know the medical history for either of my parents." Angie twisted the hem of her uniform shirt in her hands. "It's possible that I might be able to track down my birth parents' medical records, but…I'm not sure I want to dredge up the past."

Jace squeezed his wife's hand protectively. "We don't have to make that decision yet. There's still time."

Wow. Jace and Angie were planning a life together that felt light-years away from anything Trent was doing. He couldn't even pull the trigger on signing an architect, let alone committing himself to not only another person but to creating a whole new family.

A whole new life.

"I'm really happy for you guys," he said, smiling. "You're perfect together. Just make sure as soon as there's a baby, the little one knows who's the cool uncle, okay?"

Angie laughed. "I have a feeling Nick and Adam will *both* fight you for that title."

"They can try." Trent waved a hand as if shooing a fly. "But I claimed the spot first. Anyway, I should be going. I don't want to leave Cora waiting too long."

His brother and sister-in-law saw him to the

door, Jace's arm still protectively around Angie's shoulders. If he was like that now, imagine how he was going to be when Angie got pregnant. Not to mention when the kid actually arrived. Jace was going to be a full-grown papa bear, Trent could picture it already.

He paused to say goodbye to the puppies, crouching down and delighting in the little pink tongues and black paws and wet noses for a full minute before he headed outside. Once he was sitting in the driver's seat of his ute, key in the ignition, Trent found himself still for a minute. The rest of his family were moving on with their lives, building their own worlds and creating futures... and he was essentially still couch surfing. Lusting over a woman he knew wouldn't be around in a few weeks. Working hard at building things for other people but never for himself.

Nick had accused him once of putting other people's needs ahead of his own as a way of procrastinating. Maybe it was true. But Nick didn't know the truth of who Trent was. Why he was scared of trusting again. Nick had never been cheated on, had never been lied to and kept in the dark. So it was easy for him to judge.

He rolled down the window and caught sight of himself in the side mirror. "What are you waiting for?"

He didn't know. It wasn't like he needed someone to deem him worthy of a full life—Trent was as self-assured as they came. He was independent to a T. He liked being free and following his whims and relying only on himself. Because then he'd be assured that no one could hurt him.

But watching Jace and Angie through the window of the front room of their house, hugging and looking at each other with stars in their eyes, grand plans swirling in the air around them, Trent wondered for the first time if he really was missing out on what life had to offer.

For some reason, that made him think of the block of land he'd bought, sitting lonely and uninhabited at the outskirts of Patterson's Bluff. It called to him. Beckoned him. Maybe it was time to start thinking about his future.

For some reason, it felt like the universe was pushing him in a certain direction…and he wasn't sure if he liked it.

• • •

"Where are we going?" Cora asked as they zipped along the coastal highway out of Patterson's Bluff. Trent had picked her up a few minutes ago from the house, where she'd been diligently working on the scrapbook.

They'd made steady progress on it, hopefully it would only take a few more nights of gluing and stamping and sprinkling to have it done.

"I wanted to show you something." Trent glanced across at Cora, admiring the way her short denim skirt showed off miles of tanned skin.

It hadn't taken long for the strong Aussie sun to give her a glow—her limbs were darker, the ends of her hair lighter, and all the freckles had come out on her pink cheeks. And now she had her window down, and the air blew her hair around her face, making her look wild and free and so beautiful, it caused his stomach to somersault.

"You look different," he said, unable to stop the abrupt change of topic.

"Do I?" A pair of oversize black sunglasses masked her eyes, but the gentle curve of her mouth showed that she was relaxed and happy.

"Yeah. Something about you seems…I don't know. Changed."

"Maybe I relaxed." She lifted one shoulder into a shrug. "Maybe the sun here finally thawed me out."

Cora did *not* need any assistance thawing out, in his opinion. There was something guarded about her, sure. Given what he knew of her past, it wasn't surprising, and he wasn't about to push. He knew what it was like to need time to work through your shit.

"Good for you," he replied with a nod.

"And don't change the subject." She twisted in her seat to face him, not that he could penetrate the thick black lenses of her glasses. They made her look like some Hollywood starlet hiding from the press. "Where on earth are you taking me?"

Trent watched the sign approaching and slowed the ute. It was easy to fishtail in these front-heavy vehicles, especially if you had nothing in the tray, and he'd seen one too many dickheads do it on the highway when they almost missed a turn. Flicking his indicator, he eased off the bigger road.

"Trent," Cora prodded, sliding her glasses down her nose to flash her baby blues at him.

"We're going to a little place called number three Bramble Court."

He navigated onto a quiet residential street, the houses thinning out as he took another turn. Then another. Number one...two...three. He pulled the ute to a stop in front of the block. It was overgrown, weeds running wild and the grass alternating patches of straw-like tufts and dry, dusty earth. Set back from the street was a rundown structure with a broken front window and a graffiti tag sprayed in black across the front door.

Cora eyed him curiously. "It's a good thing I know you're not the murdering type. This place is..."

"In need of some work," he supplied.

"I was going to say the perfect place to bury a body." She wrinkled her nose.

"Nah. There's way too many nosy people around these parts." He winked. "You don't know gossip until you meet some of the folks in Patterson's Bluff. They make it a sport watching people out of their front windows. I swear, they've uncovered all kinds of secrets—affairs, divorces, secret business arrangements..."

Cora made an adorable snorting sound. "But no murders?"

"We're a chill people here; the ocean is a very calming influence." He pushed open the door and stepped out onto the road. "And I hear murder is a whole lotta work."

Cora followed Trent up the driveway, which was little more than a section of dirt loosely paved with gravel. The building was a complete eyesore and vastly different from how it looked in the photos from the online listing, which had used clever angles to hide the worst of it. But he'd bought it anyway, seeing the potential others might not. He'd need to get a demolition crew in and have a thorough cleanup. After that, save for a few towering gums, which he was adamant about keeping, it would be a clean slate.

He held up his hand, covering the shambling building so he could see nothing but the land around it. The block looked long and a little narrow, but it flared out at the back. It was an odd shape, but he could make it work.

He walked onto the plot, his boots crunching over dead grass and twigs and gum nuts. There was a sliver of ocean at the back, the slight incline of the land giving enough height to see the thin blue line over the back fence. If he built a two-story house, he could put a balcony out back and watch the calm waves roll in from the bay side of his hometown.

"I assume you're going to get rid of the murder hut?" Cora said, coming up beside him.

"It's got a certain charm to it, don't you think?" He couldn't keep the amusement out of his voice.

"If that charm is crack-den chic, then yeah." She wrinkled her brow. "Should we even be here? Isn't this private property?"

"You're a stickler for the rules, aren't you?" he said with a grin. "And you're right. It is private property. *My* private property."

She raised an eyebrow. "You brought me to the place where you want to build your home?"

When she said it like that, it sounded…intimate. Beyond the unspoken boundaries they'd laid around them. For some reason, bringing her here, showing her his plans—he felt proud for the first time in a long time. Maybe it was seeing Jace and Angie so loved-up and future-focused and happy.

It had been a long time since he'd wanted those things for himself.

"The view is really pretty," she said, taking a look around. After her initial reservations, she seemed to warm to the place, especially when she spotted the magnificence beyond the backyard. "You could build a two-story house facing… What?"

"I was thinking the same thing," he said with a grin.

The last couple of times Trent had come to check out his block of land, he'd felt this caged sensation. Like there'd been vines creeping up his legs and arms, wrapping around his wrists as though the place wanted to claim him. Hold him prisoner. It was a strange thing to *think* you wanted something, only to experience a very negative physical reaction when presented with the opportunity to achieve that goal.

But now there was nothing but the rustle of leaves and salt-drenched air and the sweetest hint of flowers. Not that there were any blooms in the immediate vicinity. Oh no, *that* was all Cora. And standing by his side, looking out at the ocean… well, it was a little too easy to take a mental pencil and sketch in the fantasy details—beautiful house, chilled beers, blanket to get hot and heavy under while the stars twinkled overhead.

Let's focus on the hot and heavy component of that, shall we?

"It's beautiful." Cora sighed, and the sound touched him somewhere deep. It was the sigh of a person releasing something into the world, the sigh of someone becoming one with a place.

"It's a good size," he said, trying to shake the uncharacteristic sentimental tone to his thoughts. Clearly, he'd let Nick and Jace and Angie get in his head. Building a house wasn't an emotional choice—it was a logical one. Dollars and percentages and decades. Squares and rooms and walls. Solid, real things. "I was worried about the narrow frontage, but I think I can make it work."

Cora made a disbelieving sound. "You *love* this place. Don't give me that crap about 'narrow frontage' or whatever."

The way she mimicked his accent—badly—made him smile. "You've got to work on your Aussie before you start tackling impersonations."

"Oh yeah, like your American is any better." She folded her arms over her chest.

"My American is, like, *perfect*," he said in his best Kardashian-type accent, which earned him a dirty look and a swat from Cora.

"I do *not* speak like that! And nice try changing the subject." Her mock annoyance faded into something softer, more observant. "You do that a lot."

"Do I?" That was Trent, evasive any time someone saw too much.

The affable, unaffected persona had developed

over the years—starting with the class-clown antics of his childhood to more subtle things as he got older that allowed him to hold people at a distance. Jokes and flirting and charisma were powerful shields, and he'd built a wall made of smiles around his heart. It was easier that way, to hide the hurt and sense of loss and the fear that he didn't belong.

"Yeah, you do," Cora said. "I think people take you at face value, but there's a lot going on under the surface. You're a complicated man."

Trent snorted. "That's the first time I've been called complicated. Ever."

"People don't look much farther than the ends of their own noses," Cora replied sagely. "*That* much I have learned in life."

"But you do."

Cora nodded, biting down on her bottom lip. There was that feeling again—the sense that she wanted to say something more. It was like a tautness in the air. What was swirling around in her head right now?

"That's because I'm a reader," she said eventually, nodding. Whatever was dancing on the tip of her tongue, she wasn't going to share it any time soon. "We tend to enjoy the study of people."

Trent wasn't sure what was going on in Cora's head, but he had the urge to reach out to her, and so he did. He looped his fingers around her wrists and tugged her to him. She came without hesitation, letting him pull her close, winding her arms around his neck and tilting her face up to his.

Trent brought his lips down to her, coaxing her open and sweeping his tongue against hers. It was sweet, burning, heady. He kissed her like he'd never kissed anyone else before, with abandon and longing and a desire to connect beyond the physical.

Bringing her here had been…stupid? Risky? Pointless?

Necessary.

There was some part of him that felt like he needed to prove something to Cora and to himself. But what, exactly? That he could move forward? That he wasn't just the funny guy with no substance? That he was capable of a life built on more than taking things day by day?

He shut the swirling thoughts out and focused on the feel of Cora's lips on his, on the way her hands curled into his T-shirt and the way her hips swirled against his.

Right now, he wanted nothing more than to drown in the physical. He could deal with his confusing swirl of thoughts about the future later.

Much, *much* later.

CHAPTER SIXTEEN

Cora couldn't get her head on straight for the rest of the evening. She was a jumble of thoughts and feelings, good and bad and everything in between. Why had Trent taken her to the place where he wanted to build his home? It didn't feel like the kind of activity for two people having fun, meaningless, great-but-going-nowhere sex.

It felt…personal. Real.

Real, like the secret she'd found out. The photo. Her revelation about his identity. It felt like a weight around her neck. More than once, she'd opened her mouth to try to broach the topic with him, but she couldn't force herself to say the words. He'd seemed so…hopeful.

What kind of person would shatter that moment?

It was none of her business, yet she felt embroiled in his life when she shouldn't be. Did he know? Had his parents lied to him? Would it break his heart if he found out?

You have to stay out of it. No good will come from meddling in his family life. Lord knows you hate it when people poke their noses into your family business.

And, in addition, seeing him open up had made her want to do the same. It made her want to tell him important things. Like her big, scary dream of being an author. She had fantasies of quitting her job at the agency and finding a quiet, beautiful place to spend her days writing. Like this vacation but…permanent.

She had dreams of sitting in a bookstore with a line of people waiting to meet her, clutching copies of her book to their chests. She had dreams of touching people with her stories, of knowing that her words had been a source of joy or healing or relief.

Those things were too terrifying to say aloud. What made her think she was so special that she could achieve something like that?

To take her mind off it, she'd settled on the couch with one of the books she'd bought from Maddy. She was halfway through and loving it enough that it whisked her away from her worries. Wasn't that the most magical thing about books? Their power to transport you to a place where you could breathe again?

"Hey, bookworm," Trent said, and her head snapped up, startling her out of her reverie. He settled down on the couch next to her. It was late now, and dark outside. "Still getting your nerd on?"

"If you're asking whether or not I'm still read-ing, the answer is yes," she said in a mock annoyed tone. "Call me a nerd all you want."

"You're a cute nerd, that's for sure."

"Maybe I think *you're* a nerd for reading *Architectural Digest*." She gestured at the magazine on the coffee table.

"Nah, I just look at the pretty pictures." Trent winked.

"Thanks for showing me your place today," she

said, closing her book and pushing herself up into a sitting position.

"I'm not sure why I did that, honestly." He raked a hand through his hair, as if suddenly bashful. "That was probably boring as batshit."

"It wasn't," she protested. "I guess it's…"

Here she was, overthinking things again. Reading into a situation more than she should. Why was it that she sought to be closer to every person in her orbit, as though it might fill some hole in her heart?

"What?" he asked.

"I don't know what our boundaries are." She looked down into her lap. "I don't know what this is."

"I don't know, either," he admitted.

"You shared something pretty personal today. Least it felt that way."

He looked away, his gaze drifting out the back window and into the dark yard. There was a tension in him—a resistance. She felt it, too. The push and pull between logic and feeling, her brain telling her this wasn't anything important and her heart murmuring its disagreement.

"I want to write a book," she blurted out. It was like the words refused to be contained any longer, like her dreams had swelled to the point that she couldn't keep them inside.

Trent's lips lifted into an amused smile. "Wanted to even the score, did you?"

"Something like that." She reached down to the little shelf under the coffee table and pulled out her laptop, opening the lid.

"*Flight of the Caterpillar*, a story of metamorphosis." His eyes scanned the screen. "What's it about?"

"It's fiction," Cora replied. "It's about a woman who packs up her whole life and moves to a small village in Italy to escape her controlling parents. She falls in love with the place, but the whole time she's fighting with the man who owns her building. It's a story about how she becomes the person she was always meant to be and how all people can blossom under the right conditions."

"Wow. Good for you."

She glowed under his words, warmed like hands turned to an open fire. "Thanks. I mean, it's no big deal unless I get it published, right? Anyone can make up a story and have it collect dust under their bed."

He shook his head. "I disagree. How many people say they want to do something and never take a single step toward their goal?"

That was true. If she had a dollar for every person she'd met who'd told her they wanted to write a book one day...

"You don't need someone else to tell you it's worthwhile," he added. "That's for you to decide."

"It needs to be better." She scrolled through the pages, her eyes scanning the Track Changes and highlighted bits of all the things that needed fixing. "But I'm determined to get there. I've wanted this my whole life."

"I have zero doubt in my mind that you will, Cora. Your passion for books is like nothing I've ever seen." He smiled at her, and this time it wasn't sexy. It was more…admiring. Holy hell, it made her feel good.

"Who knows, maybe one day I'll have my face on the inside of a cover just like this book." She held up the romance novel and showed Trent where the author's picture was in the back. "I'm up to chapter twelve now and it's getting good."

"Providing some good inspiration?"

"Oh yeah, and the hero is a total cinnamon roll. I didn't even know that that was a term, but it means the hero is totally sweet and kind and good-hearted and delicious…" She grinned. "I'm learning so much."

"I never thought I'd meet a person who loved reading more than my dad, but here we are."

"Books are my whole life. That entire torturous time I was at the music conservatory, books got me through it. Having Alex call off our engagement… books made it easier to face the day. I want to create a story that gives that same escape to other people when they're having a hard time."

Something flickered across his face, but it was difficult to read. Suddenly everything felt so serious, and Cora wasn't sure she should be going down this path. She liked Trent. Maybe too much.

And liking him too much wasn't part of the plan for a distracting holiday fling.

"And besides," she said, steering the tone of the conversation away from anything too real, "I could learn a few moves from these books. Reading is sexy."

Trent snorted. "Maybe it's sexy when *you* do it…but that's got nothing to do with the book."

"You wouldn't say that if you could see what was written on this page." She wriggled her eyebrows.

"Oh yeah?" His tone challenged her to keep going. "Try me."

Challenge most definitely accepted.

"I'm going to prove you wrong," she said, her voice low and sultry. Around Trent, she felt comfortable enough that some of her awkwardness started to disappear. Or at least, went into hiding. "'Jenna touched herself again, circling her fingers over her most sensitive part and letting out a soft groan. Not too loud—because she didn't want anyone else but him to see. But it felt so good with his eyes on her.'"

Trent faked a yawn, but his eyes were glittering. Taunting. He wanted to play.

"'His mouth went slack, and he palmed himself through the towel wrapped around his waist,'" she continued. "'Jenna wished it were his hands on her. She let herself imagine it—what would have happened if he'd stayed and stripped her out of her tights and her miniskirt instead of turning her away.'"

Despite his disagreement, Trent's eyes grew dark. Who was she, being so forward and so bold? Being a seductress?

He brings out the best in you.

Under Trent's hot, steady gaze, she felt powerful and beautiful and like she didn't need to try so damn hard. She could say what she wanted, claim what she wanted, without rejection lurking around the corner. Today had sparked something inside her—a connection to him. A bond.

"'She imagined what it would have been like if he'd taken her to bed and laid her down, peeling the underwear from her body and sliding his hands along her thighs, thumbs tracing circles on her skin. Getting higher, higher, higher…so close.'"

Trent was now totally focused on Cora, watching the way her lips wrapped around each word and the way her voice grew softer and breathier. His pupils were wide and dark, and when his eyes flicked back up to her, she had to bite back a groan.

"'Jenna's eyes fluttered shut, and she was lost imagining his big body covering hers, knees pushing her legs apart and mouth seeking hers. The fantasy played out in vivid color in her mind, and a tremor rippled through her. Everything was wound tight like a coil as she touched herself.'"

Dear *Lord.*

Cora knew exactly what she was doing to him, and it made her feel like a goddess. More powerful and in control than she ever had before. It was like she was a new person. Reborn. Better. Stronger. More capable.

It would be way too easy to become addicted to how he made her feel. But she had to remind herself that their time would come to its inevitable close.

"You don't play fair," he said, his voice gravelly.

Life wasn't fair. The people who thrived were the ones who didn't let fear of rejection stand in their way. But that had always been Cora's driving force—trying desperately to win approval, trying desperately to make her parents proud, trying desperately to be the perfect girlfriend or fiancé.

And what did she have to show for it? A job that didn't fulfill her, a lonely apartment filled with memories of failed relationships. A relationship with her mother that was beyond repair.

It's not too late. You can take risks. You can change.

If she could be with Trent now and *enjoy* herself—no expectations, no deeper emotions, no strings—then that would prove she'd changed. She didn't have to seek his approval or his love; she could simply indulge in his body and the way he made her feel, take the gift he offered her, temporary as it was.

If she could put every worry out of her mind— about the photo, about her novel, about what was waiting for her back home—and just *be,* then maybe Cora could finally grow some wings.

. . .

Cora slid her bookmark between the pages and let the book drop to the floor.

"So," she said with a shy smile. "You seemed to enjoy that scene about the guy watching."

"Hell yeah, I did."

"Is that something…?" Her eyes lowered. Trent could tell Cora was pushing out of her comfort zone, and it made his heart sing.

Not your heart, your body. Big *difference.*

"Maybe we could…" Her eyes flicked up to his. They were beautiful eyes, ice-blue and framed by thick golden-brown lashes, and they told him a story. Unlike so many people, she didn't hide her feelings away.

"Only if we head straight to the shower."

"Are you dirty?"

"Always."

He pushed up from the couch and held a hand out to her. She took it willingly, her eyes never leaving his.

"Maybe I should get into the shower first?" She sucked on the inside of her cheek. "We could replicate the scene before you wash the day off."

What good karmic deed had he done that had brought him this incredible, sexy, blossoming woman?

Cora had looked so broken that first day, and yet every day since, she'd shined harder and brighter and more brilliantly. There was a toughness inside her. A resilience. And it was like the sun and sea air and his kisses had helped bring that part of her back to the forefront. For some damn reason that made Trent feel like the king of the world.

"You'd better be careful," he said. "I might start making you read to me every night."

"I'll make you a romance reader yet," she said, walking ahead of him to the bathroom, wriggling her butt so sexily that he almost tripped over his own feet.

Yeah, this woman was going to unravel him.

"Finish working on your story," he said, coming up behind her and wrapping his arms around her waist. "That's a book I want to read."

"You would?" The hope in her voice was like the soundtrack in a movie, a note of danger ringing through the air to warn that things could turn bad. Why was he making promises he might not be able to keep? Cora wasn't going to stick around, and he didn't necessarily want her to.

This was nothing but a distraction—a very sexy distraction.

"Yeah, of course I'll read it." The promise stuck in the back of his throat, but as Cora stepped into the bathroom and out of his grip, her hands immediately going to the fly of her jean shorts, he decided that worrying was pointless.

Here and now was what mattered. Not tomorrow or the day after or the one after that. Just now.

Cora pushed the jean shorts over her hips and down her thighs, letting them slide to the ground in a soft, blue puddle. She wore simple pink and white striped underwear, which was trimmed with a touch of lace and a small, flat bow right under her belly button. They slid down her legs, too. Then went the floaty pink and yellow top, and her bra— something equally soft and feminine—until Cora was naked in front of him. She was beautiful beyond words, every part of her like a feast for the senses. Wild, wild hair tumbled down her shoulders, golden from the sun and brushing her pink-tipped breasts. Her tattoo stood out starkly against the slightly paler skin on her thighs. She let him look, basking in his attention.

There was no bashfulness about her now, just glowing confidence and sensuality. Unlike the first time they'd kissed, when she'd been eager and hesitant in equal measure, this time there was nothing holding her back.

"Stay there," she said, sliding the shower door open and turning on the taps. Water filled the stall and quickly heated, causing steam to billow into the bathroom.

Cora stepped into the shower, reaching her hand under the water to test the heat. Then she let the stream run over her body. Seeing her naked and wet, hair growing dark and damp, cheeks flushed with wanting, was enough to bring him to his knees. Trent felt himself grow harder and harder behind the fly of his pants, a sense of aching flooding his veins.

He wanted Cora more than he'd *ever* wanted another woman.

It was almost painful to wait and watch, and he palmed himself in restless anticipation.

Cora didn't miss the action, and it quirked her lips up, as though his anxiousness to join in the fun fueled her. She reached for the soap, lathering it between her hands and then sliding the bar over her skin. It circled her breasts, coating them in creamy lather, before dipping down over the plane of her stomach to foam the skin of her inner thighs. Trent groaned out loud.

"You're killing me," he said.

Her smile was damning. "Stay right where you are."

"You're getting off on my pain, wicked woman." He took a step forward, but she held a hand up in warning.

"I get the impression you were never very good at following instructions." The bar circled over her thighs, higher and higher. Then she took one hand

and brought it up between her legs, grazing her sex.

"I'm not," he growled. In seconds, his jeans and T-shirt were on the ground. His socks followed soon after. Then his jocks. "And if you think I'm going to miss out on the action, then you're dead wrong."

Cora laughed, her hands working over her body slowly. Sensually. He tracked the movement with hungry eyes, hovering at the opening of the shower. Steam fogged the glass walls and made her look like something out of another realm. She was unworldly and ethereal, so beautiful she couldn't possibly be human. So beautiful she couldn't possibly be real.

"I don't want you to miss out on the action," she said, reaching for him. Her hand curled around his wrist, and she tugged him closer. "Because then I'd be denying myself."

"You want me, huh?" He swaggered toward her, pinning her against the wall. She gasped as her back hit the tile, the sound turning from shock to pleasure as he rubbed against her.

"Yes, I want you," she said, looking up at him, her icy blue eyes wide and absorbing. "Too much, I worry."

"Too much?" He brought his lips down to hers, kissing her hard and deep. She curled her arms around his neck and pressed against him, breasts flattening to his chest, hips swirling against his in time with the sensual sweep of her tongue. "No such thing."

"I think there is," she whispered. Her voice was almost lost in the rush of the water, to the drumbeat of his heart. "I'm not supposed to care this much."

So she was having the same reservations at him, worrying that they were treating it as more than what it really was. He wasn't sure if that comforted or unnerved him.

"Let's enjoy this for what it is," he said, peppering her neck with kisses, licking the water droplets from her skin. Letting his body burn to cinders in her arms.

"Which is?" Her head rolled back against the tile, her mouth open in a silent moan.

"Fun." He slid a hand between them, feeling for the curve of her hip and down farther until he reached the spot that made her croon those delicious sounds. On cue, she gasped and pressed in to his touch. "Temporary."

"Temporary," she murmured as his fingers worked her sex, playing her like a guitarist coaxing music from strings.

"Yes, temporary."

Cora was hot and wet, and when he pressed a finger at her entrance, she was ready for him. Every part of her was responsive. Eager. Their bodies were so in tune, it was almost like they'd been lovers for years instead of days. Trent loved women and sex, loved the mutual pleasure of finding a partner who was as hot for him as he was for her. But this...this was something else, no matter how much he tried to label it as temporary.

"I don't want it to hurt when this ends," she whispered against his ear, hanging on to him so tightly, it was like she thought she might fall without him there to hold her upright.

"It won't," he replied. "I promise."

She arched against him, fingers tightening in his hair, nails dragging along his scalp. The sound of her crying his name bounced off the tiled walls of the shower as she came, shuddering against his hand.

"It won't hurt a bit," he echoed. But as he said it, he wasn't sure who he was lying to more—Cora or himself.

CHAPTER SEVENTEEN

The next twenty-four hours were pure bliss. Trent had rushed home Friday night after work instead of going for beers at the White Crest with his mates—aka the only thing he loved *more* than cricket—and had herded Cora straight into the shower. They'd made love for hours. Up against the tiles, tangled in the sheets of his bed, on the couch after they'd stopped for nourishment. Then later, when it was dark and they were both exhausted, he'd reached for her again. She'd come so willingly—sleepy, but willingly—into his arms that it satiated something deep inside him. Knowing she wanted him as much as he wanted her, knowing that they didn't seem to be tiring of each other…it was new. And wonderful.

This is dangerous. You're not treating it like a temporary thing.

Hell, tomorrow was the surprise birthday party for her. He'd been fussing over every detail with Aimee's help. She'd worked a miracle, pulling it all together in a week. They were going with an Australian kid's party theme including fairy bread, Vegemite scrolls, and party pies. Of course they were giving it an adult kick with two signature cocktails—a Manhattan, as a nod to Cora's hometown, and a Dark 'n' Stormy with Aussie flare, using rum from far north Queensland.

His folks had graciously agreed to host. Their

ginormous backyard had been the scene of many a party over the years, and his family lived life with an open-door policy. He'd invited a group to help Cora celebrate—the cricket gang, Jace and Angie, big brother Adam and his wife Soraya. Maddy had helped him select a perfect gift, a book by a local author, which she'd gotten signed. Everything was going to be perfect tomorrow. A Sunday afternoon birthday adventure.

Except…

Well, except he couldn't shake the feeling that something was wrong with Cora. And he certainly couldn't shake the feeling that he was getting *far* too involved for his own good. Despite the hot sex, she retired back to her own bed at night. And during the day, he kept catching her looking into the distance as though something was bothering her. Frowning, like she was occupied by some worrisome thought.

That's none of your business. Temporary, remember? That was the boundary you *set.*

And temporary didn't mean getting involved in each other's personal lives. He had plenty of secrets, and he hated when people pried. So he wasn't about to be a hypocrite and do that to her.

"You're thinking too much," he muttered to himself as he stepped back from the bathroom to survey the final result. Cora had been working on her book all morning, and he'd been feeling guilty about how he was spending more time with her than working on Liv's renovations.

So all the new tiling had been completed *and* the new vanity was installed. Yesterday he'd had one of his electrician mates come around and check the wiring for the new light fixtures. Thankfully, that was one aspect of this house that seemed to be in tip-top condition. Now the bathroom was illuminated with the glow of two high-end sconces he'd splurged on for Liv.

By some weird cosmic snap of timing, a FaceTime call flashed up on Trent's phone screen. It was Liv. He ducked out of the bathroom and into the hallway before answering so she wouldn't see any of his work.

"Hello from New York." Liv's face was half covered by a wool hat, and her cheeks and nose were pink. When she breathed, puffs of cold air made wispy clouds of condensation come out of her mouth.

"Hello from…your house." He grinned.

"So it's true, then—you're squatting." She shook her head, laughing.

"Who spilled the beans?"

"Nick. He's got a big mouth." She laughed and fogged the screen for a moment. "You could have given me a heads-up! I told you I had a guest coming to stay and she might not be comfortable having my big brother there."

Trent did his best to keep a straight face. He wasn't about to tell Liv what had been going on between him and Cora—they were both consenting adults able to make their own decisions—and for some reason, putting it out in the open felt dangerous. Like speaking the words aloud would make it all feel even more real.

"I offered her to stay at Adam and Soraya's, but

she didn't mind having a roommate." Yeah...
roommate. "And I wasn't fully aware you had a
guest coming to stay."

"You mean the group text, email, *and* Facebook
post updates weren't enough?" Liv huffed.

"C'mon Liv, you know I don't go on Facebook.
Or check my email."

"Or read group chat messages." She rolled her
eyes and laughed. "My dear brother, you're incor-
rigible. Besides, why aren't you staying with Hale
anymore?"

"Long story, but it starts with A."

"Aaah, lovely Aimee." She giggled and clamped
a gloved hand over her mouth. "My God, it's cold
here. I don't think I've ever been so bloody freez-
ing in all my life."

"So how is it? New York, I mean."

"Magical." His sister sighed. "And manic."

"And the internship?"

A strange look passed over her face. "Not what
I expected. But that's a story for when I get home.
In the meantime, I wanted to make sure you
weren't planning on staying at my place forever.
Cora might be fine with a roommate, but *I'm* not."

His sister was only half teasing. As the baby of
the family, she'd always craved independence. It
couldn't have been easy having four big brothers
watching over her at all times.

Adam always helped her with her homework
and made sure she wore sunscreen before going
outside. Nick had taught her to swing a cricket bat
and pushed her hard to pursue her dreams. Jace
had been there when she'd needed peace from the

rest of the family. And Trent had been the fun brother, always ready to hoist her up onto a flying fox or encouraging her to do a wheelie on her bike.

Liv loved them all with the ferocity of a lion, but she craved the ability to forge her own path. And while she was hacking away the jungle leaves of life, pressing forward no matter what, Trent was still standing at the fringe, watching as everyone raced ahead of him.

"Nick told me you still haven't started work on your place," Liv added. "I'd hoped without me being home to distract you, maybe you'd be getting a move on that project."

Trent glanced at the newly decorated bathroom. "I've got lots to keep me busy."

"Doing stuff for other people?"

Instead of making him feel better, her comment stuck like a thorn under his skin. He was trying to help her, trying to make her life easier because she was his little sister. "I really wish Nick would stop discussing my life decisions with everyone."

"Ah, don't get your jocks in a twist. You know what Nick is like—standing still is the worst thing in the world. He gave me a hard time for coming to New York for an unpaid internship when I could have been on the hunt for a full-time position back home."

Trent frowned. "I didn't know that."

"Yeah, he thinks I'm letting corporate sharks take advantage of me." She shrugged. "But I've always wanted to come here and see more of the world, so it served my purpose. I'll find something when I come home, no worries."

Trent had always appreciated his sister's positive, optimistic outlook on the world. She was a good influence like that.

"Looks like Nick gets stuck into us all," Trent commented.

"He wants the best for everyone, you know that."

Sure, Nick wanted the best for everyone, but only if it lined up with his idea of what that person *should* want. But he wasn't going to get into that now. Ultimately, he knew Liv would take Trent's side, if only to protect her spare bedroom from an unwanted tenant.

"Anyway," Liv said. "The reason I was calling is because there's something I need you to do for me."

"What's that?"

"There's a box in my bedroom that has the scrapbook I made for Mum and Dad's anniversary," she said, and Trent cringed. Before he had the chance to wipe the expression off his face Liv's eyes widened. "What was that look?"

"Nothin.'"

"You gave me a look."

"No, I didn't." But denial was pointless. Liv was looking at him with all the practiced suspicion of a sister who knew her brother was up to no good. She'd had *years* of catching him out.

"Don't lie to me, Trent Andrew Walters! I *know* that look." She pulled the camera even closer to her face so all Trent could see was the furrow of her brows over narrowed eyes. "What. Did. You. Do?"

Shit. No way was he getting out of this now.

"There was…an incident."

Liv let out a sound of frustration. "What kind of incident?"

"A flooding incident."

"You flooded my house? What the hell?" Her cheeks were pink now, a key sign that his little sister was about to go apeshit on him. Bloody video calls. He could have kept things on the down low if she hadn't been able to see his face. "Tell me what happened and don't scrimp on the details."

"I was fixing the pipes to get rid of that rattling sound and…I left the mains on. It was a rookie mistake." He wasn't going to throw Cora under the bus. No way. "It's totally my fault."

"And what's the damage?" She cringed as if unsure whether or not she wanted to hear the answer.

"Nothing too major. The carpet soaked a bunch of it up, but we got it dried out quickly." Hmm, how to word the rest of this story delicately?

"You're not telling me something."

"The scrapbook may have sustained some damage."

She wrinkled her nose like she always did before she was about to swear, but she bit back her angry response. "How much damage?"

"It's done."

"Done?"

"Ruined."

"Trent!" She let out a long breath, and the background changed suddenly, like she'd entered a building. Liv yanked her hood back. "I worked on that thing for *ages*. It was supposed to be a really special present."

"I know, Liv. I'm sorry. It was an honest mistake." He held up his free hand to halt any further freak-outs. "But Cora and I have worked our butts off to put it all back together."

"Excuse me, what?" Liv blinked.

"We remade the scrapbook."

"You? The boy who once told me arts and crafts were for people who didn't know how to have fun?" She shook her head. "No, even better, the boy who once glued his own hand to his face while making Christmas ornaments."

"Don't remind me." The Great Glue Accident of 1996 was somewhat of a family legend.

"You really remade the scrapbook?" Liv looked at him through the small screen, her disbelief palpable. "I almost can't believe it."

"Believe it. Cora helped, of course. I didn't do it on my own."

"I bet that's just what she wanted to be doing on her holiday." Liv rolled her eyes. "How's she doing, anyway?"

"Good." He wasn't sure exactly what his sister was getting at.

"Boys, always *so* detailed." She laughed. "Does she seem in good spirits, I mean? I know the holiday is supposed to be some time-out for her. She had a nasty breakup, and I know she really wanted to get away. I've been worried about her, but every time I check in, I get the same canned response that she's fine."

"She's having fun," he replied. They were having

some of the best sex of his life—what *wasn't* fun about that?

Abort. Do not think about that while on the phone with your sister.

"I convinced her to come play beach cricket with the team."

"Oh, you did?" Liv beamed. "That's great. Thanks for including her."

"Of course. The girls were missing your epic swing."

"Flattery will not make me forget that you flooded my house *and* decided to stay there without telling me." Liv wagged her finger at him. "I don't know if Cora told you, but it's her birthday tomorrow. I'm sure you probably have plans and stuff, but—"

"Don't worry," Trent replied, biting back a smile. "I'll make sure she celebrates."

"Thank you, seriously," Liv continued. "And tell her to call me when she can. I tried her before I rang you, but she didn't pick up. Her ex stopped by the apartment concierge to drop off something that she'd left at his place, and I overheard him, so I stopped to pick up her stuff. He asked me to pass on a message."

At the mention of Cora's ex, Trent's muscles froze. "What did he say?"

"To call him. I got the impression he regretted ending things." She shook her head in disgust. "Honestly, after he told me what happened... God, no wonder she wants a break. Her parents sound horrific. Imagine your parent coming on to your partner in public!"

"*That's* what happened?" Cora had told him about her mother interfering and causing tension between her and her ex, but *that* particular detail had been left out of the story.

"Her ex broke it off after Cora's mother tried to kiss him. She got drunk and propositioned him, Trent. For sex. I can't even…"

"That's fucked up."

"Right? Anyway, I've got to run." Her eyes darted offscreen, something snagging her attention. "Can you keep an eye out for Cora? I've been worried about her."

"Of course."

"Thanks, Trent."

His sister disconnected the call. Trent leaned against the wall, agitation flowing through his bloodstream. Her ex regretted ending things…

It was none of his business. None at all. And yet that didn't stop the sinking sensation deep in the pit of his stomach that told him he was in *all* kinds of trouble. Because the only reason something like that would bother him was if he didn't want to lose Cora. But how could you lose a person you didn't have in the first place?

This whole thing shouldn't involve feelings of jealousy, and that was most definitely what he was feeling right now.

"Were you talking about me?"

Cora's voice snapped Trent's head up, and he caught sight of her standing at the end of the hallway. The disappointed expression on her face was beaten only by the sad tone of her voice.

"Liv called…" he said. "She was worried about

you, that's all."

"I've been gossiped about my whole life, you know." Her lips pressed into a flat line. "And yes, my fiancé left me because my mother has a need for attention that's so deep-seated, she'll crush anyone around her to get it."

The words were like a blade over his heart, the pain in her voice like fingers digging into his skin. Nobody should have a parent make them feel like that. But he knew what it was like, to be betrayed.

To feel like you were less than.

"If your fiancé left because he wasn't man enough to stand up to her, then that's on him," Trent said bluntly. "Not on you."

"It wasn't just that." She shook her head. "I thought at the time it was all my mother's fault, but in reality...he and I weren't a good match. I don't think he ever saw what I was capable of. In some ways, I wonder if he liked that I was a bit damaged. He wanted a project, only he got frustrated when I didn't turn out the way he wanted me to after all that polishing."

"You're not a fixer-upper, Cora." He walked toward her, unable to stop himself even though he knew he was standing on a cliff's edge. "You're a beautiful, perfect caterpillar."

She ducked her head, cheeks pink and smile burgeoning. "And *you're* going to give me a big head."

"Good. Someone should." He pulled her to him, wrapping his arms around her shoulders and holding her tight. "He was looking for you."

"Alex?" She tipped her face up.

Trent nodded. "Apparently he regrets ending things."

There was a tightness to his voice, though he tried to hide it. Jealousy wasn't an emotion that he actively engaged—in his mind, being jealous was useless. There would always be someone faster/better/smarter/more. Trent didn't need to be number one the way Nick did. In fact, he was pretty sure being number two was even better—most of the glory, way less work.

But right now, being number two behind Cora's ex felt like last fucking place. Would she go back to him? Pick up the phone in the hopes of reconciliation? Was Alex like the fancy, big-city guy his ex had craved? The one she'd cheated with?

"*He* ended things," she clarified. "But I owe him for that."

"You think?"

Cora stared up at him, eyes wide as the open ocean. He could stare into that icy gaze all day long—because he knew now there was *nothing* cold about Cora. She was warmth all the way through. Warmth and goodness and burning, passionate heat.

"I know," she whispered. "I'm not going back to him. Ever."

For a moment, Trent wondered if this were what it felt like to be a king—to be proud and sure and to feel like you could take on the world. That's how Cora made him feel. She boosted him, made him fearless. Because seeing her grow and change inspired him. Seeing her stand her ground and make good choices for herself made him want to do the same.

What's the good choice here, pining after a woman who's got her exit strategy booked and paid for? Falling for a woman who's going to grow her wings and fly away from you?

It's what Rochelle had done. It's what his siblings had done. They were all soaring toward their goals and their dreams, and he was still standing on the ground with his head craned toward the sky.

Maybe Liv was right. He *was* doing so much stuff for other people that he neglected his own life.

"Come on," she said, her hand curling into his. "You promised me another reading session."

And with the saucy twinkle in her eye, all his thoughts and worries vanished. Overthinking never did anyone any good.

CHAPTER EIGHTEEN

The next day Cora sat at the kitchen table and tried her hardest to concentrate on fixing her manuscript. Ever since she'd found that photo of Trent in his real mother's arms, she'd been fighting the urge to confess. It felt like a betrayal to keep it a secret.

How did you feel when you overheard him talking with Liv about your life?

Not great.

It wasn't fun to be the object of someone's gossip, and she most certainly didn't want him to feel like she'd been spying. Or prying. Cora sighed. If only she had a crystal ball that would tell her the best course of action. The last thing she wanted to do was hurt him…

No matter how much she tried to come to a conclusion on that problem, her mind spun around and around like a hamster wheel. Moving fast but going nowhere.

Maybe part of it was selfish. She didn't want to lose the time she had left with Trent. When she was with him…

Everything felt right.

Even her novel was flowing. Maybe it was all the sexy reading sessions with Trent. Maybe it was fresh air and sunshine suddenly reviving her creative juices. Maybe it was being away from all the toxic bullshit in New York.

"How about option D, all of the above?" she muttered to herself.

Whatever the reason, she was happy for the boost of creativity. *And* to make things even better, she'd finally figured out what was missing from her story…romance! Reading to Trent had sparked the idea that there was a reason her main characters were always at odds. They were hot for each other, and totally mismatched in the best way possible.

Romance had been lacking in her own life for so long—even while she was with her ex—that she hadn't even seen it as a solution until now. But Trent had changed that. Her lips quirked into a smile as she watched him working. He was in jeans and a tight white T-shirt that showed his muscles off to perfection as he used a screwdriver to change the knobs on a big cabinet sitting alongside the far wall of the living room.

"Stop perving on me," he said over his shoulder. "I caught you looking in the mirror. You're supposed to be working."

She laughed. "Then stop bending over. That peachy ass is a distraction."

"I'm being objectified right now, you know that, right?"

"Yeah, and you're loving it, too." She dragged her gaze back to her laptop. Her manuscript was now a sea of Track Changes as she tried to fit her new romance plotline into the story.

Instead of reading to Trent from her latest romance book, she had read to him from the book she was *writing*. It had been terrifying to share her words with him, to expose something that was part of her. She'd had good feedback before from her professor, but her father's rejection had dinted her confidence. Yet Trent had looked at her with wide, smoky eyes and told her that she was talented and gifted and that her future was bright. She wanted to believe him with all her heart.

But what if her father still thought her book was unpublishable?

The cursor on her computer screen blinked at her. Every time she thought about her dad reading her manuscript again, she seized up. She wanted so badly for him to love it. If he let her join the agency as a client rather than an employee… God, that would be like a sign that he thought she had what it took. That he was proud of her. That he wanted to see her succeed.

But if he rejected her work again…

Then you'll try again. You'll keep trying until you get it right. Because only quitters lose.

Cora might not be the best at a lot of things, but she didn't give up easily.

"How's it going?" Trent asked as he slid one of the drawers back into place.

"Good. I think the romance subplot is exactly what it needed."

"Lucky you've got some inspiration for that." He winked at her, and a lock of his sandy hair flopped over his forehead in a way that was so rakishly handsome, it could have been staged.

"Yeah, that book series I'm reading is *great*," she teased.

"Hey! I was talking about me."

"I guess you're okay, too." She grinned.

He slapped a hand to his chest. "You wound me. I thought that thing I did with my tongue last night was *very* worthy of some character inspiration."

Cora flushed and ducked her eyes, pressing a cold glass of water to her heated cheeks. In the throes of passion with Trent, she didn't feel inhibited at all. In fact, he brought out a wildness in her that she didn't even know existed. But talking about it in broad daylight was a whole other thing.

"It was great," she admitted. "*More* than great."

"You'd better dedicate that book to me." He stood and shoved the screwdriver into his back pocket. "I want to see the words *to Trent, thank you for the orgasms* right there in the front of the book."

"Want to be commemorated in print, huh?"

He swaggered over to her, with that panty-melting roll of his hips that mimicked the way he made love—slow and liquid and so damn hot, it singed her brain cells. "I want you to remember me every time you open the cover of that book."

"What if I don't get published?" She bit down on her lip.

"Then I'll come to New York and tell each of the publishing houses that they've clearly never seen talent before."

A smile split across her face. "How do you know I'm any good?"

"Because passion shines out of you, Cora. It would be mighty unfair for someone to have that much passion without any talent to back it up." He planted a hand down on the table. "Finish the book. Send it back to your dad, and I will eat my own hat if he doesn't love it."

"I hope he does."

"He will." Trent held out a hand. "But first, I'm taking you out for lunch. I'm starving."

As if on cue, Cora's stomach grumbled. "Looks like I am, too. What do you have in mind?"

There was a sparkle to Trent's eye that told Cora he had something planned. Maybe a nice restaurant, or maybe a picnic on the beach. Being with Trent meant expecting anything at all times—he was prone to doing things on a whim, without planning. It was the total opposite of dating Alex, who scheduled every moment of his day from sunup to sundown.

You're not dating Trent, remember? When is that going to stick?

Only it felt like they *were* dating. They made love, kissed and touched without fear or inhibition. They talked about real things—like her literary dreams and all the things he wanted to have in his perfect house (deep tub and heated bathroom floors, yes please!). They cared about each other.

Too much. You're not supposed to care about him.

But how could she not? He treated her with kindness and consideration and a permanent mischievous twinkle in his eye. Around him she was lighter, unburdened. A fling didn't give a person those things.

A fling didn't *change* you.

Absently, she reached down to where the caterpillar was etched into her skin. Was she really changing now? Or would this lightness evaporate when she went back home, leaving nothing but a hazy memory of the person she was here?

Can you trust him?

She didn't know. Could she even trust herself? Also an unknown. She'd made so many mistakes in the past, but she was still here. Still working. Still trying.

They ducked into his bedroom and changed, and she had to wriggle out of his grip, convinced if his eager lips touched hers, then they wouldn't make it to lunch at all. To teach Trent a lesson, she put on her most enticing outfit—a short dress made of soft black silk with a ruffle across the bust and a tie at the waist that always made her feel like a million dollars.

Trent let out a long, low whistle as she slipped a pair of flat sandals onto her feet. "Maybe I shouldn't take you out for lunch after all."

"Too much?"

"I'm worried you'll give everyone in town whiplash and then we'll have a class action on our hands."

They walked out to the car, teasing each other and holding hands. Trent agreed not to blindfold her but still wouldn't give up what he planned for lunch. It wasn't until they turned down a familiar street that a knot formed in Cora's stomach.

"We're having lunch at your parents' house?" She blinked. This was *not* what she'd expected.

She'd had a *very* brief introduction to Mr. and Mrs. Walters the day they'd almost been caught getting photos for the album, but Trent had whisked her away before they had time to talk much. Now he was bringing her back. Was this an "official" introduction to the parents? They hadn't talked about where this thing between them was heading, but it seemed…serious.

After all, you didn't introduce a fling to your parents.

"Trust me," he said. It was a weird echo of the thoughts that had been swirling in her head back at the house. Did you trust a fling?

This isn't a fling and you know it.

But if it wasn't that, and yet it wasn't a real relationship…then what was it? Cora felt a panicky feeling take hold of her chest, squeezing like a fist determined to crush the air in her lungs. She wasn't ready for this.

Hell, she'd chosen the wrong damn dress. It was too short and too sexy and too silky. Oh my God, they'd probably think she was some big-city floozy, flashing her legs all over their quaint small town.

Calm down. One, this isn't Victorian England. There's nothing wrong with showing off your legs. Two, it's lunch. You can handle lunch.

"Cora." Trent laid a hand on her arm. "Stop freaking out. I promise you'll have a good time."

Why was he doing this? She wasn't ready for other people to know her business again.

"I don't know about this." She shook her head. "I…"

"I wouldn't do anything to hurt you." When he said things like that, with such clarity and such resonance, it made her heart flutter. Trent made her feel so *seen*. So important. "Please trust me."

She nodded. "I do trust you."

When she said the words aloud, she knew it was true. Trent hadn't done anything but good things for her, so why would he turn into an asshole now?

"Good." His smile was like pure sunshine. "Come on, then."

They got out of the car, and Cora forced herself not to tug at her dress. The breeze swirled the hem around her thighs, and her loose hair ruffled around her shoulders. Trent's parents would have to take her as she came.

He jabbed at the doorbell, but when no one came to greet them immediately, he stuck his key into the lock. The door popped open, and he motioned for her to go ahead of him. The entry was quiet, without a sound of life inside. She'd expected something—music or footsteps or the clatter of dishes in the kitchen. But the place was silent as a tomb.

"Go ahead," Trent said, closing the door behind them. "Dad's probably asleep in the lounge."

Her sandals slapped against the tiled floor, echoing eerily in the house. What on *earth* was going on?

She rounded the corner, with Trent close behind, and all of a sudden there was a booming *surprise!* Cora shrieked, startled at the sudden noise. A dozen smiling faces shouted her name and cheered, blowing party horns and clapping. A shiny silver banner displaying the words *Happy Birthday* hung across the wall. Cora spotted the cricket team, Trent's parents, and a few new faces as well as a collection of adorable black puppies.

"Oh my gosh." Her head swung to Trent. "How

did you know?"

She hadn't said a word to him. Hadn't wanted to make a big deal.

"I overheard you talking to Liv. This is a party to make up for all the ones you never had as a kid." He slipped an arm around her shoulder. "It's a proper kid's birthday party. We have Aussie party food, a jumping castle, and all the red food coloring your child heart desires."

Tears immediately sprang to her eyes. Mortified, she blinked them back. "Oh my God."

He kissed her cheek. "Happy birthday*s*. Plural."

The crowd came forward, and Maddy shoved Trent out of the way and threw her arms around Cora's shoulders. There was a chorus of people shouting well wishes and even a table with brightly wrapped presents. The whole scene was totally and utterly overwhelming.

In fact, it was almost TV sitcom perfect.

An older woman came forward. It was Trent's mother, Melanie, and she had a warm smile on her face. "I know we didn't get to talk much the other day, but we're so happy to meet one of Liv's friends. She told us all about how you were letting her stay in your apartment for her internship and what a good friend you've been, Skyping all the time and checking up on her."

Cora wasn't sure she could speak for all the emotion in the back of her throat.

"It's so good to have you in our home." Then Melanie leaned forward and embraced Cora in a perfumed hug. "Come on out back, we've got all the food set up, and the birthday girl always gets first dibs."

The group trailed out into the backyard, and what Cora found took her breath away. Trent hadn't been joking about the bouncing castle—it was big and yellow and had Big Kid Bounce written on the side. Clearly there was a market for adult bouncing castles. A long table was set up with all kinds of food and drinks. There was a cocktail station, some kind of a game with bats and a ball on string.

"I don't know what to say," she said.

"It was all his idea, you know," Melanie said. "He said no one should be deprived of a birthday party. That's my son in a nutshell; he always wants everyone to be included."

Son. The word stuck in Cora's mind. How could such a kind, warmhearted woman keep such a secret? Head swirling, Cora didn't have time to process her thoughts because Maddy sidled up close to her along with Dean and Nick.

"Right," Nick said, rubbing his hands together. "It's time for Aussie party foods 101."

Cora brushed her worries away, determined not to let Trent's kind gesture go to waste. "I'm ready to learn."

"Party pies and sausage rolls." He pointed to the first plate. "An Aussie classic. They must be eaten with tomato sauce."

"Or dead horse," Cora said, winking at Dean, who pumped his fist into the air.

"Number two is fairy bread, aka white sliced bread with hundreds and thousands."

Cora looked on at the little white bread

triangles that were covered in round sprinkles. "You feed this to small children?"

"Why not? It's got all your essential nutrients," Dean said. "Sugar, simple carbohydrates, whatever the hell margarine is made out of."

"Chemicals," Maddy supplied with a shake of her head. "And it's definitely not an everyday kind of food. Special occasions only."

"Next is…" Dean made a drumroll noise. "Vegemite."

"I've heard about this." Cora wrinkled her nose as the traffic-sign-yellow label on the jar of mysterious dark brown stuff. "Tell me, do Aussies really eat this or is it a mean prank you play on tourists?"

Nick gasped and pressed a hand to his chest. The gesture was so similar to what Trent had done before they left the house that she had to laugh. "Excuse me," he said, "but Vegemite is a national delicacy."

Maddy wrinkled her nose. "I'm not sure I'd call it a delicacy."

"What is it made out of?" Cora watched as Nick unscrewed the lid off the jar.

"Yeast."

Cora blinked. "Yeast?"

"Yep, yeast." Nick proceeded to get a piece of bread and smooth a generous layer across the surface, which caused an argument to erupt. Apparently, there was indecision about the correct way to consume the spread—with butter or without, how much to put on, whether you toast the bread or not, cheese or no cheese.

Unable to help laughing, Cora watched the friendly yet spirited argument spread to more and more people, who came to see what the commotion was about. There were definite camps, Team Toast and Team Cheese and Team Butter Is For Quitters. Cora felt like she was getting a lifetime's worth of Aussie education in one hit, and she couldn't remember ever having a birthday party that made her feel so happy and so included before.

As Dean tried to wrestle the Vegemite jar out of Nick's hands, Cora's gaze slid across the yard to where Trent stood, watching her. The corner of his lip twitched in amusement at the scene before him, and he looked so incredibly loving and indulgent that Cora knew this was *exactly* what he'd hoped for.

She mouthed a quick *thank you*, her cheeks already hurting from smiling so wide. And when he blew her a kiss, Cora pinched herself. He was too good to be true. Way too good to be true.

So good, she knew she couldn't believe it.

• • •

A few hours into the party, the mood had mellowed out perfectly. People were chilling around the yard, some sitting on the grass while others had dragged the outdoor chairs into a big cluster around one end of the table where all the food was.

Cora was full, everywhere. Full heart. Full belly. She nursed a plastic cup with the remains of one of the cocktails, the ice creating condensation on the glass that was pleasantly cooling to her hands. Skye and Maddy sat with her.

"You have a…" Skye leaned forward and brushed something from Cora's cheek. "There we go. You had sprinkles on your face."

"Thanks."

"So, are you missing back home?" Maddy asked.

"I'm enjoying having a break from the real world," Cora replied, although in the back of her mind, the answer was a resounding *no* with multiple exclamation points. The knowledge of that sat unevenly in her stomach, but she brushed it to one side. Who *wanted* to return home from a vacation? Nobody. That was totally normal. "It's nice to take some time away."

"I hear you." Skye leaned back and rested on her elbows, her face tipped up to the sun. Her blond hair hung in two long braids down her back. "I'm *well* overdue for a holiday. But damn that overtime is too good to pass up."

"Skye's a workaholic," Maddy added. "To her detriment, I might add."

"Nah, I'm just being fiscally responsible." She grinned and put her sunglasses on as the sun shifted out from behind a cloud. "Besides, I got a little one to take care of. That mouth isn't going to feed itself."

Cora blinked. "You're a mom?"

"Yeah, I got a little girl named Annemarie." A dark expression filtered over Skye's face. "I'm lucky to have family help me out, because it's not like her dad stuck around to give a shit about her."

In moments where Cora was trying to find the good in her situation, she was thankful that Alex broke things off *before* they got married and had a baby like she was planning. Things were always so much more complicated when children got involved.

"I'm so sorry," Cora said.

"Don't be." Skye shrugged. "I don't need a man to complete my life. My family is all I need. Without them…I have no idea what I'd do. But it makes me sad that my baby girl won't get to know her dad."

For some reason, that comment made her think of Trent—he'd never know his real mother. Did he even know what he was missing? Or had his parents kept it a secret for that specific reason? Hard to miss someone if you didn't know you'd had them in the first place.

She couldn't let go of the memory of that photo. It was stuck in her head, like a slide image that refused to budge. A puzzle with a piece missing. A mystery with no conclusion.

It's none of your business. Maybe they all talked about it and everything is fine. Just because your family is all kinds of messed up doesn't mean everyone else's is.

"Anyway," Skye said. "This isn't good birthday party chatter. We need something more positive."

"Maybe Cora can tell us how the romance novels are going," Maddy said. "Like the one Trent bought her for her birthday."

Skye's eyebrows shot up so fast that Cora was surprised they didn't launch right off her head. About an hour into the party, Trent had pulled her inside the house to give her the present he'd bought her—a romance novel by a local author that had been signed in sparkly pink pen. He'd kissed her cheek so sweetly and told her he wanted to know as soon as she read it, in case there was any "inspiration" to be found inside.

"Excuse me, what?" Skye shook her head. "Maybe I'm not hearing right. Trent purchased a book? Like one of those things with a front cover and a back cover and pages full of words in between?"

Maddy grinned. "Yep, one of those exactly."

"Trent Walters, the man who once petitioned to get out of English class because quote, 'nobody cares what some dead dude thinks about life.' Spoiler alert, that dead dude was Shakespeare."

"Oh God, I remember that. Mr. Langly was *pissed*." Maddy slapped her thigh, laughing. "Typical Trent. He'd say anything to get a rise out of a teacher."

Cora cringed but couldn't help laughing, imagining Trent doing exactly that. It was so him. "I imagine Shakespeare is turning over in his grave at being called a *dude*."

"Well, I'm impressed." Skye sat up and brushed an ant off her leg. "He must be even more smitten than I first thought."

"Than you first thought?" The question popped out before she had adequate time to consider the consequences of encouraging this conversation.

"Skye called it that first week, when Trent brought you to cricket," Maddy said.

"I sure did. I said I hadn't seen Trent taken by a woman like that in quite some time. Probably not since..." She made a noise of disgust. "Rochelle."

"His ex?" Even thinking about his ex—about the photo that was like looking into a mirror—made her stomach churn.

"Yeah. I never liked her, to be honest. Even Maddy wasn't a fan, and this little marshmallow likes *everyone*."

Maddy made an indignant squeak. "I do *not* like everyone. I have discerning taste, thank you very much."

Cora stifled a laugh. Despite Maddy's uber-cool appearance, she totally *was* a marshmallow. Which was exactly what Cora liked about her.

"Oh yeah?" Skye teased. "Who don't you like?"

"Well...I had a rude customer the other day. I didn't like him very much." Maddy wrinkled her nose, and her piercing winked in the sun. "But he *did* seem like he was having a rough day, so maybe he's not normally like that. Oh, and I never liked that dog that Greg used to have. He growled at me once."

"Now you're reaching." Skye caught Cora's eye and shook her head. "100 percent marshmallow."

Maddy made a *hmph* sound. "Excuse me for being nice."

"Anyway, I would like to state for the record that I was correct. Trent *does* have a crush on Cora." Skye grinned. "Clearly he has a type. You look exactly like his ex, you know."

Maddy swiped at Skye and rolled her eyes. "You're unbelievable."

"What?" She shrugged. "It's true."

"Please excuse my friend, Cora. She's got a big

mouth." Maddy rolled her eyes and folded her arms across her chest. "And you're nothing like Rochelle, so it doesn't mean a thing."

"I saw a photo of her," Cora admitted. "It was a little weird, but he said that had nothing to do with…"

Shit. Two pairs of hawk eyes were trained intently on her. Now she'd done it. Cora and Trent hadn't even set any boundaries about what they were going to tell people, if anything. Likely he'd want to keep it a secret…at least she thought he would. And she wanted to keep it a secret…didn't she?

She knew one thing for certain—she didn't want it to get back to Liv without Cora being the one to tell her.

"Go on," Skye said.

"Nothing to do with…" Dammit. Her brain was like a spinning top, going round and round and round without any signs of stopping. "Uh…"

"Oh my God, you're fucking him."

"Skye! Bloody hell, you're so *blunt*." Maddy snorted. "And can you not say stuff like that with his family around? Geez."

Skye chuckled. "Don't think you're getting out of this, Cora. The gossip gods demand their sacrifice."

"You don't have to tell us anything," Maddy said to Cora, then she turned to Skye. "And *you*, you're as subtle as a sledgehammer and nosier than my grandmother."

"I like to think of myself more as a pickaxe, thank you very much. Precise and lethal." Skye sniffed. "And don't you dare say a word against your grandmother—that woman is a national treasure."

The friendly, affectionate banter tugged on something deep in Cora's chest. How was this town so perfect? People seemed to thrive here, to build lasting relationships and show genuine care toward one another. They were relaxed and happy and able to enjoy the time they had on this earth.

You're romanticizing this place, like how people romanticize Manhattan.

It was true. Outsiders thought her city was a wonderland, a magical place of New Year's wishes and Christmas miracles and meet-cutes on every corner. But she knew the city to be a cold, silver landscape of shiny, beautiful things and locked doors. Of secrets and betrayals.

But what could Cora do about that? Manhattan was her home. Her family was there. Even if she'd had enough of her mother's drama, she still loved her father and wanted a relationship with him. She wanted to cling to her belief that she could have that perfect family if only she kept trying...

You've tried so damned hard already.

But anything worth having was worth fighting for, right? Just like with her novel. Sure, writing challenged her and hearing her father's rejection was difficult...but she wasn't about to give up. She wasn't going to quit. Which meant she would be heading home to New York once her vacation was over, and she would keep trying to impress her dad with her dedication and hard work.

"So?" Skye prompted.

"It's…" Cora sighed. "It's a vacation romance, nothing more."

Every word felt like a burning lie. Her connection with Trent was like nothing she'd ever experienced, but letting herself revel in a fantasy about them falling love and making a life in this cute little town would do nothing but end up with her getting hurt. Even if he wanted her to stay—which she highly doubted—she wasn't about to give up on her family.

She had to go home.

"He seems to really like you," Maddy said quietly.

"I like him too; he's a great guy. But I'm not looking for anything," Cora said firmly. "I have a life in New York that I need to get back to."

Neither Maddy nor Skye said anything in return, but they exchanged a look that Cora couldn't quite decipher. Maybe they didn't believe her. It didn't matter, one way or the other. She couldn't let herself get caught up in this place, no matter how much the warm sun and friendly people and sexy men had gotten under her skin.

Sexy man. Singular.

Trent was a great guy and an amazing lover—but that's where she would have to leave it. Her life plans didn't include uprooting herself for a relationship.

Which meant her sexy Aussie fling would have to stay exactly where it was.

CHAPTER NINETEEN

Trent hung back and let Cora enjoy herself for a good portion of the party. Not that he could have gotten close if he'd tried; she was holding court—laughing and tossing her sun-bleached hair and generally sparkling like the brightest star in the universe. His mother had come past to say what a "delightful young woman" she was, which filled Trent with a burst of pride. Seeing Cora come into her own in the last two weeks had been like watching a flower open to the sun.

It was a *stark* turnaround from the opinion his mother had about Trent's ex.

Melanie Walters might seem like the dictionary definition of the caring, tough but kind mama bear, but she had a bullshit radar like nobody else. Though the rest of his family bought the story about him growing tired of Rochelle, his mother had said a quiet "you're better off without her" when he'd announced the split. She knew him better than anyone. Knew when he was lying or hiding something, knew when he was trying to pull a fast one.

He shouldn't really care what his family thought of Cora, but he did.

Only there was bringing a girl home and *bringing a girl home*. He wasn't sure which of those two things was happening right now.

Just as Trent was trying to sift through his

thoughts, Adam wandered over. "Looks like the party is going well," he said, taking a swig of his beer.

Cora was having a ball with Jace and Angie's little black fluff balls. She was sitting on the ground while the tiny beasts yipped and pawed at her, and Cora's laugh carried across the backyard.

"Aimee did an awesome job setting this up," Trent said. "Seriously, she put in all the hard yakka."

"So you're working on scrapbooks together and throwing her birthday parties. That's very familiar for a temporary visitor." Adam's tone said he wasn't about to buy any bullshit Trent might consider peddling.

"I'm nothing if not familiar," he replied with a wink.

"I overheard her telling Nick you'd showed her your block. Even *I* haven't seen it."

Trent raised an eyebrow. Adam might be the typical overprotective older brother always keeping watch on his siblings, but he was generally a pretty open and trusting person. It wasn't like him to be wary of someone without reason.

"So?"

"I don't know, seems a little intimate. You've been cagey as hell about letting *anyone* see it and then suddenly you're taking some woman there." Adam took another swig of his beer. Something was under his big brother's skin, that was for damn sure. "Bringing her home to meet everyone…"

Trent nailed his brother with a stare. "If you want to say something, then say it."

"I don't want to see you getting hurt by some high-flying chick."

"What's *that* supposed to mean?" Trent wasn't sure he was going to like what was about to come out of Adam's mouth. "You think she's too good for me?"

"She's a big-city person, like Rochelle was. They don't want the kind of life we have here. And I know you keep telling everyone that *you* called it off, but the second you broke up, she hauled her stiletto-wearing ass to Melbourne with that guy."

Okay, so maybe his story about losing interest hadn't stuck as much as he'd hoped.

He folded his arms over his chest. "Why does everyone around here feel the need to keep telling me to watch my back? One minute I'm the town charmer and the next minute I'm supposedly putting myself in the firing line? Sounds like a load of bullshit to me."

Adam frowned. His big brother had that expression that foreshadowed him dishing out advice. Trent felt himself tense up in anticipation. Not that Adam didn't have useful things to say, but Trent had always felt like everyone assumed they knew what was best for him. That they knew what he needed.

Fact was, they knew nothing.

Not his friends, not his brothers and sister, at times not even his parents. Nobody knew who Trent was deep down. And that wasn't an accident. Trent played his cards close to his chest because he knew that the second you loved someone, you gave them the power to hurt you.

He knew that everyone had the capacity to lie.

"She made it clear you were just fooling around and that it wasn't anything serious for her," he said. "She was chatting with Maddy and Skye before and I overheard her."

The words were like a fist to his solar plexus. "She said those exact words?"

Damn, simply by asking that question, he'd given something away.

"Close enough. This isn't anything serious to her." Adam looked genuinely worried. "Now, you know I don't like to stick my nose into other people's business—"

"Which is *exactly* what you're doing," Trent pointed out.

"But when I see one of my brothers headed straight for a repeat mistake, how can I not say something? I've got nothing against her, truly. But I can tell you're treating this like more than…the physical."

He scoffed and shook his head. "How'd you figure that out? Crystal ball?"

"Uh, what about all this?" Adam waved his hand around to indicate the birthday party.

Trent's gaze landed on Cora, who was chatting animatedly with Angie while playing with the puppies. The two American women appeared to be hitting it off, and Cora was giggling as one of the black fluff balls jumped up and tried to lick her face. If he was being totally honest with himself, he *could* see this being his future—Cora, a dog, driving back to the fantasy house overlooking the ocean.

You're in too deep.

"Since when is it a crime to throw someone a birthday party?" He rolled his eyes, frustrated more by himself than by his brother's observation. He didn't want to feel anything for Cora, but the fact was…he did. And that was a problem. Still, in his opinion a private problem was better than a public problem. "Maybe you wouldn't worry so much if you minded your own bloody business."

Adam scowled. "I'm looking out for you."

"I don't need anyone to look out for me," he snapped. "And I find it ironic that people have been quite happy to joke about me charming women into my bed all over the place and yet the second you think I like someone, it's a red flag. Newsflash, it's sex. Nothing more. But just because I'm not planning a future with her doesn't mean I can't do something nice."

When he looked back over to Cora, she was staring at him—brows furrowed. She was too far away to have heard any of their conversation, but he got some weird feeling that maybe she knew what they were talking about. Not that it mattered. Trent believed Adam—he had no reason to lie, and his oldest brother was as honest as they came.

It was one of the reasons Trent had always looked up to him. Adam was a rock of stability and integrity in their family. A pillar they'd all leaned on over the years. That's why the words cut, because he knew Adam was telling the truth.

This doesn't mean anything to Cora. So it shouldn't mean anything to you.

But what if it did? Could Adam be right? Was Trent falling for the wrong woman all over again?

• • •

Later that night, they were back at the house, extra fairy bread and leftover meat pies stacked high in plastic containers that his mother had forced on them. She'd fussed over Cora, squeezing her with hugs and complimenting her in not-so-subtle whispers to Trent. She was exactly the kind of woman his mother always wanted him to bring home—sweet, friendly, eager to be part of the group.

Cora had even tried to help his mum clean up by sneaking into the house and washing the dishes before she got found out and shooed away. Rule number one, the birthday person *never* had to do the washing up.

But talk about the way to his mum's heart…

"Your family is *so* delightful," Cora said as she flopped down on the bed, still in her party dress but with feet bare and eye makeup a little smudged from all the laughter. Her hair was a wild halo, frizzed out from bouncing up and down in the jumping castle for a good portion of the afternoon. She'd taken to it with gusto, laughing and encouraging everyone to join her. "I had a good chat with your brother Jace and his wife. They were telling me all about his comics, and I'm hoping to put him in touch with someone from the agency. We've got some of the publishers looking for more graphic novels, and he's so talented."

"I hope they don't send him a letter like the one your dad sent you," Trent replied. "I'm not sure how well Jace would do with the rejection."

The comment came not from any doubt of his brother's talent—Jace was blessed with more talent in his little finger than most people had in their whole bodies. But rather, the feeling came from a deep-seated protectiveness he had for his siblings. He hated seeing them hurt.

Cora propped herself up on her forearms and watched him closely. Her expression was difficult to read, like a frozen lake trapping all her emotions beneath the surface. "My father is very direct with me because he knows I can take it. But rejection *is* part of publishing."

"Even from your own father?" Trent asked.

"Yes," Cora said. "And I prefer it that way. I'd rather know if I'm any good than waste my time because he was filling my head with lies just to be nice to me."

There *had* to be a middle ground between those two things.

"Why is he the person to determine whether your work is good or not? Isn't creative stuff all… subjective?"

It wasn't like building a house, where the lines of good and bad were more clearly drawn. If your walls didn't line up or your foundation wasn't properly set, then it was bad. Easy call. But like he and Jace would argue about which Marvel movie was the best until they were both blue in the face, there was no right or wrong answer when it came to art.

Cora's gaze slid away from him, and she pushed herself up to get off the bed. "He's been a literary agent for over thirty years. He knows what he's doing, and I trust his opinion."

Trent wasn't sure whether that was the right move. Why should one person—no matter how experienced—have the right to tell someone their work wasn't good enough?

It had given Trent flashbacks to one dragon of an English teacher he'd had back in year seven. Her comments, scrawled in red pen across his essay, had made him feel small and stupid. But when Trent had shown his father, *he'd* pointed out all the areas where Trent had made good arguments.

It had been an important lesson in subjectivity.

Maybe that was one of the reasons Trent had always preferred building things over writing essays. The boundaries and goalposts were clear.

"You could always have my dad read it," Trent offered. "He's been teaching literature for just as long, and he's been a lover of books his whole life. I'm sure he'd be happy to give you a second opinion."

She turned away from him and tugged at the zipper of her dress. "You can't compare teaching with publishing. They're two different worlds."

Trent had always hated that phrase, *different worlds*. Rochelle had thrown that term at him more than once, and he'd never understood it. Were they not all human? Were they not all made of flesh and blood?

Why did people feel the need to draw these artificial lines around themselves?

His mind flicked back to the earlier conversation with Adam. Maybe this was nothing about "different worlds" and everything about Cora trying to distance herself.

"That sounded harsh, I'm sorry. I didn't mean it as a criticism." Cora sighed. "And I appreciate the offer. I'm sure your dad would have some great wisdom to share, but I need to get it across the line with my father before I show it to anyone else."

"Why?"

"Because…" She slid the zipper down her back, and Trent watched the fabric peel away from her skin. "I want to know if it's any good before I let other people see it. What if I *am* a horrible writer? I don't want to embarrass myself."

"But you're not."

"You don't even read," she said with a soft laugh. "I heard all about your disparaging remarks about Shakespeare today, by the way. Nobody cares what some dead dude thinks about life…really?"

He raked a hand through his hair. "Hey, just because I don't appreciate the classics doesn't mean I don't know passion when I see it."

She shot him a look over one shoulder as her dress slithered down her skin, creating a whispering *whoosh* as it fell to the floor. Underneath she had black underwear and no bra, and Trent's throat was suddenly tight.

"Passion is all good and well, but I don't want to be like those fools you see on *American Idol* who think they can sing because their families haven't had the heart to tell them they sound like a dying cat."

"A little encouragement wouldn't hurt." He came up behind her and wrapped his arms around her waist, pressing his lips to the back of her neck. "Everybody deserves to be encouraged."

"I deserve the truth." She sagged back against him. "And doesn't the truth matter more than protecting people's feelings?"

Did it? How many times had he told a white lie to make someone in his family happy? Like that time Liv baked ANZAC biscuits that were hard enough to split a tooth clean in half, but he'd dunked them into his coffee and swallowed them down with a smile on his face.

Wasn't protecting the relationship worth *more* than the truth?

You didn't think that when you found out what Rochelle had been hiding.

Yeah, but that was different.

"I can tell you don't agree with me," she said.

"Relationships are important."

"Says the town charmer," she teased. "I bet you like having everyone wrapped around your little finger."

She made it sound like a source of power for him, but truthfully, he'd never known any other way to be. Making people smile and helping others out was how he'd been raised. It was his personal currency.

"Have I got *you* wrapped around my little finger?" He swept her hair to one side and kissed the tender spot behind her ear. The resulting sigh was enough to send blood charging through his veins like a stampede of bulls.

"I'm worried about it." Her hands slid behind her, clutching his thighs as she pressed back against him. "I'm worried you're twisting me inside out and upside down."

"Maybe I'm simply adjusting your worldview."

She turned, planting her hands against his chest and shoving him so that he stumbled back and hit the bed. He dropped down, eyes wide as she stood proud and magnificent before him. Regardless of what she thought, Cora *had* transformed. Her time in Australia was a metamorphosis—because she was confident and sure and in charge.

She stepped toward him, eyes smoky and dark as she lowered herself to straddle him. She rubbed over his lap, giving him the barest hint of contact. It was enough to fully ignite him—turning him to ash and bone. Hardening him all over. Making him hers.

"I don't need my worldview adjusted," she said with a wicked smile. "The view is pretty damn perfect right now."

He chuckled. "That so?"

"I've got a hot man at my mercy, a long sexy night ahead of me…" She pressed down, rubbing herself against Trent. He let out a soft moan and tugged her face to his, nipping at her lower lip with his teeth. "Another week and a half of bliss before I have to be an adult and face the real world."

The words turned his stomach to stone. She was already thinking about the end. Her leaving.

"I want to make the most of this while we can," she said, grabbing his hands and bringing them to her breasts, encouraging his greedy fingers to take, take, take. She moaned when he palmed the firm mounds, softly at first. Then harder. "Trent…you're incredible."

"So are you," he whispered. More words hovered on his tongue, things he *shouldn't* be saying to her. Words like "stay" and "more" and "future." Words like "I need you." Words like "You're fucking incomparable."

Her lips found his neck, and she pushed him back against the bed, taking charge of his body. He rolled his hips up against her. She was so hot, bare breasts pressed against his chest. Sexy little black underthings left most of her glorious backside free, and he let his hands take full advantage.

"And the man who doesn't like Shakespeare has all the best words." She kissed him, her tongue sweeping the inside of his mouth while her body writhed on top of his. "Who would have thought?"

"Not me."

"You *are* a charmer."

He bristled at the description. "I don't care about charming anyone else, Cora. Not now. Now it's…you. Only you."

"It's only you, too," she whispered, something flickering in the depths of her eyes. Something wary and wonderful and raw.

"I want you to stay in my bed tonight. The *whole* night." He brushed her hair back and glided his thumb over her cheek. Cora nodded, bringing her mouth back down to his and kissing him like the air in her lungs depended on it.

His words were true. He thought of her day and night. Only her. He wanted *her* in his bed, in his arms, in his shower. He wanted *her* lips brushing his ear as he fell asleep and *her* fingers entwined with his. And he wanted to wake up next to her as well.

Nobody else would satisfy him.

And he never thought he'd feel like that about a person ever again.

CHAPTER TWENTY

Her desperate heart wanted so badly to read into his words—to believe she was special.

But she, Cora Cabot, was *not* special.

Never had been, never would be. Special was for people who were born talented and beautiful and exceptional. Special was for the select few. And she'd learned the hard lesson over the years that she was absolutely and thoroughly average. Not bad, but average. Not ugly, but average. Not unintelligent, but average.

In fact, her father's website called it out specifically: *our agency is founded on the rigorous pursuit of exceptional literature.*

And he'd rejected her manuscript. Meaning it wasn't exceptional.

That stung. But Cora wasn't one to indulge her ego nor the delusion that she was above the norm, despite Trent trying to woo her with such words. She could not be suckered into believing that this whirlwind vacation fling was anything more than scratching a primal, physical itch.

Even if her heart didn't believe a single word of the protection plan her brain was laying out.

She'd almost crumbled when he'd offered for his dad to read her manuscript, when he said she deserved encouragement. It was a tempting cocktail and he seemed to know, better than anyone, how to reach her.

Which was all the more reason to hold him at a distance.

"You'll forget all about me the second I'm gone," she said, smoothing her hands up and down his chest.

Trent's skin was honeyed and warm, deepened by the day spent in the sun. His hair seemed even lighter, strands of it almost pure white gold. But his blue eyes were no longer a calm ocean; they were a storm—dark and direct and unwavering.

"I won't," he said. "Even if I wanted it more than air, I wouldn't forget you."

"Please don't." Her voice shook.

"Don't what?"

"Make this out to be more than it is."

She pressed her face to his neck, moving her body to draw his mind to the physical and away from the emotional. It would be only more painful when she had to pack her bags. When she had to walk out that door. Because Trent had marked her, and the truth of it was, she would never *ever* forget him.

These memories would follow her to her grave.

"And what is it?" His voice was like flint.

"We're having fun... Aren't we?" She chanced a look at him.

Trent held his arms tight around her, the press of his hard muscles a comfort she never thought she'd crave. To be trapped in a man's arms like this... She felt safe. Secure. Wanted.

"Yes, we're having fun," he replied, burying his face in her hair. "But if you think I'll happily skip on to the next woman the second you walk out that door, then you're wrong."

What was she supposed to make of that? It was a trap. A rocky, crumbling cliff face luring her to emotional ruin. His secret was a wedge between them, her baggage wrenching that space even wider.

There were too many obstacles, too much bad timing. Too many things that would result in both of them being hurt.

"I told you to stop." She pulled away.

"I thought you said the truth was the most important thing." His hands roamed her body, dulling the sharpness of her mind, thawing her heart. Hushing her worries. "And the truth is…I want you more than anything."

"Then be quiet." She pressed a finger to his lips and shimmied down his body, her hands finding the button of his fly and pushing it open. He was hard inside his jeans, and it made her blood pulse eagerly in her veins. "And let me show you how much *I* want *you*."

She drew his zipper down and palmed him through his boxer briefs. Trent's moan cut through the quiet room, sharp as a blade. When her hand connected with his warm flesh, her insides flipped. And as she lowered her head, her hair brushing his stomach and his fingers threading through the curling strands, she forced herself to focus on the physical.

He tasted of salt and skin, and the slide of him along her tongue was more erotic than any time she'd done this before. Because deep down she knew this was something different. Something more. At least to her, it was. But she'd seen how quickly people could turn—like when her ex's declarations disintegrated once things got too difficult. Words didn't mean a damn thing.

But action…action meant something. And she *would* show Trent what he meant to her, how he made her feel emboldened and empowered and transformed. Only recently, she'd pulled away from their first kiss, afraid to proceed. Now she was in charge, controlling their passion. Charging it and churning it up.

"Cora." He moaned her name.

She took him deep, using her hands as well as her mouth, and for now, she was relieved that he could only say her name. Because walking away from Trent—from this great, explosive pleasure— would be torture. But her heart could be shattered only so many times before she might not be able to put it back together.

She had to go home and figure out her life. Figure out her head. And now, because of him and this incredible, beautiful place, she felt strong enough to do it.

"If you keep going…" he warned, fingers tightening in her hair. But she wasn't going to listen. This was her time to be in charge.

She felt his thighs tighten beneath her as his orgasm swelled, saw the muscles clench beneath his white T-shirt. The change in him was breathtaking—the raw sounds coming from the back of his throat, the feel of the bed shifting as he thrust into her mouth, the taste of him as he exploded, crying her name like it was a prayer to every god that ever existed.

• • •

The next week followed a similar pattern — Trent would try to talk to Cora about what was going to happen at the end of her vacation, and she would distract him by any means necessary. This had resulted in another sexy reading session, blindfolding him with a silk Hermès scarf that she usually had tied to one of her purses. Another time it had been touching herself in the bath, hands diving under the bubbles and letting her head roll back while he watched, enraptured. Last night she'd stooped even lower — anticipating that he'd bring the subject up after dinner, so she'd gone into the kitchen to "get dessert" and had come out wearing nothing but whipped cream and strawberries.

Trent was starting to get suspicious. And frustrated. Thankfully, he had the sex drive of a bull in mating season, so she'd ruthlessly used that to her advantage. But tonight they were supposed to work on the last few pages of the scrapbook in time for Liv to return home the following Wednesday and to present it at the Walterses' big anniversary dinner. Cora would be long gone by then.

Gone.

She brought two mugs of coffee to the table and hoped that Trent couldn't see how her hands shook. The milky liquid sloshed up against the sides of the cups as she set them down. It was impossible to think that merely a month ago, they were complete strangers. Now…

Now he felt like a key piece of her world.

Despite her trying to maintain the distance early on by retiring to her own room, she couldn't tear herself away anymore. She slept every night in his arms and woke struck with how magnificent he looked with the sunlight streaming over him. They cooked dinner, laughed at inside jokes. He encouraged her every day, doling out caring words like they were limitless and unconditional even though she knew such words always had strings, even if you couldn't see them at first.

"I can't believe we've almost finished this bloody thing," he said, flipping through the scrapbook. In reality, it wasn't as good as Liv's work—there were dried bits of glue on some of the pages, random specks of glitter that refused to budge after the "glitter incident," and some pretty shoddy washi tape application. But it was filled with love in every page, in every photo, in every dotted *i*.

She settled into the seat next to him. Then she made a snorting sound. "God, I couldn't even imagine what my parents would say if I presented them a handmade gift."

"They wouldn't appreciate it?"

"Darling, true gifts come from Fifth Avenue," she said in her best impersonation of her mother. "How do I know it's love if the price tag doesn't have at least four zeroes?"

"She sounds like a nightmare," he said, reaching for his coffee. With his other hand he fanned a section of ink where he'd glued down some gold stars.

"You know, I've tried really hard to understand

her over the years." Cora sighed. "My mother came from nothing. Her family immigrated to America when she was a little girl, and she shared a bed with her three sisters until they were teenagers. She worked her ass off to get through school, juggling cash jobs on the side to help keep her family afloat. They were dirt poor. She decided that nothing and nobody was going to stop her from having a future."

"So that's an excuse to be narcissistic?"

"I guess the fire to succeed was ultimately what became her downfall. Too much of any trait can be a bad thing." Cora bit down on her lip. "Add to that a drinking problem and a tumultuous marriage… I don't think parents ever *mean* to hurt their children."

Cora looked at the scrapbook's open pages, which contained pictures of a young Trent with his arms around his parents. She swallowed back against the words clogging her throat—he looked so happy in that picture, and he so easily labeled her mother, but did he have any idea *who* his mother was?

"Why do you let her treat you poorly?" he asked. "It's unacceptable, even if she doesn't hurt you intentionally. You deserve so much better than that."

Her eyes prickled, but she wouldn't let him see her cry, because this conversation sounded *way* too much like the ones she had with Alex. He didn't understand why she kept trying with her parents, didn't understand why she craved their love even after all her mother's antics and her father's adultery.

But maybe she needed to see this with Trent. It was proof that all relationships would turn out the same way no matter how good a partner you had. Alex wasn't perfect by any means, but he was a good person. He cared, he was smart and attentive. Trent…well, Trent was on a whole other plane. His heart and soul were like beaming rays of sunshine.

And yet they had circled around to the same place, thinking she should quit on her family because things were tough.

"Is it so wrong that I'm a forgiving person?" she asked.

He shook his head. "No, but…isn't there a line somewhere? Will you ever get to the point where enough is enough?"

No.

The word came out of nowhere into her mind, quietly, as though whispered. It frightened her. Was it really true that she would keep trying to build a strong relationship with her parents no matter how many times her mother hurt her? No matter how much her father didn't believe in her talent?

"If you say no, I'm… I don't even know," Trent said, placing his coffee cup down with a dull *thunk*. "Parents should lift you up and help you with your dreams, and they should want you to have every good thing in life instead of trying to hold you down."

He saw her now. The real Cora. Not the Cora who existed in Australia with carefree hair and her suntan and her ready smile and her sexy writer persona. No, *this* was who she really was—sad, lonely, unloved. For the first time since meeting

Trent, she felt truly ashamed, but she didn't want him to pity her. She didn't want him to see her as the sad, pathetic creature she was.

"Your family isn't perfect, either," she said, shaking her head, letting her defensive walls shoot up. Her emotions were swirling now, creating a tornado inside her. Why had she said anything? She should have known this was how it would end. "Everyone has skeletons in their closet."

"What's that supposed to mean?" Trent's shoulders drew back.

Oh shit. Why did she always go into verbal diarrhea mode whenever she felt attacked? If only she'd never seen that picture…

"I'm just saying, I'm sure your family has its flaws."

"That's *not* what you said." His eyes were on hers, searching and searching. Seeing too much. Peeling back her layers. "What skeletons are you talking about?"

Now the tears came with more force, filling her eyes, and she turned away, trying to blink them into submission. Was she self-sabotaging now, the way her mother always did? Sure, this wasn't getting drunk and coming on to someone inappropriate, but she was trying to ruin something with someone she cared about by opening her big damn mouth.

"Cora." Trent touched her arm, and she flinched. When she turned back to him, the hurt was splashed all across his face as vivid as red paint. "Talk to me."

"I should never have said anything." A tear splashed onto her cheek, and she whisked it away with the back of her hand, shaking her head in frustration. "It's none of my business, but when you said those things about my family, I felt vulnerable and…"

"And?"

"It was like staring down the barrel of how things ended with Alex." She sucked in a big breath. "I said too much."

"You can't say a little and then stop." His brows were furrowed, knitting above his perfect nose and perfect blue eyes and crinkling his perfect tanned skin.

God, if her issues weren't enough to end things between them, then *this* certainly would be. But she'd mentioned the skeletons in the closet; now they were creeping out and shaking their bony limbs in time to the "Monster Mash." No way she could stuff them back in there now.

"I saw a picture…" She scrubbed her hands over her face. "When we were doing photocopies for the scrapbook. I noticed that your mother had the same exact picture with your brothers and sisters in the hospital bed, a blue teddy bear sat with her, and…"

When she looked up, Trent's face was impassive. His eyes were frosted over and his hands curled around the coffee cup, still, as though he weren't a man but a lifelike rendition in marble.

"I noticed there wasn't one of you," she said, gulping.

"And?" His jaw twitched. "Were you snooping?"

"No!" She shook her head vehemently. "It was an accident. In trying to rush and clean everything up the day your parents came home early, I knocked a box off the shelf and some documents spilled out. There was a picture in there…"

"With my real mother."

He knew.

Cora almost couldn't breathe as she waited for Trent's reaction. Was he going to yell? Cry? Leave? Would he push her away? The sound of the outside world intruded on their moment—the sound she'd come to know as warbling magpies filling the air with their unique song. The rustle of trees, the laugh of a kookaburra. She wanted to tell them all to be quiet.

"I found out when I was twelve," he said eventually. "I'd always suspected I was different. Even Jace, with the challenges he had growing up, felt more similar to the rest of them than I did. They all thought the same, they were logical and ambitious and good at school and I…wasn't."

"How did you find out?" she whispered.

"I was doing a school project about family trees and noticed that same photo missing as I trawled through the family albums. When I asked my mum, she told me there was a whole album missing. Water damage, ironically enough." He shook his head.

Cora bit down on her lip.

"But there was something about her answer that didn't sit right. All the albums were stored in the same place, so how could only one be damaged?" He shook his head. "I went looking, and I found that photo. I started asking more questions about my real mother."

"What did you find out?"

"That nobody knows who my real father is. My birth mother refused to tell anyone. Maybe it was a one-night stand? Short of hoping for a hit on AncestryDNA or one of those things, I have no way of finding out who he is. As for her…" He let out a big sigh. "She died in a car accident when I was three months old. She'd left me with her sister so she could run some errands. It was dusk, a kangaroo jumped out in front of the car, and she swerved and went off the road, straight into a tree."

Cora clamped her hand over her mouth, her eyes so blurred by tears, she had no hope of keeping them in. "Oh my God."

"My mother had a will, and she wanted her twin sister to take custody of me. Ever since then, I've called Melanie my mum." He raked a hand through his hair. "It sounds tragic and horrible, and I guess it is, but…I've had a good life. I love my parents and my siblings. I love my life here."

It made sense now, why he did so much for his family. Why he always seemed to put other people's needs before his own. Was he trying to earn his place? Make sure he was loved for what he did rather than who he was?

"Does she know that you found out?"

He nodded. "I kept it a secret for a long time, and I think deep down she knew. But it was like neither of us wanted to say anything because we were afraid if we did, everything might fall apart."

"What about your brothers and sisters?"

"They don't know. We've never told them." He

bit down on his lip. "That's my decision, and my mum and dad respect it. If Liv and my brothers suddenly saw me as less than one of them, I'm not sure what I'd do."

"Family isn't just about sharing the same biological parents. You've grown up alongside them." Cora's chest was almost full to bursting. This man, his positive outlook and spirit, had caught her deeply. If everyone in the world was half as good a person as he was, life would be very different.

"I know, but sometimes when things are so good…"

She nodded. "You have more to lose."

"Yeah." He reached out and tucked a strand of hair behind her ear. "Some days I feel like I have everything to lose."

"Is that why you don't date seriously?"

He sighed. "It's hard not to assume that everyone lies, even the good people. Even for good reasons. I tried dating and thought I understood what love was, but…she lied, too. So I figured there's no way to be lied to if you don't get too close."

Something lingered in the air, a snapping, sizzling thread between them that drew Cora to Trent like a magnet. It was almost as if the universe was telling her that they *were* close, that they'd crossed that line together.

That they had something to lose.

It *was* terrifying. Because Cora knew that loss was inevitable. That history repeated itself until you finally learned the lesson you were meant to.

Until you submitted to your fate.

"Maybe you deserve more than secrets," she said.

"I'll admit to that only if you also admit you deserve more, too." He brushed the hair from her face, his fingertips sending sparks skittering along her skin.

"I never meant to pry into your life," she said. "I promise. It was an accident."

"I understand."

She shook her head at him, eyes holding his. Unwavering. Unflinching. She couldn't tear herself away.

"How are you so strong?" she asked, wonder tinting her voice. "How did you go through that and still have such a whole heart?"

"I'm not going to say I handled it perfectly, because I definitely didn't," Trent replied with a laugh. The sound held so much weight and feeling, she reached out and pressed her palm to his cheek. "Nor the breakup with Rochelle. I've made a lot of mistakes. I've had *so* many false starts."

That made her sad. Because Trent deserved everything good in this world. He was a bright light. He could easily have turned bitter and resentful and angry from what had happened to him, but he'd taken it all and soldiered on with his life.

"Do you think we're too broken to make good on this life?" she asked softly.

"No." He rested his forehead against hers. "I think we're just two regular old caterpillars."

She laughed, and a tear plopped onto her cheek.

This time she didn't brush it away, because Trent was there first, catching it with his thumb and whisking it off her cheek.

"Come on," he said, straightening up. "We've got a scrapbook to finish."

CHAPTER TWENTY-ONE

To: Cora.Cabot@CarsonCabotLiterary.com
From: Anderson.Cabot@CarsonCabotLiterary.com
Subject: Manuscript revisions

Cora, thanks for sending through your revisions last night. I can tell you worked very hard on them.

I don't know how to say this…

While I know you have a great deal of passion, I cannot represent you simply because you are my daughter. That is not what's best for my business. Nor, I think, is it what's best for you. I also worry it would be unfair to lead you on, knowing that you'll be hurt. Maybe I have indulged this dream too much. Only a very small percentage of writers get published, let alone have the talent and stamina to sustain a career in this industry.

The last thing I want is to see you end up like your mother, tortured and twisted by criticism. I don't think your writing is at the right level, and I'm honestly not sure if further work will get it to that point. I worry that your beautiful spirit will be broken by this. Maybe it's time to think about how you can direct your efforts inside the industry in some other way. Perhaps we could talk about training you to be an agent instead.

Your father,
Anderson.

Trent shouldn't have looked at Cora's email. It was wrong, an invasion of privacy…yadda yadda yadda.

But he did. He looked. And he read. And his blood boiled as though he were plugged directly into the core of the earth. How *dare* he try to crush her dreams. How dare he tell her that no amount of work would be enough.

How dare he tell her that she couldn't grow.

Without thinking, Trent emailed himself a copy of the manuscript file, because Cora's heart could *not* be shattered without a second opinion. His dad would be more than happy to read her book and give some honest thoughts. And while Trent himself wasn't much of a reader, he was certain Cora had talent. There was something musical about her words—the way she spoke and wrote, the way she described things. Plus, that English professor of hers had urged her to write.

That had to mean something, right?

For whatever reason, Anderson Cabot didn't seem to want to help his daughter. Yet every time he tried to talk to Cora about it, she clammed up and made excuses for him. The whole cruel-to-be-kind thing? Bullshit. If he wanted to help Cora, he wouldn't tell her not to write. Anyone could see she was passionate about books, and what right did her father have to tamp that down?

Sure, Trent's family wasn't perfect. They'd kept a *huge* secret from him for his entire childhood. Finding out his parents weren't his real parents had been…well, devastating. He still remembered the day, clear as a bell, still remembered the tears in his

mother's eyes and the choked-up voice of his
father.

He still remembered that sick feeling in his gut
and the question swirling in his mind: *What if
Adam and Nick and Jace and Liv decide I'm not
one of them anymore?*

He understood why it was hard for his mother
to talk about losing her twin sister, and he knew
without a shadow of a doubt that his adoptive
parents loved him. So much so, that he didn't ever
think of them as adoptive. They were simply Mum
and Dad.

Yet he still hadn't plucked up the courage to tell
his siblings the truth. The longer it went on, the
harder it became to think about voicing his big
secret.

Which meant Cora knew more about him than
most people. He'd never discussed it with *anyone*
aside from his parents—not even Rochelle, when
he thought he was in love. It was the card he kept
closest to his chest. Maybe he should have been
happy that Cora was going away, taking the
information with her to the other side of the world
where it couldn't upset the easy balance of his life.

But he couldn't be happy about it. Not when it'd
become obvious that he couldn't watch her walk
away without saying something. Without making it
damn bloody clear that this *wasn't* a temporary
fling to him.

The only problem was…how to tell Cora? When
it came to their bodies, they had no problem
communicating. Sex came easily and was always
good for them. They fit together physically. But

emotionally and mentally?

That was a whole other ball game.

Shaking his head, Trent headed out of the house and hopped into his ute. With the window down, he cruised through Patterson's Bluff, watching all the houses blur by. All these people had put a stake in the ground, built something for themselves. A space, a home.

They'd forged a life.

What the hell had he done in his thirty years?

Trent leaned his head back against the seat and pulled his car onto the highway. Sea air streamed in through the window, bringing back memories. Patterson's Bluff was already his home. So why had he been so afraid to make a commitment by finally getting started on his house? Why did the thought of him chasing after what he wanted fill him with ice-cold fear?

He pushed Cora to chase her dreams, saying she deserved encouragement. He *believed* she could do anything and that she didn't need anyone's approval.

"Easier to give advice than to take it," he muttered to himself.

The ute zipped along the coast, eating up the distance, and before too long he was easing onto the off-ramp, entering Sorrento.

Sorrento was kind of like Patterson's Bluff's older, more popular big sister. It was a wealthier town, with a bustling tourism industry, streets dotted with fancy sports cars, and shops selling random trinkets and foodstuffs that were hideously overpriced simply because someone had slapped a label on it calling it "artisanal." It was a beautiful town, but not really Trent's kind of scene.

Today, however, he was here on business.

Personal business.

Nick had pushed him into setting up a meeting with an architect whose specialty was designing modern homes with a coastal twist. Their company mantra was all about sustainability and protecting the environment, which Trent appreciated. And while he'd resisted the meeting, eventually he'd broken down and looked at the website. Nick was right, their designs were amazing.

How can you tell Cora to go for it and then hold yourself back?

He couldn't answer that question without sounding like a hypocrite. Being with her, seeing her battle against her fears and grow her confidence, had shown him something important—it was easy to stay still. To be stagnant.

To let the past bind you to one spot.

It was harder to push through all that and be honest about what you truly wanted. And after talking out in the open about his big secret, after being with a woman whose courage inspired him, Trent could honestly say that he wanted more.

More from life. More from himself.

He parked the ute in front of a row of sleek shop fronts. The architect's office was on the second floor, apparently right above a jeweler. He walked along the quaint strip, past the fashion boutique and an antique store and a hipster coffee place full of dudes with man buns.

Then he found the jewelry store. To its right was

a single glass door leading to a staircase. But something caught his eye in the glittering window of the shop. There were clusters of fancy-looking things—diamond rings the size of marbles and watches that probably cost more than he spent on his first three cars combined.

But it wasn't any of that flash that got his attention. It was something far humbler. At the bottom right-hand corner of the display was a cluster of gold necklaces so fine, a subtle breeze might snap them in two. Each one had a thin gold disc hanging from it, with a simple image engraved. There was one with a flower, one with a seashell, and one with a star and moon.

But it was the one with the caterpillar that had him rooted to the spot.

Metamorphosis. Change. Growth.

These were Cora's ideas, and the things he'd shied away from in the past. But she'd shown him that it was possible to keep moving, even in the face of bad things, while he'd clung to his unaffected smiles and flippant charm as a way to keep the world at arm's length.

I don't want her to go.

The words circled around in his brain, chasing themselves like a puppy chasing its tail. What if Trent took a leap this time? What if, instead of pretending he didn't care or that he wasn't affected, he told the truth?

What if he told Cora that she meant something to him? Like, *really* meant something? Not sex or laughs or a fun time. Not a temporary fling. But something more. Something…real.

Looking at his phone, he knew he was going to be late to his meeting. But the architect would have to wait. Trent had to make a purchase.

• • •

He waited until Cora's last day in Australia, oscillating between blurting out his desires and driving back to Sorrento to return his gift. But, for once in his life, Trent *wasn't* going to take the easy route.

"Don't think about the negatives, think about the positives." He looked around at what he'd created—the perfect romantic scenario in which he could reveal how he felt about Cora, hopefully with a positive response.

Emphasis on the *hopefully*. Because romantic gestures weren't Trent's forte. He was a simple guy—a steak and two veg guy, a small town, enjoy a few beers and watch the stars kinda guy. Maybe Cora was used to private limos and champagne dinners and little blue boxes.

But to Trent that wasn't love.

Love? You're jumping straight to love with a woman you've known only a month?

But this month hadn't been any ordinary month. They'd lived together, played house, and gotten to know each other in ways he'd never known another person. They'd shared their dreams. Shared secrets about themselves.

It was like cramming a whole year of a relationship into thirty days.

He walked out onto the back deck and stepped down onto the grass of Liv's backyard. A red and white checked picnic blanket was sprawled out, with a basket of food from all the best local vendors—bread from the Wattle & Oat bakery, wine from T'Gallant, fruit from the local market, and his mum's town-famous lamingtons.

"You beauty!" Joe the cockatoo arrived with a squawk and a flap of his wings, settling down next to the blanket and doing his little waddle across to where the cheese sat.

Trent clapped his hands. "This isn't for you. I've got something very special planned here and I don't want your grubby little claws messing it up."

The cockatoo craned his head up as if to say, *Who, me? I wouldn't do that.*

"Yeah right, I know better than to trust a scavenger." Trent tried to shoo the bird away, but Joe would not be so easily scared from the feast of all feasts. "Come on, this is a special night. I don't want you messing it up."

"Arrrk! Bugger off." Joe bobbed his head.

"No, *you* bugger off." Trent crouched down to meet the bird at eye level. "Seriously, mate. Do me a favor, okay?"

Joe cocked his head. *"Pretty boy."*

"I've got a special lady staying tonight, and I want it to be romantic." Trent reached for a cracker and snapped it in half, the bird's beady black eyes laser locked on the tasty morsel. "I'm going to pour her a drink, feed her some delicious food, and ask her…"

His gaze flicked to the back door, catching movement inside the house. A glimpse of Cora's long legs and wild hair could be seen as she dropped her bag and keys onto the dining table.

"I'm going to ask her to give us a chance." Trent sucked in a breath and gave the cracker to the bird, who munched happily, sending a shower of cracker crumbs all over the blanket. Sighing, Trent gave him the other half and brushed the mess away. "So give me some space, all right? This is a big deal."

Understatement of the century. Trent never thought he'd be in this position again, liking someone enough to put himself in the firing line. Sure, there'd been other women he'd crushed on and dated briefly—but none of those times had felt real. They were pleasing distractions. Enjoyable detours from adult life. Not something that would stop him in his tracks and make him question everything he thought he wanted.

But Cora did.

And tonight he was going to ask her to give them a chance. "Got any advice, old bird?"

Joe the cockatoo stomped around, swinging his head from side to side. The crest fanned out, showing off brilliant gold feathers.

"I don't know what that means, but I'll take it as a sign of encouragement." He laughed. "You'd like it if she stayed, wouldn't you, buddy? Yeah, me too. It's unexpected, but she makes me…"

The back door swung open, and Cora emerged, a floor-length cotton dress in yellow and white swirling around her feet. Her fluffy cloud of hair bounced around her shoulders as she walked, and the smile on her lips was brighter than the most brilliantly polished diamond.

For a moment Trent wondered if his heart had

stopped. "She makes me wild."

"*Bloody oath!*" Joe bobbed up and down as Cora came closer.

"What are you two whispering about?" she asked, her gaze swinging from bird to man and back again. Trent gave a cavalier shrug, belying the anxious knotted sensation in his stomach. "I don't know which one of you is more trouble."

She walked straight over to Trent and slipped her arms around his neck, rising up on her toes and kissing him. His muscles automatically tightened, sealing her body to his, telling her what he wanted without words.

But the kiss was broken up by the absolute silence at foot level. And where Joe Cockatoo was concerned, silence was the most concerning sound he could make. Trent pulled away and dropped his gaze to the red and white checked blanket.

Joe froze mid-lunge, his open beak hovering over a cubed piece of cheese as though someone had suddenly cast him in stone.

"Don't you dare," Trent said in his most authoritative voice.

There was a tense standoff as time slowed down, then the bird made his move. He snatched the cheese and scuttled across the blanket, knocking over a punnet of strawberries in his great escape before flapping his wings and launching himself into the air. He settled in a tree at the side of the yard, gloating over his prize.

"Bloody bird," Trent muttered.

But Cora watched the exchange with pure and utter joy, her blue eyes sparkling and cheeks flushed with happiness. "You leave my Joe alone. He's doing what's required to survive."

For some reason, the words struck him as more than an observation about a greedy, scavenging bird. But Trent would not be deterred from sharing his feelings with Cora. Too many times in his life he'd stayed quiet—the years after he found out the secret of his birth, all the times he'd suspected Rochelle was cheating on him but didn't want to confront her. Every time someone called him the town charmer, not knowing it was a fabrication.

He smiled and shrugged it off as a joke, hid behind his charming smile and flippant tone no matter how much he was hurting.

Yet being with Cora made him feel like, for the first time in his life, maybe he didn't have to censor himself. The way she wrote, with such passion and honesty, had inspired him to speak his own truth.

"What's all this for?" she asked, taking a step back and surveying his work. "I thought we were going to grill some sausages and have a quiet night in, since we've got a big party tomorrow."

The cricket team had wanted to send Cora off in style—with beers and Aussie staples like parmas and chips at the White Crest. They'd also invited Trent's siblings and partners, the staff at Just One More Chapter, and everyone else whom Cora had befriended during her holiday. But Trent was hoping it was going to be more of a surprise party than a send-off: *Surprise! Cora isn't leaving after all.*

Or, more realistically, maybe she'd be leaving for a short while and then coming back with more than one suitcase. Was it crazy to ask a person to upend her life? To take such a big chance on something so fresh and new?

But Trent had reasoned that Cora was miserable in Manhattan. She worked a job that didn't fulfill her, had a broken relationship with her parents, no partner or pets waiting for her return. After all, *she* came *here* looking for an escape.

Their life could be amazing. Building a house together while she focused on writing her book. Building a life that healed them both from the past.

"I wanted to do something special," he said, taking her hand.

"You're not going to make me cry, are you?" Her brows pinched. "To be honest, if there was a way for me to slink off without saying anything, I would. I'm terrible at goodbyes."

Trent tried to ignore the stone settling in the pit of his stomach. There was no point being scared. All he had to do was man up and say it.

Don't chicken out now—you know she's one of a kind. This is one of a kind.

"So don't say goodbye." Each syllable was like digging a spoon into his chest and scooping out chunks of his heart.

Yeah, it sounded a bit gross. But that's exactly how it felt.

Cora blinked, shaking her head. "You really think I should have left without saying anything?"

"No, not that." Ugh, so much for being smooth. How had his famous charm deserted him now? "I mean, there's no need to say goodbye if you don't go. So…don't go."

She opened and closed her mouth for a second,

like a stunned goldfish. A cuter than hell stunned goldfish. "I…"

"Stay." He filled the gap with his desire. With his wish.

"Here, in Australia?"

"Well, I was hoping specifically in Patterson's Bluff." He raked a hand through his hair, desperate to do something with his hands. He'd always been better with his hands than with words. "With me."

"With you?" she squeaked.

For a moment there was nothing—no sound coming out of her mouth, seemingly no blood in her veins—if her pallor was anything to go by. Okay, so she was shocked. That wasn't a total surprise. Shock wasn't a bad reaction… Was it?

Shit. What the hell are you doing?

"Is that such an outrageous suggestion?" He jammed his hands into his pockets. "I thought you had a good time here."

"Oh my God, Trent. Of course I did. I had an *amazing* time with you." Her features softened. "But I can't pack up my whole life and move to another country because I had good sex."

The words were like being slapped across the face. "I'm not asking you to stay for sex, Cora. I can get that anywhere."

She winced. Okay, so that's not how he'd wanted that statement to come out.

"I'm aware you can have any woman you want," she said stiffly. "Although I'd rather not think about you with anyone else, to be perfectly honest."

See, *that* was a sign she felt something for him.

"That came out wrong. What I'm trying to say is

that we're *more* than good sex. You'd be staying for *more* than good sex…" Why was this so hard? He'd seen enough of those cheesy romantic comedy movies to know the whole big declaration at the end was what won a person over. He couldn't beat around the bush now. "Cora, I like you a hell of a lot. I like *us*. I like the way I am with you and the way you are with me. I like holding you and listening to your dreams and getting excited over things I'd never be excited about on my own."

Her eyes were glassy, and she clasped her hands in front of her pretty yellow dress. "I like us, too."

"So stay. Move here and work on your novel and…be with me." There it was, the thing he wanted most out in the open. Soft and squishy and fearing the worst. Another word hovered on his tongue, a word he'd sworn he'd never say again.

Love.

He loved Cora. Against every fear in his heart and every scrap of logic telling him it was utterly and completely ridiculous, what he felt for Cora was real. It was forever. He wanted to build them a house and a life. He wanted to see her soar.

"I…I can't stay." She shook her head. "I have a life in New York, an apartment. I have a job."

"A job you don't like."

Her eyes cast downward. "Not forever. My dad has been talking about maybe making me an agent and…"

She smiled like she was happy about this offer, but Trent could hear the pain in her voice. It wasn't what she wanted.

"I could help other writers achieve their dream

of being published," she finished.

"What about *your* dream?"

"I'm still working on it. But that's why I need to go home."

"It doesn't have to be that way," he said. "You told me you wanted to have a beautiful house by the water one day, somewhere to write and create. You could have that here."

"But what about my family?" she asked. She was barely looking at him now, her hands white-knuckling one another. "I can't leave them."

"Your family, who treats you like dirt."

"They're *still* my family."

It made his blood boil the way she clung to her loyalty when it sounded as though they'd done nothing to deserve it. "Family is what you make it. I know that more than anyone."

"And where would I live, in your sister's house?" She gestured to the back door. "A few weeks ago, you didn't even seem to care where you would sleep after Liv came home, and now all of a sudden you want to plan a future?"

She was freaking out; he could see the wildness in her eyes. Hear it in the heightened pitch of her voice. Maybe he'd gone too hard, too soon. Perhaps he should have eased into this conversation more.

If she wanted to stay, she wouldn't be freaking out.

"Now I have a reason," he said. "I want to build it for us."

"Trent, everything you do in life is for someone else." She shook her head. "You have to want to do things for *you*."

"What are you talking about?"

"Instead of building your home, you're here doing things for Liv. Whenever Nick calls you for extra work, you drop whatever you're doing. If I asked you to give me the moon, you'd find a way to get a lasso around it."

He blinked. "Am I missing something? I thought it was a good thing to be kind to others."

"Not when it *always* comes at a sacrifice to yourself." She bit down on her lip. "You act like you have to earn your place, but the fact is, people love you here. You don't need to earn anything."

"That doesn't have anything to do with me asking you to stay—you're deflecting."

She sighed. "My point is…we're still caterpillars. We still have so much work to do, so much growth we have to experience before we're ready to be butterflies together. We're not…we're not ready."

Trent glanced at the ground, to the little wrapped box that contained the gold pendant, and frowned.

"The way you see yourself, you'll never be a butterfly," Trent said. "You think you're so broken and so unlovable that you've *become* that way. It's a self-fulfilling prophecy."

"I don't think that." She folded her arms across her chest.

"Why else would you go back to the parents who've done nothing but belittle you? You don't think you deserve any better." He clenched and unclenched his hands. This was *not* going the way he'd hoped. "Don't you think it's possible for two people to grow together? To change together? If you had to be perfect to be worthy of love, then nobody would ever be loved."

"You forgave your family for lying to you for more than a decade, yet you can't understand why I keep hoping that I can turn things around with mine? That's hypocritical."

"He wants to crush your dreams, Cora. For crying out loud, he basically told you to give up!"

The second the words left Trent's mouth, he wanted to snatch them back. Shit. He hadn't planned to broach the topic of the last letter from Cora's father in such an emotional fashion.

"You read my emails. Wow." She took a step backward, shaking her head.

"I didn't go looking. Your laptop was on the table and it was open…" Okay, and maybe he'd nudged the track pad so her screen would light up. But he hadn't done anything more than that… except sending his father Cora's file without her permission. Crap. Okay, so maybe he'd majorly overstepped. But it all came from a good place. "He should never have told you to quit."

"That's *none* of your business." Her cheeks were bright pink now, her eyes blazing like twin blue flames.

"If it's hurting you, then I want to make it my business. He has no right to bring you down like that. Why can't you see how toxic they are?" It was like beating his head against a brick wall. It made absolutely no sense to Trent that she would leave a place where she could be loved and included to go back to a place that by all her accounts was cold and unwelcoming. Back to people who were happy to cut her down with their words. "Are you so desperate for a family that you'll go back to them simply because they're related to you?"

Her eyes widened as if he'd slapped her.

"I'm sorry, that came out harsher than I meant." He held up a hand, but something told him the damage had already been done.

"It's *not* your place to tell me what my family should be like," she said quietly. It was as if the flames had been extinguished with his carelessness, and for some reason the quiet felt so much worse than her anger. "You of all people should know that family isn't always perfect."

At least my parents love me.

He bit back the words because, even though they were true, they felt spiteful. And he didn't want to treat Cora like that—he'd hoped that by showing her what it might be like to be part of a cohesive unit, she'd want to stay. That she'd see how much better her life could be.

But he'd clearly underestimated the pull her parents had on her.

"Bloody hell, Cora. I care about you." Now he was laying it all out on the line, opening himself up further when she'd given him no reason to. No encouragement.

If she walked away now, it wouldn't be because he'd kept his feelings a secret—and that meant he'd live without regrets. Because, for the first time ever, he was showing someone all his cards. Leaving nothing unsaid.

For too long, he'd kept secrets like rocks in his pockets, not telling people about his true identity for fear they'd reject him. And maybe Cora had a point; he *did* put other people's needs first. A lot. He could say it was the "Walters Way," as his dad liked to espouse, helping those around them without pause.

But if he was being truly honest with himself, that was the easy cover. The fact was, he *did* feel the need to earn his place. To buy people's love with good deeds, instead of being himself and trusting that his siblings would love him anyway.

It sat uncomfortably in his chest, as though she'd revealed a part of him he'd wanted to ignore.

"You're not supposed to care about me," she said, shaking her head.

"I know," he said. "But I do."

• • •

It was like a bad dream and the best dream she'd ever had rolled into one. Cora couldn't think straight, because her head was so stuffed full of battling emotions that there wasn't space for logic. For reason.

Trent cared about her.

And the hard truth of it was, she cared about him, too. A heck of a lot.

More than she'd ever cared about Alex, she realized on reflection. Because Alex had never known her the way Trent did, he'd never encouraged her the way Trent had. He'd never seen her tiptoeing around her dreams and shoved her in the right direction no matter how terrifying and thrilling it was.

But she couldn't stay here. Because that would mean sacrificing her *other* dream—the one she'd had since she was a girl, staring at her bedroom door and willing one of her parents to come and save her battered little heart. If she left her life in Manhattan behind to move to Australia, then her father would forget about her. He barely made time for her now, despite them working in the same office and living a block from each other. If she left the country…

Well, he might forget that she existed altogether.

"You're killing me, Trent." She swung her gaze over the beautiful picnic he'd put together—from the ripe, sweetly scented strawberries to the bottle of wine and the little paper bag from the bakery she'd grown to love during her time here. "Why can't we appreciate this for what it was and walk away with some good memories?"

"Because a good memory of you isn't enough. I don't want to *remember* you, like it was some happy blip in my life." He was so sincere, it radiated out of his face, his goodness gripping her heart and squeezing. "I want us to *keep* making memories."

This wasn't how her trip was supposed to end. "I never came here looking for forever. It was supposed to be a distraction from my real life."

"And this wasn't real?"

"This was a vacation fantasy, where I was going to lick my wounds in a beautiful place and get my head back on straight so I could go home and fix everything."

"Fix everything?" His nostrils flared, and

something dark and sharp cut across his face. "You're planning to go back to your ex?"

Had she wanted that reconciliation? Maybe for a moment as she'd packed her bags back in Manhattan. Maybe a bit during the flight over when tears burned her eyes. But after that? Not once.

Alex wasn't the guy for her.

Trent had shown her that. The way she'd felt in his arms, waking up next to him, walking around his block of land and listening to his plans... She'd felt true passion for the first time ever. Alex was a good person, but he hadn't made Cora's heart soar the way Trent did. He hadn't believed in her the way Trent did.

"No, I'm not. It's over, completely." She sucked in a breath, her chest protesting the movement as though her heart was physically bruised. "But my life is still in New York."

"What life?" He threw up his hands. "That's the part I'm having trouble understanding. Everything you've said about that place has painted an ugly picture, and yet it seems to have this hold on you."

Maybe it did. Maybe it was because it felt like leaving Manhattan for good would mean admitting failure, whereas if she kept trying...

But for how long?

Cora's heart felt weighed down. Heavy. She'd failed at everything she'd ever tried to achieve—her music performance career was a bust, she'd never been able to hold down a relationship, she wasn't speaking to her mother, her manuscript was a disaster, her father didn't think she had potential to succeed as an author...

You can keep trying.

Being the caterpillar meant working hard for change, and she still had such a long way to go. Her fingertip drifted over the top of her thigh, to where her tattoo was hidden behind the length of her cotton dress.

"Am I…am I seeing something that isn't here?" Trent asked.

For a second she thought about lying. It would be easier to say she felt nothing for him. To say that leaving wasn't going to shatter her heart into a million pieces. To push down her emotions and protect herself with falsities.

But what kind of person would that make her?

"I care about you, too, Trent. A lot." She blinked back the prickly feeling in her eyes, determined to be honest but strong. "These last few weeks have been incredible."

"But?"

"I can't stay." Her voice trembled. "I know you don't understand the relationship I have with my family. It's messy and imperfect and…yes, it's difficult. For someone who had such loving parents, of course you would find my situation strange. But all my life I wanted to make my dad proud, and even though it never seems to turn out right…I can't give up now."

He shoved his hands into his pockets. She could see he was closing himself off, shutters going up and locks engaging and walls fortifying around him. "I understand."

"You don't, really. But that's okay." She attempted a watery smile, but her lips refused to turn up. Inside, it felt like her heart was slowly being chipped away, each word cleaving off another piece until there was nothing left but an unrecognizable lump. "It's something I have to do for myself."

Something that looked a whole lot like respect flickered in his eyes. "So this is it."

"It's okay if you don't want me in the house tonight," she said, biting down on her lip. "Maybe I could crash at Maddy's place. I can pack up and—"

"No, this was supposed to be your holiday. Not mine." He reached out and touched the side of her face, and for a second Cora wanted to snatch all her words back and promise him everything. "I'll head out tonight and give you some space to pack. I can take you to the airport the day after tomorrow."

"You don't have to do that," she said softly.

"I know. I want to." He dropped his hand. "Someone needs to see you off."

That was Trent in a nutshell. Even after she'd rejected him, pushed him away…he was still here, helping her. Being a good person. It was a good thing she wasn't staying, because Trent deserved someone who would sacrifice everything for him.

"You're going to make someone very happy one day," she said.

But Trent didn't reply. He simply nodded and walked toward the house, leaving the beautiful picnic spread behind him as though it now meant nothing. A sinking sensation settled in the pit of Cora's stomach. Saying goodbye would be brutal, but it was for the best.

This was never meant to be anything permanent, and all the wishing in the world wasn't going to change that.

She knelt down onto the picnic blanket and began to pack up the food. It seemed like such a waste to leave it there, though she was sure Joe would have enjoyed the feast. She put lids on the dips and closed the strawberry container. As she was cleaning up, she came across a slim black box. It was beautifully flocked, and the velvet almost melted under her touch.

Cora's gaze drifted to the house. Should she open it? Or would it only make things harder in two days when she would leave Australia for good?

She couldn't find it in herself to peek. Because her control was balancing on a knife's edge as it was, and her grip on her childhood dream felt looser and more precarious than ever. If she looked and her heart exploded…

No, she couldn't stay. The hard part was over; now it was time to go home and think about how she could put her life back together.

CHAPTER TWENTY-TWO

Two weeks later…

Trent had been wandering around like a sleep-deprived zombie ever since Cora had left. He'd put on a happy face at her going-away party and forced himself not to drag her out of the check-in line at the airport. Ever since, he'd been exhausted. Not to mention that he was couch surfing again now that Liv was home.

Despite her teasing him about squatting in her house, she'd offered for Trent to stay a while longer, but everywhere he looked he saw Cora—in the shower, in the spare bedroom, at the dining room table, on the quaint little chairs under the veranda out back. He sketched her into any room with vivid details so realistic, he could almost smell her perfume in the air.

It was a cruel kind of torture, to see a person everywhere while knowing you'd never *actually* see them again.

So he'd taken up residence at Skye's place for the next little while, sleeping in her spare room. Her little girl was over the moon, since "Uncle Trent" was the fun uncle, and he was more than happy to listen to her babble for hours about whatever her latest obsession was—yesterday it was asteroids and space. Today, unicorn battles.

However, sleeping at other people's houses couldn't be a permanent setup. Not only did he not expect Skye to give him space forever, but now the couch surfing thing felt a whole lot *less* appealing than it had in the past. Instead of making him feel free and spontaneous, it had the opposite effect—caging him to a life that was without roots and direction. Without purpose.

Trent shook the thoughts from his head as he walked up the driveway to his parents' house. Nick's Merc was parked there, followed by Liv's little hatchback. Jace's car—the same one he'd had since forever—was on the street. It looked like Adam and Soraya hadn't arrived yet.

Trent sucked in a lungful of air to try and pep himself up. But it was useless; he was miserable without Cora. Every day felt like it had a great big gaping hole in it. He missed her sunny smile, her deep and insightful thoughts; he missed the way she read to him in that husky, sultry voice. He missed seeing her eyes light up when she told him about a change she'd made to her manuscript, or when she'd read a sentence that took her breath away.

He jabbed at the doorbell as though the small button had personally offended him. All his actions were like that lately—jerky, filled with bristling frustration.

The door swung open, and Trent's dad stood there, a beaming smile on his face. He was dressed in a white T-shirt and beige cargo pants with white runners—typical dad attire.

Frank embraced him in a warm hug, because his family was never shy in doling out affection. "Son! Come on in."

"Hi, Dad. Happy anniversary."

"Thank you. It means so much that you kids want to celebrate it with us." He smiled, and it caused his bushy mustache to bob. Sound floated through from the back of the house, Liv's laughter like a sparkling bell and Nick's groan at something she'd said.

"I was hoping I could talk to you before we go out back," Frank said, scrubbing a hand over his jaw.

Trent raised an eyebrow. "Everything okay?"

"Yes, everything is fine. It's about that book you sent me."

Cora's book. Trent's heart clenched on her behalf…not that it would matter what anyone in his family thought now. It's not like he was going to contact her to pass on the feedback. "Okay…"

"It was…marvelous."

In spite of knowing that it meant nothing, Trent's heart soared for Cora. He *knew* she was talented, and his dad was a fussy reader. He also wasn't the kind of guy to blow smoke up someone's ass if he didn't truly mean it.

"Her writing is very crisp, and the way she wove that relationship into the story…" Trent's father shook his head. "Beautiful."

"I'm really glad you liked it. Cora would be thrilled."

There was a strange pause in the conversation, the kind of pregnant pause that Trent immediately knew meant there was something more going on than what his dad was saying.

"So…" The older man bobbed his head. "I did something."

Oh shit. "What?"

"Remember Mark, the guy I went to university with who moved to Sydney about ten years ago?"

Trent scanned his memory. He had a vague recollection of a guy with a wide, charming smile and thinning hair.

"Anyway," his father continued. "He's an editor now in Sydney."

Trent's blood ran colder than a glacier. Oh no. If Cora lost her shit because he'd read her father's email, then how would she feel knowing that he'd passed her book on to his dad, who'd then passed it on to an editor?

"Dad!"

He offered a sheepish shrug. "The book was so good, and Mark and I bumped into each other at that literary fair in Melbourne a while ago, so we've been talking more often and...well, I sent it to him."

Trent scrubbed a hand over his face. Cora was going to kill him. It was a total violation of her privacy, of her trust. He couldn't believe he'd *ever* done something like that, but he'd been so fired up about her dickhead father's email and...

You know that's no excuse.

Maybe Trent and his dad could keep this little secret between them. Cora didn't have to know, did she? Ugh, of course he was going to have to tell her.

"I can't believe you did that," he said, though whether it was directed at his father or himself, he wasn't totally sure.

"I know, I know." His dad threw his hands up in

the air. "But there's good news to hopefully smooth over the fact that I didn't tell you first. He wants to talk to your friend."

"The editor?" Trent blinked.

"Yep. He told me he read it in one day and he *loved* it. Said there's some work to do, of course, like with all new authors, but he wants to help her."

"Holy shit." Trent shook his head. "That's amazing."

"Yes, so I'll email you his details and you can pass them along. Please tell her how much I enjoyed the story. It's so invigorating to see young people going after their dreams. I hope she's not too angry with me."

"I'm sure she'll forgive you," Trent said with a smile.

And hopefully me, too.

Trent's dad slapped him on the back in a hearty Walters family fashion and then led him out to the backyard. Nick looked up and waved with his free hand, the other turning the snags on the barbecue. There was some salmon there, too, and long skewers holding prawns and chunky slices of capsicum and red onion.

"Hi, Trent." Liv waved and came over to give him a hug. Her long hair was tied into a bouncing ponytail and she wore a printed blouse with denim shorts and wedge heels. "I have to say thank you again for fixing the shower at my place. It works like a dream now. In fact, it was so good, I managed to drain my entire hot water tank with one shower."

"I'm forgiven for squatting in your house,

then?" He shot her a cheeky smile.

"Totally." She leaned in and gave him a big hug, but there was something sluggish about her movements. Dark shadows circled her under-eye area.

"You okay?" he asked.

"Uh-huh, just tired." Liv smiled, but it didn't seem completely genuine. "Cora was messaging me yesterday saying she's working super-long hours, too. The post-holiday backlog is a killer."

He swallowed against the lump in his throat. He'd been doing the same—drowning himself in work, so the memories would stop playing on repeat.

"Thanks for taking good care of her," Liv added. "She told me that you really made her feel welcome. I can't believe you threw her a birthday party."

"It was nothing." And by nothing, of course, he meant everything. Now he was going to have to contact her, like that wouldn't be awkward as shit.

Ugh, how do you get yourself into these messes?

"It *wasn't* nothing. It was a really sweet gesture. You're good people." She squeezed his shoulder. "And I still can't get over all the things you fixed in my house. I'll pay you back for everything."

"No, you won't. It was a gift."

"But that's *so* much money, Trent. You're supposed to be putting it all toward your own place." She looked at him with a crinkled brow and worried eyes. "I mean, I know you tradies seem to earn more money than us white-collar folks these days, but still. I didn't expect you to go all *Grand*

Designs on me."

"Probably more like one of those dodgy cable renovation shows, if we're being honest," he joked.

Liv swatted him. "Stop it. Those lights in the bathroom were magnificent; you have great taste. I can only imagine how beautiful your house is going to be when you build it. Emphasis on the *when.*"

"Don't you start, too. You've been back in the country a few weeks and already you sound like Nick."

"Sorry." She held up her hands in peace. "It's easier to think about everyone else's future sometimes instead of worrying about your own, you know."

Did he ever. "You've got nothing to worry about, Liv. You've got four walls and a roof to call your own...and a cockatoo who won't leave you be."

She grinned. "Don't you dare say anything bad about my baby Joe."

"Ha, baby nothing. That guy is a stone-cold food-motivated master manipulator."

At that moment, the final guests arrived. Big brother Adam and his wife, Soraya, walked through the back door into the yard, waving and calling out their hellos. Usually, at family gatherings, Trent felt a sense of restorative peace. His family was the most important thing in his world, and he loved spending time with them.

But today, for some reason, he felt disconnected.

"Hi, Trent, good to see you." Soraya came over and gave him a hug, scenting the air with her signature rose perfume. She wore a long skirt that swept the ground and a white top that tied at her waist. "Liv, welcome back."

The two women hugged, and Liv immediately started chattering about the amazing shopping in New York—his little sister and sister-in-law were as close as if they were born related, rather than being linked through marriage.

See? And nobody views Soraya as less than family. DNA isn't the most important thing.

He couldn't seem to shake the past. For years, he'd worked desperately to conceal his secret from his siblings, convincing his mother and father to help him hide the information of his birth. They'd agreed, telling him the information was *his* to share, whenever he felt ready. Yet years had passed, and no such urge had surfaced. It wasn't until Cora had accused him of always putting others before himself, of needing to earn his place and earn their love, that he'd started to wonder whether his secret was holding him back.

She'd shown him that dreaming was good. And what greater dream did he have than building a house and creating a life inside it?

He watched his family bustle around him—Dad and Nick on the barbecue, always the first to offer a helping hand to others. Soraya, Angie, and Liv were laughing and joking, bringing light and happiness to every gathering. His mother was fussing over the table settings, working hard to get everything "just right" for the family she loved so much. Jace and Adam were constructing a new banana lounge, showing how they cared with their actions.

He *was* part of this family.

Would it change if he told them the truth? Would they treat him differently, view him as less?

"Lunch is on," his dad called as he and Nick carried platters of cooked meat, veggies, and seafood to the table.

The rest of the table was set, wine and beers chilling in the Esky beside the table, a place for everyone set with plates and cutlery. His mother and father sat at opposite ends of the table and everyone else was scattered between them. Jace dropped down next to Trent.

"How's…everything?" Trent asked as he leaned forward and piled some salmon onto his plate.

"No news yet," Jace said quietly, a disappointed look on his face. "But apparently it can take a while for some people. The puppies are keeping us plenty occupied anyway. And work is busy."

"That's good. You're living the dream, bro."

Jace laughed. "My dream, maybe. Probably sounds like a nightmare to you."

He and Jace were the most opposite within the family — Trent had never taken himself too seriously, and Jace was *Mr.* Serious. But the fact was, his brother inspired him. Jace had smashed down every barrier that people tried to place in front of him, never letting his autism define what he could achieve. *All* Trent's siblings inspired him in different ways, and for too long he'd felt like he could never inspire them back.

"So, Mum and Dad. Forty years of marriage." Adam raised his glass and everyone followed, shouting congratulations and hear, hears. "Any words of wisdom for us whippersnappers?"

"Your mother is always right, even when she's making no bloody sense at all," his dad said with a chuckle.

"Communication," his mother replied, rolling her eyes but still smiling. "There's nothing that can't be overcome by a strong relationship, and communication is a key part of that. Never go to bed on a fight, and don't keep secrets."

Don't keep secrets.

The words stuck on repeat in Trent's head, swirling and swirling. He'd never felt so stuck as he had in the past week.

"Good advice," Nick said with a nod. "Here's to forty more."

"Please God, no." Their father clutched as his chest dramatically, and the table cracked up laughing. "Seriously, I couldn't have asked for a better wife or family."

"Awww." Angie pressed into Jace and looked up at him lovingly. "That'll be us in forty years."

"Well, since it's such a special occasion…" Liv reached down to grab something from under the table. "I made a present for you to commemorate the milestone."

She glanced across the table at Trent and winked as she handed over the scrapbook to Mum. Dad came around the other side of the table to see what was going on. Trent's mother immediately teared up as she began to look through the pages, oohing and aahing over the photos capturing all her favorite memories.

"Oh my gosh, look at little Adam." Soraya leaned closer to her mother-in-law and clapped her hands together. "You were so cute."

"Then came Nick." Melanie flipped the page.

"I was the biggest baby," Nick said to Angie, who was sitting next to him. Trust Nick to find a way to make it a competition.

Trent's chest tightened as the pages were turned. After Nick came Jace. Then Trent. The picture on this page showed Trent and his mother at home, rather than in the hospital—his mother was smiling, but she looked tired. Only Trent and his parents knew the dark circles weren't from being up all night because of a crying baby.

Don't keep secrets. Don't keep secrets. You're living your life for other people.

The words spun around and around and around, choking Trent. Smothering the air in his lungs and making his blood feel thick and sluggish in his veins. The story being told by the scrapbook was a lie.

"That's not what happened." The words left his mouth before he could think any further about the consequences. "It's not…"

His parents exchanged worried looks but said nothing. As always, they had never prevented him from doing anything he wanted to do or from making his own decisions.

"I was going to tell them, Trent," Liv said with a laugh, waving her hand. "But I wanted them to look through the book before I told them about the mishap."

She thought he was upset about not getting any credit for the scrapbook. Sweet Liv had no clue what was coming. "There's something else I need to tell you all."

Now everyone at the table was looking at him. The backyard had gone quiet, as though he'd commanded the attention of every living creature, every blade of grass. Even the flies had the decency to stop their incessant buzzing for a moment.

"I…" Oh God, why did it feel like he was standing naked in front of everyone?

His mother reached out and grabbed his hand, love shining from her eyes. His father stood quiet and strong as a stone pillar, hand resting on his wife's shoulder. They both knew what was coming.

They'd been waiting for years.

"I've been keeping a secret from you." The words were strange and heavy on his tongue, years of lies making the truth feel foreign and uncomfortable. "Mum and Dad aren't actually my mum and dad."

For a second, there was a silence so deafening that Trent wondered if he'd spontaneously lost his hearing.

Liv shook her head. "Is this a joke?"

His siblings looked at one another, confused and uncertain. They knew he was a joker, but even *he* wouldn't try to derail an anniversary for the sake of an inappropriate laugh.

"My birth mother is Aunt Linda," he said. "I'm her baby. That's why there are no photos of me in the hospital with Mum…because she didn't give birth to me."

The hushed silence was like a boulder crushing his chest. He wanted them to do something—yell, scream, cry, get up and walk away. The staring was physically painful. The fear of not knowing what would happen next was a fist around his throat.

"I don't know who my birth father is," he continued, sounding a hell of a lot more together than he felt. "But as far as I'm concerned, these two people here are the only parents I need in my life."

Jace frowned as though the information wasn't computing. "So you're…my cousin?"

"Actually, he's your adoptive brother," Trent's mother said, her lip trembling. "We officially adopted him when he was a baby. It was my sister's dying wish that we make him part of our family and treat him no differently than the rest of you."

"I can't believe you never told us," Liv said, her eyes bright with unshed tears. "How could you all keep this a secret?"

"It's a pretty big fucking secret," Nick replied. He raked a hand through his hair.

"I don't see what difference it makes," Jace said, shaking his head and looking a little befuddled by all the fuss. "It doesn't change anything."

Angie reached for her husband's hand and squeezed, without saying a word.

"Who decided not to tell us?" Nick asked.

Trent sucked in a breath. "I did."

"But we had kept it from him when he was young, and truthfully…we let it go on too long. I never knew when he would be old enough to understand what it meant, and I was so worried about losing him." His mother bit down on her lip. "It took me a long time to accept losing Linda, because she was my best friend. The other half of me. And then I was scared I'd left it too long to tell the truth."

It dawned on Trent now that had he been born in Patterson's Bluff, the secret may not have been kept as long. But, since they had lived in a much bigger place closer to Melbourne back then, not moving to Patterson's Bluff until he was in school, the secret had been much easier to keep.

"So you found out by accident?" Adam asked, eyes wide.

Trent nodded. "Yeah, I came across an old photo and put the pieces together."

"Why didn't you tell us?" Nick asked. "Did you think we'd kick you out of the house or something? Vote you off the island?"

Trent laughed in spite of the somber turn of the afternoon. "Something like that."

"Well, that's insulting." Nick crossed his arms over his chest. "A Walters family member is a Walters family member, doesn't matter whose blood you've got in your veins."

"Technically he has his own blood in his veins," Jace said with a serious expression. "Unless you've had a transfusion recently."

Nick rolled his eyes. "You know what I mean."

"It got to the point that I wasn't sure what to say and I didn't want it to…" Wow, being vulnerable was the worst. "Affect things."

I didn't want to lose you all.

"And lots of people say things like blood is thicker than water, but I—"

"You're *not* water, Trent." Liv was almost vibrating with anger. Out of everyone, he'd expected her to take it hardest—being the two youngest, they'd been thick as thieves since they were kids. He'd kept her safe at school and threatened any bullies who might try to pick on her, and she'd always looked up at him with wonder and respect. "If you ever say that again, I will literally lose my shit."

"Well, if you say literally—" Jace began, but Angie shushed him.

"You *are* one of us and you have been the second you set foot into this house," Liv said, eyes blazing. "I'm really hurt that you didn't think we'd accept you, and while I understand why you were scared, I wish you could have trusted us. I will say this, however. If anyone thinks even for a *second* about treating Trent any differently, they'll have to go through me first. I will fight you. All of you."

That was his little sister, warrior and voice of their family.

"No one is going to fight you, Liv," Adam said softly. "And no one is going to treat Trent differently. We're not that kind of family."

"Why tell us now?" Nick asked.

"I had a bit of an epiphany recently thanks to the help of a very wise lady." This time when he smiled it wasn't in spite of anything—it was *because* of everything. Though losing Cora hurt him more than he'd ever anticipated, he now knew that one decision wouldn't have to dictate his whole life.

If there'd been any doubt left in his mind that Cora was like his ex, this would obliterate it. Cora's whole idea of metamorphosis was catching. She'd changed him. Before her, he couldn't even *think* about confessing his true parentage to his siblings, let alone have the guts to actually stand up and say it. But now that it was out in the world…he felt free.

And it was all thanks to her.

"Cora?" Liv asked with wide eyes.

"Yeah." Trent nodded. "She's special."

Too special to let go. He would reach out to her and maybe they could talk. Maybe they could try the long-distance thing. Maybe he could even visit her in Manhattan.

Who knows, the future was suddenly a blank slate for him to paint anything he wanted.

They all looked at him for a moment, and then Nick reached down to the Esky that was sitting beside the table. "Who wants a beer? I feel like we all need a drink now."

And just like that, the family lunch returned to normal.

CHAPTER TWENTY-THREE

To: Cora.Cabot@CarsonCabotLiterary.com
From: Trent.Walters@regularmail.com
Subject: News

Cora,

I know I'm probably the last person you're expecting to hear from. I also know you're possibly going to hate me for what I have to tell you next…

I gave your manuscript to my dad and he loved it so much, he passed it on to a friend who works in publishing. The editor wants to speak with you about the book. His email and details are below. I hope you get in touch with him. And I hope you don't blame my dad, because if it wasn't for me, he wouldn't have read your manuscript in the first place. Let me know how it goes. I'd love to speak with you some time.

Give yourself a chance, even if you're not sure you can do it. We believe in you.

Trent

_____

Dear Ms. Cabot,

I had the pleasure of reading your novel, Flight of the Caterpillar, and would very much like to speak with you further about it. I have some feedback that will fortify the plot and make your natural voice shine even more. You have a great amount of talent, and with the right editorial *guidance, this could be a phenomenal story. I want to discuss the terms under which we might work together.*

Do you have a literary agent you would like to involve in this process? If so, please provide their details and we can set up a group call to discuss your submission.

Kind regards,
Mark Nicholls
Editorial Director

Cora's hands shook above the keyboard on her laptop. Was this really happening? A publisher wanted to talk to her about her manuscript. And Trent…Trent! She wasn't sure whether she wanted to scream at him or hug him to death. Probably a bit of both.

Sagging back into her office chair, she spun around to face the view outside. It was a frosty Manhattan winter day—with snow and sludge and little puffs of condensation coming from everyone's mouths. She longed for the Aussie heat and the perfect blue of the ocean right on Patterson's Bluff's doorstep.

More than that, she longed for Trent.

Cora opened her desk drawer. Inside was a slim black velvet box…the same box she'd found the day of the ill-fated picnic.

She'd found it upon her return home, when she'd started unpacking her clothes. He must have slipped it in when she'd stepped away from her packing. It had been sitting for weeks in the desk at her office, unopened. Every time she even thought about seeing what was inside, her fingers froze.

She missed him so much. Each passing day, the feeling grew stronger and more aching, memories snapping at her with sharp teeth. She couldn't escape them—not at night, not during her endless workdays.

Heart in her throat, she pulled the box out of the drawer and ran her fingers over the velvet. It was buttery soft, luxurious.

Open it.

Holding her breath, she pushed the lid up. Inside was a superfine chain in gold and a small disc, with a tiny caterpillar engraved onto it. It was the most thoughtful, personal gift she'd ever received and with shaking hands, she drew the thin chain around her neck, securing the clasp under her hair.

The gentle weight of it was like being embraced in a warm hug. In his strong arms.

Cora bit down on her lip and read the email again and again and again. After what felt like the hundredth time, she drew her eyes away and toyed with the necklace.

Would her dad want to represent her now? Maybe with the offer from an editor on the table…?

It's not an offer, it's a phone call.

But it was close, right? This sounded like a prelude to an offer. A discussion with serious interest. This would *have* to make her dad see that she had potential.

A knock at her door startled her, and she swung back around, her stocking-covered feet searching for the shiny black Louboutins she kept under her desk. She slipped the pretty deathtraps on and called for the person to come in.

"Cora?" Her father's executive assistant poked her head around the door. "Have you got a minute?"

"Sure." Cora motioned for the other woman to take a seat. But the second she started talking about business—some new hire who needed an office tour and something about a printer needing a service—Cora completely zoned out.

Her mind had been swirling for days. Her father had promised to make time to talk about her becoming an agent for the firm, and he'd asked her to think about what kind of clients she might want to represent. To do some market research and think about the list she wanted to build. But every time she tried to think about it…

Her mind went to her story. To her characters.

She wanted to tell stories…not sell them.

Her gaze drifted across her desk, catching on the artfully arranged trinkets—the little succulent (fake) in the marble pot, the Tiffany pen (real) that she only ever used for signing office birthday cards, the silver-framed photo of her family (the photo was real, but the smiles were fake). Her father stood stoically behind Cora, his hand resting on her shoulder. In the past, she'd looked at that photo and felt comfort in seeing his solid grip. But now… now it felt like a padlock on a cage.

"Cora?" The other woman waved her hand. "Are you okay? You look like you're somewhere else."

"Sorry." She shook her head. "I'm still waking

up at odd hours."

"That's all right. I'm sure it's going to take a little while to get fully caught up."

"Does Dad have many meetings this afternoon?" Cora asked, glancing at her schedule on her laptop screen. "It would be good to debrief with him, too."

"He hasn't seen you yet?" The assistant frowned. "Strange. I put a two-hour meeting in his schedule three days ago so you could talk."

And yet her father had brushed her off when she'd come back to the office, saying he had too many meetings. "Oh."

"I'm surprised he didn't tell me to reschedule. Oh well, he's got a break now until the leadership meeting starts. If you go, you can catch fifteen minutes with him."

Cora rose up from her chair almost as if pulled by some otherworldly force. She snapped the lid of her laptop closed and picked it up. "Thanks."

Without waiting a beat, she walked out of her office, leaving the bewildered assistant behind, still sitting in the plush leather chair. The walk to her father's corner office took mere seconds, and despite that, she could go days without talking to him.

With each step, her pencil-thin heels clicked against the polished boards. It was almost a strange sensation after a month of nothing but flip-flops slapping against her heels. Oh how she longed to have sand between her toes and the sun beating down on her shoulders and Trent's arms sliding…

No, stop that. You will not think about him.

But how could she avoid it? The whole reason she had the email of a lifetime burning in her inbox was because he believed in her enough to risk her being furious with him. He believed in her enough that he said the difficult things and kept encouraging her even when she didn't believe in herself. When she wasn't strong enough to accept his love.

You think he loves you? Even if by some slim chance he did before, he certainly doesn't now.

She caught a glimpse of herself in the shiny reflection of an ornate mirrored piece of artwork hanging on the wall in the main office area—Trent wouldn't recognize her here, hair straightened to within an inch of its life so it hung around her shoulders in a glossy kink-free sheet. She had on red lipstick and pearl earrings, skyscraper stilettos, and a pencil skirt so tight she couldn't eat more than a few pieces of sushi for lunch.

It was as if coming back to New York had transformed her back into her old self, not the carefree, happy person she'd been in Australia.

Cora paused outside her father's office and observed him through the slight gap in the door. They shared some features—both of them had a tendency to bounce their leg while they worked, they shared a taste for coffee strong enough to punch you in the face, and they both hated cilantro with a passion. Growing up, she'd collected those similarities like baseball trading cards, filing them away and growing her collection as if it was a substitute for them having *actual* things in common.

She raised her hand and knocked on the door, the action nudging it open farther. "Dad?"

He waited one beat, then two, before looking up at her. There was no delight in his eyes, none of that blossoming warmth she got from the people in Patterson's Bluff whom she'd started to consider her friends.

Watching him now was like watching a stranger.

"Yes Cora?" His tone, as usual, had a clipped sound. Time was money in New York, and niceties weren't worth the energy.

"I saw you had a break between meetings and I was hoping we'd be able to catch up, since I got back from my trip almost two weeks ago." She couldn't keep the sting out of the last few words, her bitterness seeping onto her tongue like a foul-tasting liquor. "*If* you have time."

"I'm busy, but come in anyway." He waved her in, still looking at his screen. He was dressed sharply as always, with a sleek charcoal suit and crisp lavender shirt. He wore more vibrant shades these days since he'd walked out on her mother. Almost as if leaving her had brought life back into his body. "I'm sorry I've been hard to get a hold of. We've got a big potential auction on the table, and it's taking all my focus."

"I understand."

"I assume you want to talk about the transition into becoming an agent. Have you done the homework I sent you?"

"Actually, I wanted to talk about my book—"

"Not this again, Cora." Now she had her father's attention. He looked at her with an expression that was equal parts concern and pity. "I know my last email must have been tough, which was why I wanted to give you space when you came back. But I really can't keep rehashing this."

"I'm sorry my dreams bother you so much," she muttered.

"I'm trying to protect you from inevitable disappointment." He folded his hands into a neat parcel at the edge of his desk. "You have your mother's idealistic spirit, and we know from the past that just because you want something doesn't mean it's the right path for you. Look at what happened at the music conservatory."

His comment stole the air from her lungs. She wanted to shout that she'd never even *wanted* to go there, that it was all her mother's pushing and pushing. But in hindsight, he wouldn't have known that, because she'd never protested too hard or too loud. She'd tried to convince her mother it wasn't a good move, but as usual, Catriona had steamrolled her.

For all her father knew, she'd wanted that dream as much as writing a book. And she'd failed, cementing his belief that she lacked talent and the fortitude to pursue a career in the arts.

"That was years ago," she said, keeping her voice steady.

"Not long enough that my wallet has forgotten being emptied for nothing."

"Gaining experience isn't worth anything to you?" she asked through gritted teeth.

"My dear, of course experience is worth something, and I want you to have a successful life." He smoothed a hand over his perfectly styled hair, which she knew he did to hide a burgeoning bald patch. "I know your mother has been a terrible example, chasing one whim after another. Therefore, I see it as my duty to steer you back onto the right path without setting you up for failure. Part of that means helping you understand what your options are."

"But you haven't even given me a chance."

"I know you're not cut out for a career in the arts. You were miserable the entire time you were studying music, even though you wouldn't admit it. But you're my daughter, and I could see the pain you were in. I could see what it was doing to you." He sighed. "I'm trying to stop you repeating that mistake and ending up in a worse position than last time."

For a second, Cora saw her father's expression soften and in it, the man she'd adored as a little girl. "I regret what I exposed you to when you were young—I stayed with your mother *way* too long and allowed you to be influenced by all her terrible behavior. It's only natural that you'd pick up some of her traits. But if I can prevent you from turning out like her, then I'll do it…even if it makes you hate me."

"I don't hate you," she said with a heavy sigh. God, her whole life she'd loved him more than anything. And she'd craved that love in return. "But I'm *not* her."

"But you could be. She wasn't always so…"

"Narcissistic?"

"Difficult," he supplied. "It came later, after we

got married. I don't want to see you going down the same path."

"My wanting to write a book has nothing to do with me being like her." She shook her head. Was he purposefully diverting the conversation? Or did he really think that she'd suffer one rejection and turn into an egomaniac?

If only he knew that she'd been suffering his rejection her entire life.

"Writing isn't about being famous or rich or any of that. I think...I think my stories could really help people."

"Why do you keep forcing me to be cruel, Cora?" He rubbed at his temples. "I can't put my reputation on the line for a book simply because you wrote it. End of story. I don't want to speak about this again."

Time away from her family had made some of her rosy view diminish, the pink fading away to gray reality. She *could* open her laptop now and show him the letter from the editor in Sydney. She could show him proof that she had what it took to write a wonderful story that would touch people. She could use these things to convince him to let the agency represent her, even if he didn't want to do it himself.

But why should she?

If he didn't believe in her, his one and only daughter, unless there was concrete proof from other people...then he would never believe in her, not really. And there was always the possibility that proof wouldn't change his opinion at all.

She didn't know which of those two outcomes

was worse.

All she *did* know was that she wasn't going to let an opportunity pass her by, simply because she'd been conditioned not to believe in herself. She knew it was conditioning now—a lifetime of her mother pushing her own dreams onto Cora, coupled with her father's misguided view that he needed to temper her ambition. It was the perfect storm.

No matter how much she tried to gain his respect and make him proud, he would always see her as the broken by-product of her mother's toxic personality. He would never understand that he was *also* toxic.

"No one is ever cruel because they're forced to be," she said, rising up from her chair, keeping her laptop tucked under one arm. "If you're cruel, it's because you get something out of it."

His mouth hung open. She'd never spoken back to him, never thrown a mirror up to his words. "You're being emotional, Cora."

She laughed, shaking her head in disbelief. Emotional? After she'd spent her whole life forcing herself not to cry and not to flinch and to smile, smile, smile? Cora was done trying to be the perfect daughter, done trying to win him over and mold herself into what he thought she should be.

She. Was. Freaking. Done.

"I quit." She kept her voice measured and quiet, and it was easy. Because she had no anger left, only pity. Only sadness that it had taken her so many years to see that no amount of trying, no amount of success or hard work, would change his opinion of her. "I'll clear my office out this afternoon, and you'll have my letter of resignation in your inbox by tomorrow morning."

Her father blinked. "What?"

"You heard me." She met his eyes with an even stare. "I've got a dream to chase, and if you're going to try to clip my wings, then I'll go it alone."

Wings. It was the first time she'd ever thought of herself as having them, since only perfect, fully transformed butterflies had wings. Maybe she *had* changed…even if she wasn't done changing yet.

"Actually, I won't be alone. But I will be with people who believe in me."

With a smile that blossomed from the depth of her soul, and a freedom that added an uncharacteristic spring to her step, she walked out of his office and down to her own, already dreaming about the things she would do once she set foot into the outside world.

CHAPTER TWENTY-FOUR

One month later…

Cora Cabot didn't make the same mistake twice. This time when she had her layover in Hong Kong, she'd showered and changed her clothes. After all, she wasn't going to get caught a second time being the stinkiest person on earth. Not when she had a very special meeting to attend.

Her stay in Sydney had been brief but eventful. She'd spent three days there, seeing all the important sights — the Opera House and the Sydney Harbour bridge and sunbathing on Bondi (which she'd learned was pronounced Bond-eye) — and meeting with the editor who wanted to work with her on her book.

But then it was time to move on to the real reason for her trip back to Australia.

The car she'd hired whizzed along the Nepean Highway, which felt totally thrilling because a) she was driving on the other side of the road and b) she could see the turnoff for Patterson's Bluff just ahead. The green and white sign indicated she was less than five kilometers away, which triggered her stomach to knot up like a set of headphone cables.

She had no plan. No steps to follow. No backups or fallbacks or other options. It was Patterson's Bluff or bust.

She understood Trent a little better now, and how he'd enjoyed living life following whims. It was exhilarating to be free of the restraints she'd put on herself previously, to be her own boss and forge her own path. Wind whipped through the car window, ruffling her curly hair. When she'd packed up her apartment for sale, she'd sold off most of her possessions and given the rest away. She'd even tossed her hair straightener in the trash, because she was never going back to being the woman who spent an hour taming her curls every day because she thought she had to.

Cora was going to be herself, unfiltered and unrestrained. Frizzy hair and all.

She hit the turn signal and slowly eased herself off the highway and onto the main road into Patterson's Bluff. Where would she even go? She had no hotel booked, though it was outside peak season and she was confident she could find a room at one of the various quaint places around town. But there was something about coming here with nothing concrete waiting for her that sent a thrill down her spine.

She was free to make her own decisions.

The car puttered along the main drag, and slowly Patterson's Bluff bloomed before her. It was Saturday afternoon and the street was bustling—the weather was balmy and mild, marshmallow clouds dotting a vibrant blue sky. She pulled up in front of the White Crest pub and killed the engine of her rental car.

Biting down on her lip, she grabbed her cross-body bag and slung it over her jeans and white T-shirt. She wore no makeup, and her suitcase was jammed into the trunk of the rental car. But Lord, did she need a break from driving. Inside, the pub was exactly as she remembered it—white paint and pale wood and those funky Edison bulbs they seemed to love in the eateries here.

She scanned the room, clutching at her bag. Some silly part of her had hoped she might find Trent there, sitting at the bar and nursing a beer. Maybe looking a little lost and sad because he was missing her.

"For all you know, he's moved right on to someone else," she muttered. After all, a man like Trent would make any woman happy, so perhaps he'd found someone smarter than Cora who wasn't about to walk away so easily.

She walked up to the bar, noting the curious stares of some of the patrons. They knew she wasn't from around here.

The bartender approached Cora. "Can I get you anything?"

"A pint of pale ale, please. Whatever is on tap." She smiled and settled into her position at the bar, dragging a book out of her bag and letting herself get lost in the story.

She hadn't quite figured out how she was going to contact Trent—she could call him. Maybe she should. Was it weird to show up in his hometown unannounced? Would that seem a bit…stalkerish? What if he didn't want to see her?

There was a tug of the old in her worries. Old Cora, who'd be insecure about Trent's feelings toward her, was rearing her ugly head. But she had no place here anymore. Cora had changed, and New Cora wasn't going to let fear dictate her actions. She would find Trent, tell him how she felt, and see where it went.

As if conjured by her deepest desires, the very man in question walked through the pub's door. He wore a pair of jeans that fit him perfectly, denim faded in patches where the fabric stretched across his muscular thighs. He had on a black T-shirt and work boots, and his face was covered in scruff like he hadn't shaved in a while.

Her heart thudded, bumping against her rib cage as she watched him, desperate desire filtering through her body. Only this time the wanting wasn't just about his rock-hard body and panty-melting smile. It was about everything, the whole package.

His life, his twinkling eyes, his giant, golden heart.

The second his eyes landed on hers, he blinked. Then shook his head. Then blinked again. His confusion was adorable, and her heart swelled in her chest.

"A wise man once told me if I was ever looking for anybody in town, I should come here," she said.

"Could you introduce me to this wise man?" he asked with a subtle lift of his lips. "I could do with some wisdom."

"Maybe I can help," she said softly. "Can I buy you a beer?"

He climbed onto the stool next to her, the scent of him twisting and turning inside her like a drug. He smelled like earth and the ocean and eucalyptus and man. He had dirt under his fingernails and his hair was askew, like he'd been working. Dust and mud caked his boots, and his skin was golden tan as ever. The T-shirt hugged his shoulders and biceps, outlining each and every muscle to fantasy-level perfection.

"So you're back," he said. "For how long?"

She lifted one shoulder into a shrug. "As long as it takes."

"For what?"

"To earn your forgiveness." She sucked on the inside of her cheek. "And to earn my own forgiveness."

His blue eyes pinned her to her seat, when all she wanted to do was throw her arms around him. But first she had to explain herself, say sorry. Let him know that walking away from him was the biggest mistake of her life.

"I've done a lot of things wrong," she said. "A lot of mistakes. Sometimes the same ones over and over."

"We all make mistakes," he said quietly.

"I made some of the biggest. Like walking out of here to go back to people who don't give a shit about me when I had someone who cared standing right by my side." She'd promised herself she wasn't going to cry, because she didn't want this to be a sad moment. This was a triumphant moment. A butterfly moment.

And she wasn't going to let a single tear fall.

"I was chasing a lie, hoping for a different result even though I'd been doing the same damn thing over and over for years. Trying to force something that wasn't going to happen."

"What happened when you went home?" he asked.

"Nothing. Not a thing had changed, except me." She looked into his eyes, hoping he could feel how sincere she was being. Hoping that those feelings he'd confessed to still existed. "I became a different person while I was here. I changed. I evolved. I finally started to figure out who *I* wanted to become, rather than only ever seeing the image my parents dangled in front of me."

"Good for you." There was a hesitation to him, a distance. She couldn't blame him for being that way, because she wasn't about to walk out of here without telling him exactly how she felt.

"I should be crediting you. I was in the deepest hole I'd ever been in my whole life, and you were the rope that helped me climb out." She swallowed. Despite her determination not to cry, tears pricked her eyes, but she blinked them into submission. "If it wasn't for you, I probably would have gone home and buried my manuscript under my bed and gone back to my old life, telling myself I wasn't good enough to chase that dream."

"That would have been a tragedy."

"Yeah, it would have. But when I got home, I saw…that life didn't fit me anymore. I'd grown too much. And that's because of you."

"You did the hard work, Cora. I only nudged you in the right direction." His hand drifted to her hair, tugging softly at one springy curl. A dimple formed in his cheek as a smile emerged.

"I'm sorry I left," she said. "But I needed to go home and see it for myself, that Manhattan held nothing for me anymore."

Trent bobbed his head but said nothing. The

bartender put a beer in front of him, without him having to ask.

"I…uh, I'm not very good at this." Cora reached for her drink and took a sip, but it tasted like sawdust. Nothing would be right until she got everything off her chest. "Usually I'm the one who gets dumped, so I've never had to try to fix things before. But I need to fix this. I came back here because I wanted to see you and tell you to your face that I messed up. I messed up so badly, and I'm so scared that you hate me for it."

"I don't hate you, Cora." He sighed and raked a hand through his hair. "Trust me, I understand why you left."

He understood, but did he forgive her? That was the question she needed answered.

Her fingers drifted to the necklace hanging around her neck, the one containing the pendant he'd hidden in her carry-on luggage. The fine gold ridges soothed her, as though each link was infused with his calming spirit.

"You found it," he said, nodding to the necklace.

"It's perfect."

"Perfect for a broken caterpillar?"

"I know I'm not broken. In fact, I think I'm stronger than I ever thought I could be. I'd just never given myself a chance before."

"No, you hadn't." He bobbed his head, keeping one hand wrapped around his pint glass. The frosted edge was wearing off, melting under the warmth of his touch. Her body ached, remembering what it was like to melt under him. To transform.

"And…I'm sorry for what I said before I left,

too." She traced a dent in the wood with her fingertip, remembering that first night in Australia when they'd eaten here together and how it felt like a million years ago. "That comment about you living to earn the love of other people was way out of line. I was scared and I lashed out, but that's no excuse—"

He held up a hand to cut her off. "You were right, though. I didn't want to hear it at the time, but you were absolutely right. I *wasn't* living for me. I wasn't putting my own goals as a priority. And the fact is...I changed, too."

• • •

Trent almost couldn't believe this was happening—he'd seen Cora's face in his dreams almost every night since she left. Now she was here, in flesh and blood. He wanted to touch every part of her to make sure it was real and not the product of too many sleepless nights. Not a figment of his overly wild and ceaselessly active imagination.

"I hope you didn't change too much," she said, with a breathless quality to her voice.

She looked like a goddess who'd come to earth to mingle for the day, hair beautifully free and eyes sincere and wide. Though she was dressed simply, she glowed. And seeing the necklace he'd bought her hanging from her neck, it made something shift in his chest. He'd never thought for a second she'd return to Patterson's Bluff. In fact, he'd put the whole experience with her down to a lesson—something he'd needed to learn about himself.

But having her here, hearing her say she wanted to make amends... Could he trust that she was telling the truth? That she was all in?

Because that's what he wanted now—no half measures or fleeting whims or passing interests. He wanted a life that was all in. He wanted commitment to a future, like the one he was creating for himself brick by brick.

"Did you come from work?" she asked.

He shook his head. "Actually, I've taken some time off work. I needed...a break."

Cora's eyes frantically searched his face, as though looking for clues into how he was feeling. There was a twitchy energy to her, like she wanted to leap at him but was holding herself back. He was holding himself back a little, too. Because this felt big. Monumentally big.

"Fancy taking a ride with me?" he asked.

Cora didn't even hesitate to slide off her stool and throw some money onto the bar, more than enough to pay for their drinks. "Lead the way."

He grabbed her hand, and feeling her fingers intertwined with his was the sweetest sensation in the world. They piled into his ute, and he promised they'd pick up her car later. But Cora didn't seem to care—it was like she'd walked away from everything, even her luggage.

The ute wound through the town, and it was like no time had passed since she left. His block came into view eventually, looking a little bit different than when she'd last seen it.

"The murder hut is gone," she gasped.

The second he pulled to a stop, she leaped out

of the car and raced up to where the driveway would be. The rundown building had been recently demolished, but Trent was saving some of the old stone and bricks for reuse in the garden. A pile had built up to one side. On the other side was a caravan.

"I know where I'm sleeping now," he said with a grin. "No more couch surfing."

Cora whirled around, her face aglow. "You're really doing it. You're building your dream house."

"Two stories, with a balcony facing the water. It's going to bleed me dry, but I couldn't be happier." And he meant it, every word of it.

"I'm so proud of you." This time she didn't hold back. She flung her arms around his neck and squeezed tight. She smelled like a perfect summer's day—sweet and comforting—and her hair tickled the side of his neck.

Feeling her body next to his was like coming home, and he could see the future so clearly. The two of them, this perfect house, a magnificent view. Making a life together. But he had to make sure she was ready for forever, because even though he wanted them to continue to grow and evolve as people, he knew now that he wanted a life of certainty and commitment.

Since telling his siblings the truth about his birth, he'd come to one conclusion: family was what you made of it. Having a different birth mother than his siblings didn't necessarily mean they were any less bonded to him. In fact, Nick had given him carte blanche to use his firm's suppliers to get the house built, and Liv had already started picking out things for him—tea towels and cutlery, despite the house being a good twelve months away. And Jace had written a comic about a dog who'd been adopted by another pack and came to find happiness in his differences.

They loved him, regardless of his secret.

Cora looked up at him, eyes shining and bright. God, he wanted to kiss her like nothing else. But he couldn't mess this up now. He *had* to know.

"I wasn't joking when I said I'd changed," he told her. "What I want now…it's different than before."

She nodded, but her expression hinted at uncertainty. "Tell me."

"I want this." He gestured around him. "I want the family life. I want to settle down and have kids and a wife and a home. I want to grow old like my parents and have a life that I'm proud of, not one that's a collection of other people's dreams."

"You deserve that, every bit of it."

He brushed her hair from her face, but the breeze whipped it right back into place. The twirling strands had shades of blond and brown and the barest hint of amber from the sun. "I know I deserve it. I'm out in the open now, with everything. I told my siblings about…you know."

She sucked in a breath. "And?"

"The world didn't end and I'm still part of the family."

"Of course you are." Cora touched her fingertips to his jaw and traced his hard edges. "They're lucky to have you."

Cora's body was like a warm blanket around him, her fingers tangling in his hair. It felt so damn right to be holding her close, to be touching her, telling her what he wanted out of life.

"I don't want to compromise anymore," he said. "Not on my future."

"Am I too late?" she whispered.

"Too late for what?"

"To be part of your future, and to have you as part of mine?" Her voice was tight, brittle. "Everything you can see, I want that, too. I want it with you, Trent. I…I love you."

His heart wanted to explode with joy. Hearing her say those words was a greater satisfaction than any he'd ever known.

"I knew when I made it back to New York that I'd made a mistake. I wanted to come back to you." She drew in a ragged breath. "I want to help you build this amazing life and keep growing with you."

"Are you sure it's not a reaction to your father?" Because if she stayed here and then changed her mind…he wasn't sure if he could survive it.

"I cleared out my apartment and put it up for sale, I quit my job and…well, my ticket was one-way. So I'm really hoping you've got room for two in that little motor-home thing." A hopeful smile lit her face.

"You mean you came all this way without knowing where you were going to sleep?" He laughed. She really *had* changed.

"It seemed to work for you, so I thought I'd give it a try," she replied with a sheepish smile. "I'd rather be here without a plan, putting everything into a hope and a prayer that you still feel something for me. Because I want to stay this time. I want to choose love, and that means choosing you."

"I love you too, Cora." The second the words left his mouth, it was like a weight was lifted off him. He bowed his head to meet hers, and the second their lips connected, she melted into him.

Her kiss was heaven, sweet honeyed heaven. And all the sleepless nights and regrets and breakthroughs of the past six weeks swirled inside him, waking him up in a way he'd never known possible. Cora was the final piece of the puzzle, a woman who challenged him and pushed him and showed him all the good bits in life. A woman who made him see he was valued and loved.

"Luckily for you, the caravan *does* have room for two," he said, planting kisses along the edge of her jaw and finding the curve of her butt with his hands. "But I'll warn you, it's a little cramped in there."

"How about the plumbing?" she asked with a cheeky wink.

"Perfect. But I think we should test it to be sure." He hoisted her up into his arms and carried her across the block, past the pile of bricks and stones, past where the house would be built, and right up to the door of their temporary home. "Which means we'd better take a shower together."

"It's a good thing you're so dirty," she whispered against his ear. "We'll give it a thorough testing."

"And then what?" He opened the door and carried her across the threshold.

"Everything. Absolutely everything." Her lips found his for a deep and searching kiss that hinted at exactly what *everything* might include.

EPILOGUE

Two years later…

The doorbell rang and Cora squealed, skipping across the tiled living room to answer it. Today was a big day. A *very* big day.

She yanked the door open and was met with cheers and hellos and arms wrapping around her. Liv was first through the door, squeezing Cora so tight, she had genuine fears that her eyeballs might pop right out of her head.

"We're so proud of you, girl. So *so* proud." Liv thrust a bottle of expensive champagne into her hands. "I hope you've got some ice for that because we are going to celebrate!"

The rest of the Walters family—now *her* family—piled into Cora and Trent's house. They were loud, like always, joking and affectionate. Her father-in-law, Frank, was the last in. He always let the kids and his wife go before him, happy to wait while his family got what they needed. He shut the door behind him and pulled Cora into a big bear hug.

"I knew you had something special, Cora. We're all so thrilled for you." His bushy mustache brushed her cheek as he planted a kiss there, and Cora had to blink back tears.

The warm, loving people had embraced her as one of them from the very moment she set foot in this town. They'd stood by her side while she and

Trent built a house together, while she toiled over her novel, riding the ups and downs of publishing for the emotional roller coaster it was. Frank had come around to comfort her when the first rejection came from a publisher and he'd been the first person to put his name down for a preorder copy at Just One More Chapter when she'd finally gotten her release date.

They'd formed a special bond over their shared loved of the written word, and he'd been her biggest champion. Well, aside from her husband, of course.

And now the day was finally here. Her book was officially out in the world.

"Where's Trent?" Adam asked, setting a platter of fruit and cheese and meats onto the oversize marble island that was where their family always gathered whenever they came over.

"He forgot to pick up the ice this morning, so he's gone to the servo."

"Hey!" Nick threw his arm around her shoulder and gave her a brotherly squeeze. "Nice use of the Aussie lingo there. We'll have you speaking like a True Blue so well, you'll forget you weren't born here."

Cora laughed. She'd had fun picking up the strange words in her adopted country, and there were plenty to learn. The Australians had quite a varied and colorful selection of slang terms. Although in her mind, a servo would forever be a gas station no matter how long she lived here.

Cora put the champagne in the fridge to start chilling while they waited for Trent to get back.

He'd spent all morning stringing up balloons in pink and gold that said "congratulations" in metallic lettering. When she'd woken up after a luxurious sleep-in, he'd led her out into the main room where he had coffee and croissants waiting, and the whole sight of it had brought tears to her eyes.

She'd never known this kind of love before. The unbridled, unconditional, unrelenting love.

And it was glorious.

"Are you excited for the signing, dear?" Melanie asked. "I've told all the ladies from my walking group to come down to the bookstore this afternoon and buy a copy or else I'll stop bringing my muffins to our weekly catch-up."

"Now *that's* a threat if I've ever heard one." Frank chuckled.

"Bloody oath. I'd better see them all reading it, too." Melanie winked.

"I'm nervous. There's nothing like throwing a party and not knowing if anyone will show up." Cora pressed a palm to her stomach to try to quell the churning. It was exciting and thrilling. She'd received a bunch of flowers from the publishing house this morning and an excited text from her agent, a sharp-minded woman based in Melbourne who'd been shepherding her through the process.

"We'll drag people in off the street," Nick said. "I won't rest until you have a line snaking out the door."

She looked around this incredible group of people and wondered how she got so lucky. The past two years had been a lesson in how to belong, how to be loved. She'd had a lot of baggage to work through and so had Trent. Dropping the bombshell on his family about his true parentage hadn't been easy for him, and occasionally his old fears still raised their head.

But he was better at putting himself first when it was required. Better at chasing things to fulfill his own dreams, while still maintaining the thing she loved about him most: his generous, giving nature...inside the bedroom and out.

Together, they were becoming the people they'd always had the potential to be.

But as she looked at the sea of sandy-blond heads and matching blue eyes in front of her, there was still the barest twinge of sadness underneath it all. Deep *deep* down, there was still a little part of her that wanted her father to be celebrating with her. Their relationship had suffered a blow when she left New York, but they'd been starting to rebuild it. They Skyped every few months, and when she'd gone back to New York six months ago for her cousin's wedding, they'd had a nice dinner. It had been a little awkward, sure, but her father had made some admissions she hadn't expected... like how he'd underestimated her.

How he understood now that she needed to follow her passion in order to be happy.

Small steps.

"You guys are the best." Her voice trembled a little, but she hid the tears pricking her eyes by ducking down to pull out some plates from the bottom cabinet. "We may as well get started. There's *so* much food. I hope you're all hungry."

Everyone dove in, eager to fill their bellies and their hearts. Liv surprised Cora with a cake that was frosted—sorry, *iced*—to look exactly like the cover of her book. The design was perfect, right down to the shimmering gold font and the violet-blue background and the stars and moon and the golden caterpillar in the middle.

Just as Cora was about to text Trent to tell him to hurry up, she heard the rumble of the ute pulling up to the house. A door slammed and a second later, keys jangled as Trent came through the front door with a huge bouquet of flowers in his arms.

"Oh my gosh." Cora headed over to him, shaking her head. "You're too much."

He planted a hot kiss on her lips, snaking his free arm around her waist and holding her tight. "No matter what I do, it'll never be too much. You deserve it all, Cora."

"How did I end up with a man like you in my life?" She touched his face, wonder filtering through her system. She loved this man so much, it made her entire body vibrate with joy. "I have no idea how I got so lucky."

"Well, don't be showering the praise on me yet." He pulled a face.

"Don't tell me you forgot the ice," she groaned. That was the whole point of his trip out. "Liv bought some nice champagne."

Trent laughed, slapping her on the butt. "I'm yanking your chain. It's in the car. Why don't you go grab it and I'll get these flowers into some water?"

"They're amazing." The bouquet was a spray of

rainbow flowers—pink roses and purple irises and yellow gerberas with green fronds. "Thank you."

"I'm so proud of you," he said, echoing the words their family had shared with her earlier. "You inspire me every day."

"Same," she whispered. They kissed again, harder this time and to shouts of "Get a room" from Nick and Adam and laughter from the others.

Shaking her head and wondering whether it would be inappropriate to kick everyone out of her house so she could drag Trent back to bed, Cora headed outside. But the second she stepped through the front door, she froze. For a moment, she wasn't sure if she was hallucinating.

Her father stood in front of Trent's truck, looking a little tired and a little disheveled, but still as well-dressed as always. "Hi Cora."

"Dad." She shook her head. "When…?"

"That husband of yours was adamant that I be here to help you celebrate." Her father came over to her and pressed a hand to her shoulder. They didn't have the easy affection of the Walters family, but her father being here was a big deal. "He called and told me that if I wanted to make up for not supporting you in the past, then I could start by flying out and coming to your book signing."

"He did?"

Her father chuckled, a reluctant respect shaping his mouth and crinkling the edges of his eyes. "He's very persuasive."

"Tell me about it." Cora was still shaking her head, like her brain couldn't quite compute what was happening. Her fingers automatically went to the caterpillar pendant around her neck, the familiar feel of the smooth, gold disk grounding her. "I can't believe you came."

The words popped out before she could think, but her father simply nodded. "I haven't given you much reason to believe I would support you. I regret that."

"I only ever wanted to make you proud."

"You did, Cora. You survived living with your mother and me while we fought like animals and spewed hate onto each other and you *still* turned out to be a strong, creative woman with a big heart. That makes me proud." He smoothed a hand over his hair. "I'm sorry it took me so long to see that my fears stopped me from letting you fly."

"You're here now. That's what matters," she said, swallowing against the lump in her throat.

"Can you forgive me?"

"Of course. We're family."

In a rare show of emotion, her father hugged her close. The gesture almost knocked the strength out of her for how many years she'd craved this— his love and acceptance. His presence at an important time in her life.

She looked up and saw Trent leaning in the doorway to the house, hands in his pockets and a smile on his lips. Behind him, his mother stood with a protective hand on his shoulder and tears in her eyes. They all knew that family wasn't always easy. It wasn't always perfect.

But the main thing a family needed to survive was forgiveness, and between them all, they had enough to heal every one of their wounds.

ACKNOWLEDGMENTS

Thank you to each and every reader who has taken a chance on me in my career. Your enthusiasm for my stories, your reviews and the emails you send… they mean the absolute world to me. Thank you.

I have to thank my amazing husband, Justin. His unwavering support, tough love, gentle love, plot workshopping, enthusiasm and genuine, unrelenting desire for our happiness and success play a crucial role in my stories. He's the reason I believe so strongly in the power of romance and the impact love can have on a person.

Thank you to Taryn, whose brainstorming genius cracked this entire book wide open! Seriously, you saved me when I was ready to scrap the whole thing and start over. Our Skype sessions never fail to revive my joy for a project or to get the plot bunnies multiplying. Thank you for being such an amazing friend, both in the writing world and out.

Thank you to all the people in the book world who help a project go from idea to printed pages. To my agent, Jill Marsal, the team at Entangled Publishing, Liz Pelletier, Stacy Abrams, Nancy Cantor, Jessica Turner, Katie Clapsadl and the production team, thank you.

Thank you to all the people in my personal life who ask how the writing is going knowing they could get literally any type of response. Mum and Dad, Sami and Albie, Melissa, Zia, Luke and Jill,

Russ and Kate, Shiloh and KG, Myrna, Madura, Aliza, Jeanette, Tammy. You're all amazing.

And, as always, thank you to my coffee machine for greeting me every morning and being a key contributor to getting my brain working enough to write. You're the real MVP.

Hilarity ensues when the wrong brother arrives to play wingman at her sister's wedding.

the
wedding
date
disaster

AVERY FLYNN

USA TODAY BESTSELLING AUTHOR

Hadley Donavan can't believe she has to go home to Nebraska for her sister's wedding. She's gonna need a wingman and a whole lot of vodka for this level of family interaction. At least her bestie agreed he'd man up and help. But then instead of her best friend, his evil twin strolls out of the airport.

If you looked up doesn't-deserve-to-be-that-confident, way-too-hot-for-his-own-good billionaire in the dictionary, you'd find a picture of Will Holt. He's awful. Horrible. The worst—even if his butt looks phenomenal in those jeans.

Ten times worse? Hadley's buffer was supposed to be there to keep her away from the million and one family events. But Satan's spawn just grins and signs them up for every. Single. Thing.

Fine. "Cutthroat" Scrabble? She's in. She can't wait to take this guy down a notch. But somewhere between Pictionary and the teasing glint in his eyes, their bickering starts to feel like more than just a game…

Smoke jumpers and a steamy romance collide in this new romantic comedy series from USA TODAY bestselling author Tawna Fenske.

the two-date rule

Willa Frank has one simple rule: never go on a date with anyone more than twice. Now that her business is providing the stability she's always needed, she can't afford distractions. Her two-date rule will protect her just fine...until she meets smokejumper Grady Billman.

After one date—one amazing, unforgettable date—Grady isn't ready to call it quits, despite his own no-attachments policy, and he's found a sneaky way around both their rules.

Throwing gutter balls with pitchers of beer? Not a real date. Everyone knows bowling doesn't count.

Watching a band play at a local show? They just happen to have the same great taste in music. Definitely not a date.

Hiking? Nope. How can exercise be considered a date?

With every "non-date" Grady suggests, his reasoning gets more ridiculous, and Willa must admit she's having fun playing along. But when their time together costs Willa two critical clients, it's clear she needs to focus on the only thing that matters—her future. And really, he should do the same.

But what is she supposed to do with a future that looks gray without Grady in it?

AMARA
an imprint of Entangled Publishing LLC